THE RESTORATION

Widow

DENISE WEIMER

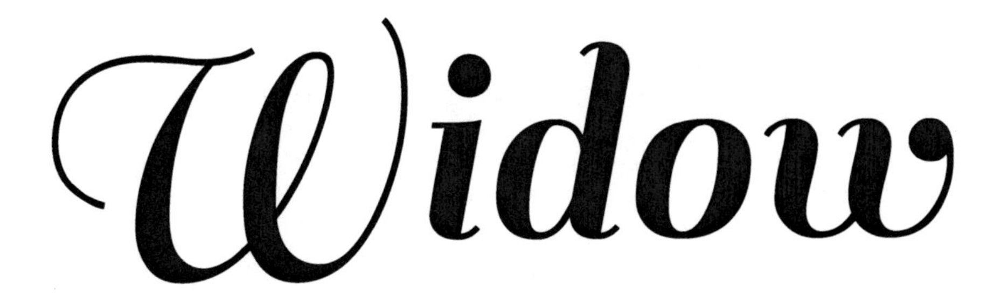

THE RESTORATION TRILOGY: BOOK TWO

Shyann-
Hope you enjoy book two of The Restoration Trilogy! And feel better soon!
Denise Weimer

DENISE WEIMER

www. canterburyhousepublishing. com
Sarasota, Florida

Canterbury House Publishing
www. canterburyhousepublishing. com

Book Design by Tracy Arendt
Front cover model: Ashleigh Roell
Front cover photographer: Phyllis M. Oleson

Library of Congress Cataloging-in-Publication Data

Names: Weimer, Denise, author.
Title: Widow / Denise Weimer.
Description: First edition. | Sarasota, Florida : Canterbury House Publishing, Ltd., [2016] | Series: The restoration trilogy ; book 2
Identifiers: LCCN 2016019873 (print) | LCCN 2016025277 (ebook) | ISBN 9780997011937 | ISBN 9780997011944 (ebook) | ISBN 9780997011944 ()
Subjects: LCSH: Historic buildings--Conservation and restoration--Fiction. | Man-woman relationships--Fiction. | GSAFD: Love stories.
Classification: LCC PS3623.E4323 W53 2016 (print) | LCC PS3623.E4323 (ebook) | DDC 813/.6--dc23
LC record available at https://lccn.loc.gov/2016019873

First Edition: September 2016

Author's Note:
This is a work of fiction. Names characters, places and incidents are either the product of the author's imagination or are used fictitiously, and any resemblance to actual persons living or dead, business establishments, events, or locales is entirely coincidental.

Permissions
Canterbury House Publishing, Ltd.
4535 Ottawa Trail
Sarasota, FL 34233-1946

Oglethorpe County, Georgia
June 1857

An angel of light stood before me, blonde, beautiful, one hand behind his back. His molded lips turned up as he studied me in his father's entrance hall. What a shame that at fifteen, lacking the discernment of Eve after the garden, I failed to see past the façade.

His voice startled me from my perusal of the portrait of a handsome man with his dark hair drawn back with a ribbon. "My grandfather, Levi.

As at our first meeting at the Lexington home of my school friend, Eliza, I could not bear to look long at Stuart Dunham's tall, muscular form encased in a trim frock coat, his golden hair slicked back from a clean-shaven face that I now fancied did bear a slight resemblance to the painting of the ancestor. When I first met Stuart, I caught myself narrowing my eyes in reflexive distaste. I thought I glimpsed the self-satisfied behind the charming smile. He'd gone on to pay court over dinner to the elderly ladies and make the men chuckle, causing me to doubt my instinct. Now, caught alone with him because I was the first one down to dinner, I determined he would not know how he affected me. I pointed to the likeness of a small, black-haired woman hung next to Levi's. "Is this his wife?"

"Yes. Verity Miller Duncan."

"She's so … frail looking. It's hard to imagine how she survived here when it was just wilderness."

Stuart gave my petite frame an amused evaluation. "And you think you'd do better, Miss Charlotte Ormond?"

"Well, no, but it's not wilderness now, is it?"

"No, it is not. Although it might seem like it to you, comin' from Athens, our state's bastion of higher education, and Lexington, womb of politics."

Indeed, the soot and noise of the train ride from Crawford, still sometimes called Lexington Depot, to Oglethorpe County, caused the journey to seem longer than it was. The wood-burning engine threw sparks like fireflies as it lurched over the rails. We'd been all too happy to spy Stuart's oldest brother Theodore waiting at the Hermon station. He told us the new engine improved on the last arrangement, when horses pulled the cars and had to be changed every ten miles.

Theodore showed us his house with pride. It lacked the panache of my family's Federal-style mansion with fan light entrance on a full block in Athens' coveted Cobbham district, or even the comforts of my roommate's father's house in Lexington, where Stuart, Theodore and their widower father Silas had first come to call. But while only two rooms with a detached kitchen, it did boast a nice porch, thirteen-foot ceilings and handsome trim work. A doctor like his father and both of his brothers, William and Stuart, Teddy saw patients in the back room. In the carriage, Mrs. Kelly commented that arrangement worked fine for a bachelor, but should he ever marry, she said with a glance at me, he'd need to add on right away. I believe even then she already envisioned the charismatic Stuart with her Eliza. I could have the more established, stocky, thirty-six-year-old bachelor Theodore, whom she had paired me with over dinner at her house.

Stuart was just that way, the iridescence of his charms appearing superior to anyone else's.

On the drive through fields of cotton to Silas' plantation, Theodore told us of his own neighbors, the Brightwells across the street, William Bugg who helped build the handsome new Center Methodist Church, and nearby, the grand estates of the Phinizy and Collier families, both established before 1800. Despite the isolation of the country, I sensed the wealth and history surrounding me, and the Dunhams intrigued me most of all. In 1840, shortly after my father, George Jones Ormond II, accepted the professorship of mathematics at Franklin College and the presidency of the fledgling Georgia Railroad and Banking Company, Stuart's father Silas sent a wagonload of gold from his plantation into Athens to bail the company out. Some people said Silas was the richest man in Georgia. For sure he garnered renown in the Southeast as a doctor who combined his traditional medical training from Philadelphia with what he'd learned about herbal medicines while growing up among the Creek Indians and African healers. Sick people rode the train from all over to be treated at his plantation and recuperate in the private cabins of his sanatorium. At considerable expense, Silas sent all three of his sons to study at Jefferson Medical College and the Philadelphia College of Pharmacy.

The Federal-style plantation house I now stood in with Stuart crowned a rise, surrounded by shade trees and both slave and patient cottages in view of Long Creek. Upon our arrival, Silas had treated us to a tour of the house and the cabin where they dried herbs and prepared medicines. I learned that the distribution of the bottles on the shelves labeled "Dr. Dunham's Blood Medicine," a formula favoring strengthening rather than letting of the blood, had greatly spread his fame.

I wanted Stuart to know I was not like other young girls, valuing frivolous amusements over lasting heritage. I clasped my hands before my tight V-bodice and said piously, "I love your county, and your home."

"Do you?" Stuart sounded pleased and surprised. "I expected you might judge it much the same as you judged me."

I felt my cheeks heat. He had indeed read my thoughts at our last meeting!

"I was right, wasn't I? You don't like me."

"I hardly know you."

"But you thought me a snob. And I did so want to meet you."

"You did? But you seemed so taken with Eliza." I slapped my hand over my mouth, mortified at what I'd just revealed.

After Eliza's parents had introduced Stuart to us at their dinner, his gaze had settled on me just as my skeptical expression betrayed me. Barely giving me a nod, he greeted Eliza instead, expressing deepest admiration of how Grove Seminary for Young Ladies had matured the lovely daughter of his host. And after dinner he asked her, not me, to dance. My stomach curled like a sick bud in my middle at the sight of my best friend in Stuart's arms, laughing at his droll observations. He didn't even look at me as they waltzed past. And the next morning, a nosegay of orange roses announced Stuart's fascination for the girl who had been closer to me than my own sisters.

At that moment, the sound of voices proceeded the Kelly family's descent down the stairs. Stuart winked at me as he moved away. "I had to get your attention somehow, didn't I?"

That trick of bait and closing trap door should have warned me. So should the conversation that followed, alerting me that some things might be amiss among the Dunhams.

The three brothers had one sister, Anne. All were present at dinner except for William, the middle son, but a brother-in-law filled his place at the long, white-clothed table. Durbin Maxwell, a younger son of a successful Wilkes County cotton planter, had moved in with Anne's family when he married her. As the plantation bookkeeper, the Dunham overseer reported to him. Silas still saw a full load of patients, and one of his slaves who also called himself a doctor assisted with the growing and preparation of herbs and medicines.

"With his help, I just manage. I will be thankful when Stuart completes his education next year," Silas told us. Indicating approval of his portion, he nodded his silvery head at the slave who served leg of mutton over his thin shoulder.

A much more solid man than his colleague, who lent the darker coloring I happened to share with his only daughter, Dr. Kelly spoke up. "Once you built the place for Teddy in Hermon, we all expected William to become your right-hand man. He showed such promise in medical school. I still haven't gotten over the shock when he went off to Atlanta."

"My middle son proved ill-suited to plantation life. He's an excellent doctor, but his philanthropic heart urges him to dispense his skills among the disadvantaged. That is best done in a city. We don't see William often."

"That's a nice way of sayin' he'd rather live in noble poverty than help shoulder the family responsibility," Stuart put in. "Some people think they are better than their roots." Acid laced his soft drawl.

"Stuart," Silas warned his youngest son.

"Doctor Silas, I had hoped to meet your sister this evening," Mrs. Kelly broke in. With her blue plaid silk dinner dress and white lace collar framing her porcelain skin and azure eyes, she looked just like the fanciest of my china dolls Mother gave me on my tenth birthday.

Anne let out what could only be described as a nervous giggle. Considering her normally quiet and composed demeanor, this struck me as out of character. Even though she was only a few years past my age, having already married and started her own family, she seemed much older. Stuart, scooping a spoonful of peas, turned up the corner of his mouth at her.

Their father cast them a censorious glance before replying to his guest. "Thank you, but Miss Selah does not partake of social life. She is quite content in the cabin our father first built on our land. I believe I pointed it out to you on the tour." He had, but had not offered to take us inside. His smile looked as melted as the chunk of ice that had started dinner in my goblet. "She, too, helps our patients with herbal remedies."

"Those who don't run on sight of her," Stuart commented in a bland tone.

Anne scolded, "Stuart, you make it sound as if Aunt Selah is deformed in some way."

"My aunt is of another time," Theodore explained to everyone else at the table. "She's not been able, like father, to move into the modern age."

"When she was young she had but one beau," Anne told us. As she tilted her head and lowered her voice as though her aunt might lurk behind a curtain nearby, her garnet earrings danced beside her dark chignon. "He went to fight in the War of 1812 and never came home. Father says after that she grew increasingly reclusive."

I blinked, my curiosity roused by this tragic romance. I sensed more lay beneath the surface and wished people would just say what they meant. With the impatience and curiosity of youth, I spurned the social morés of verbal discretion and mistook Stuart's reckless tongue for the honorable sort of honesty. I liked that I could trust him to tell me the truth about things.

That night, Stuart insisted on teaching me a new card game. He situated us at a table for two by a full-length window. The balmy breeze the open portal allowed provided welcome relief for the dampness congregating under my corset. I think my heightened temperature had as much to do with Stuart's proximity as the June humidity. We did very little playing cards. When he was not peppering me with compliments, he was fishing for information about my life back in Athens. I explained Eliza and I liked to spend our summers at her house because we were positively underfoot among my four siblings in Cobbham. But we did miss our brothers and their college friends serenading us on Friday nights. And some of the adventures of living in a university town.

"What type of adventures?" he prompted.

"Well, the boys at Franklin College are quite young, oftentimes away from their families for the first time. President Waddel uses his spy glass to determine when groups of them try to escape to Watkinsville to see the militia drills and court cases, or Lexington, for political events. He's been said to fetch them back himself. But we ladies know to never go to certain sections of town in the evening, because they're notorious for food and cane fights."

Stuart frowned with a disapproval that evidenced his twenty-two years.

"Oh, that's hardly all." I ran on like a rocky brook, terrified of awkward silence. "One time Eliza and I went to William White's for sheet music and stationery, and on Broad Street a group of boys had tied tin cans with buckshot inside to the tail of a poor, stray dog and yelled at it to make it run. Some man had hitched his horse on the sidewalk, forcin' us to pass around in the street. The dog tore straight under the hooves of John Jacob Flournoy's mule—"

Stuart held up a long-fingered hand. "Wait, the man with the long white beard and India rubber overcoat who's been publishin' his views on religion and slavery and announcin' candidacy for the legislature in the newspapers for the past fifty years?"

I stifled a laugh behind my silk fan. "The same."

"Oh, dear, what happened?"

"Well, as you can imagine, it took off brayin'. Right toward Eliza and me. She was closest and tripped over the sidewalk in her haste to get away. I caught her, but the next thing I know, she's shriekin' and jumpin'. The mangy dog had taken refuge under her skirts!"

Stuart's laugh rang out, attracting the attention of the others clustered in the middle of the parlor. Eliza's dark brow winged down.

"Shh," I whispered, tapping Stuart's card-holding hand with my fan. "She'll think we're makin' fun of her."

"You really love her, don't you?"

"She is more like my sister than my own sisters, an' so she has been since the first day we met at school."

"I can see that." Stuart smiled at me as though I'd just come back from nursing service in the Crimea. "Between all that activity in town and your siblings at home, no wonder you prefer the peace of Lexington."

I smiled and played a card. "We stay busy there, though."

"Lots of invitations, I'd imagine." Why did Stuart's mobile lips turn down at that?

"Yes. We spend a lot of time at Woodlawn and The Cedars." I hoped that would impress him without making him worry that we were fast, in case he tested to see if we had many other beaux. Woodlawn was the former home of William Crawford, the famous politician, judge and presidential candidate, now owned by the Dr. Willingham family. Mrs. Willingham's garden boasted the rarest plants, including seventy-two varieties of roses. Former lawyer and governor George Rockingham Gilmer owned The Cedars. Although his ill health forced him to retire from public life, Mrs. Eliza Gilmer maintained the love of the townsfolks from the years she threw tea parties on her lawn for local children. Governor Gilmer's collection of Indian relics, petrified animals and even a sword hilt taken from DeSoto on his march to the sea still held a bizarre fascination for Eliza and me, even at our age.

It was Stuart's turn to smile. I don't know why his approval already felt so important. "It sounds like you're keepin' good company. It just so happens that I have business in town next week. May I call on you while I'm there?"

My lips parted, then I bit down on the bottom one, chancing a sideways glance at my best friend. From her vantage point with her ruffled skirt spread out on the sofa around her, she directed a full-on glare in my direction. "Um, Eliza and I would be happy to receive you," I murmured, moving my cards around so I wouldn't have to focus on Stuart.

"It's not Eliza I want to see."

I looked up, but jerked back just as he reached out to tuck back a strand of hair that had come loose from my ribbon-tied ringlets to curl over my cheek. His fingers felt like fire on my skin.

"What did you say to him?" Eliza wanted to know on the way home. "In the foyer, before we came down?"

"Why, nothing. We just talked of his family," I insisted.

"You said something, to turn his attention to you. He hardly noticed you in Lexington, but now he can't take his eyes off you." She turned her face to look out the carriage window, unwilling to talk further.

If only the envious concern of the Kelly family had urged me to greater caution when Stuart became a frequent guest that summer. Stuart took both of us out on buggy rides and escorted us to musical evenings, but I laughed at his cleverly implied humor, matched him at lawn games and followed him through the woods in search of herbs and berries. He dearly liked to teach me and was pleased when I did not grow bored as he named the trees and wildflowers and the uses of their barks, buds and roots. Eliza would stand in a clearing brushing away insects with her hankie and reminding us of the heat and time.

It never occurred to anyone that Stuart courted me to my doom. One expects a rotten apple when the whole barrel is rotten, but at some point, that first fruit goes bad, doesn't it? It starts with a simple spot that no one notices.

Stuart made every person his path crossed feel important, even the boy who fell out of a tree in the neighbor's yard. Stuart halted the caterwauling by pulling a magic penny from behind the child's ear, and by the time he set the bones Stuart had praised the boy's bravery so highly he barely noticed the pain. Such glowing moments overshadowed hints of darkness in Stuart's character. So I considered his snide comments so infrequent as to be overlooked or so deserved as to be excused. If his humor condescended or came at someone's expense, I told myself such a sunny smile accompanied a good-natured intention. If he lapsed into a moment of roughness with a slave, I reasoned he spurned laziness, not abused his authority.

Blinded by Stuart's brilliance, I allowed him to write when we both returned to school in the fall. That correspondence eroded my intimacy with Eliza. When she went off more and more in the company of others, I comforted myself that friends could always be found, but marriage to a man like Stuart met my ultimate goal. However, my mother reminded me that until we spoke binding words, I shouldn't make assumptions about Stuart's intentions. So I received a few callers that fall, all of whom proved dull.

One Saturday I read *Paradise Lost* on a carpet of golden leaves under a tree when I heard horse hooves on the pebbled drive. Knowing Father expected a business acquaintance, I didn't even look up, not until a pair of dusty boots appeared before me. I followed them up a lean body to the face of summer's happiness.

"Stuart," I cried, jumping up with my skirts inflating around me like coiled springs. "What are you doing here?"

I was not expecting his expression to be dark and unhappy. "I'm here," he said, "because I had to come see for myself if your heart lies with another."

"What are you talkin' about?"

"I hear George Wilkins calls on you frequently."

I shook my head. "He's come by a few times, but I hardly think I've done anything improper."

"Maybe not improper, but I thought I made my feelings for you clear before the school term began."

"I—you … don't tell me you came all this way over this, when you could have written a letter."

"A letter would not tell me what your face will."

"But how …?" My distraction transformed suddenly into understanding, and a sick feeling of betrayal filled my stomach. "Eliza," I said aloud.

"It doesn't matter how. What matters is, do you care for me like I care for you, Charlotte?" Stuart claimed my attention, clasping both of my forearms in a tight grip.

My eyes floated up to his. Always so careful with me before, his intensity and forwardness surprised me now. Before I could answer, he further shocked me by drawing me to him and kissing me. It was a hard kiss but brief because I jerked away.

"How dare you? How dare you take such a liberty?" By trained reflex I both answered and raised my hand to slap him.

But he caught my wrist, and his voice sounded as cold as a knife blade. "Don't."

I tried to wriggle away, but he held me. His breath came fast as he buried his face in my neck. When I realized pain, not anger, fueled his abrupt actions, and I smelled the spicy scent of soap on his cheek, I softened. He felt it and gathered me against him. "Forgive me, Charlotte. That was out of line. I'm afraid I stewed all the way from Pennsylvania. When I heard a man here made advances while I was away, and I imagined you encouraged him, I didn't … I couldn't … I was not prepared for how upset that made me. It told me how much I truly cared for you. Will you forgive me?"

When he drew back and I saw the moisture in his green eyes, the last bit of my resistance melted. I nodded and placed my hand alongside his sideburns. He nuzzled it, and I allowed myself to kiss his cheek in a comforting gesture, then I stepped back quickly lest he get the wrong idea. Kissing remained off limits for good girls until the reading of engagement banns.

I took his arm and walked him in, and he knew if I had not cared for him I would of course have sent him away. After that, Stuart's propriety and respect convinced me his boldness merely testified to the strength of his feelings. And that made me giddy as I imagined the passion for me he must hold in check.

I didn't even confront Eliza with her tale-bearing. I merely informed her in a passing way that Stuart had come all the way from Philadelphia to surprise my family with a wonderful visit, and he sent his regards. Ha. Take that.

By Christmas, no question of me being invited to Lexington remained, but that was all right. A more serious meeting in Athens approached, that of Stuart with my parents. The tragic death of his brother Teddy that fall, his neck broken in a fall from his stallion, made a proposal premature but the time ripe to clarify Stuart's intentions. Sitting before a crackling fire beneath a mantel trimmed with holly and ivy, Stuart told us that he'd received his father's blessing to take up the practice in Hermon upon his return from Philadelphia the next spring.

The concept of living in the small house in town with a constant flow of sick and needy people knocking on the back door, demanding my bridegroom's attention, appealed far less than taking up gracious residence at the plantation, but I began to imagine our future reality nonetheless. I would nurture the herb and vegetable garden established by Theodore, searching with Stuart for new specimens on long, romantic walks in the woods. In Lexington, I would purchase silk and lace for curtains, and bamboo runners I would sew into summer floor mats. I would oversee Stuart's servants with a kind but assured hand and hostess elegant al fresco dinners for the neighbors. And soon enough, we would hire carpenters to make the Hermon house as comfortable as the plantation.

That March, as faithful members of the denomination, my family attended the Methodist camp revival in town. We had heard the power of God was showing up there, not in loud and forceful demonstrations, but in a quiet, soul-searching manner where people left introspective and changed. It was true. In the meeting, I felt something I never had before, like a warm and heavy and holy presence hovering over the crowd. I understood in a new way that God had a plan for my life, and that walking closer to Him would give me strength and peace. I went forward to pray at the altar that day.

By April, the revival spread to the Baptists and even to Franklin College. I felt sure that my decision represented a step toward becoming a mature woman who would make a better wife. When I thought of seeing Stuart after that, however, I felt uneasy. I did not know why. I attributed it to his long absence.

The country barreled toward sectionalism and war in 1858, with politicians like my neighbor Howell Cobb and Robert Toombs of Washington, Georgia, at the forefront of the controversy, but Athens acted blissfully unaware on May Day. According to annual tradition, local militia and the two fire companies paraded and drilled at Grove Seminary, and this year proved no exception, despite murmurs that by winter session the school would lose students to the prestigious new Lucy Cobb Institute under construction on Watkinsville Road. Droves of people turned out. But one stood out among all others, even above the gaudily uniformed dandies. Stuart surprised me with an early return to Georgia. All the girls recognized him. Gazes of unparalleled envy followed as I moved about on his arm. Then he whisked me through a trellis into a garden alcove. Pungent boxwoods as high as my head surrounded us.

"You are more beautiful than I even remembered, Charlotte," he told me. He smoothed the evenly parted hair under my silk bonnet and ran his thumb next to my lips. "I've known since last summer you were the girl for me, and now that it's time to set up a household and practice in Hermon, you're the only one I can picture there beside me. Please let me call on your father to ask for your hand in marriage."

I placed my hand over his and laughed with joy. *Caution*, something inside me whispered. But I was too flattered, and he was too handsome. My parents told me I could not make a better match than this. "Oh, yes. Of course you may."

"Oh, Charlotte, I've missed you so much." He darted his head down to mine and sealed my lips with his. My indignation that again he had not asked melted in the heat of his fervor. His kiss left no doubt that I would soon be his, all his. As I knew little of such things, the idea both excited and terrified. Weak-kneed and breathless, I pushed back on his chest when I heard voices coming our way.

We set our date for that October. Upon my graduation, an explosion of wedding planning, trousseau shopping, sewing and social calls began. Stuart's sister Anne would be my bridesmaid. I tried not to think about how much fun it all would have been had Eliza been in that position instead. But as a wife of five years and the mother of two tiny sons, level-headed Anne could teach me many practical things about my new life.

A gala event at Dunham Plantation introduced me to the local gentry. Certain rooms of the house were given to toilette ministrations for the women and card games for the men. The dining room table groaned under all manner of elegant refreshments: raw oysters called kickshaws, fricassee of chicken, shrimp, Chantilly cheese, brandied and pickled peaches, nuts, sweetmeats, and sorbets. On the lawn a string ensemble provided music for dancing, the trees sparkling with lanterns.

My new ruby-colored silk ball gown and the family garnets Anne clasped around my neck for the evening pleased Stuart, but somehow I kept losing my intended. I told myself that in the place of his mother, his sister saw to her job of introducing me, while Stuart made the gentlemen welcome. But I wanted him to hover over me and ensure my comfort. All the names and faces made my head spin. So did the polka I danced with Durbin. While he went to fetch me a glass of punch, I stepped around the side of the house where I could collect myself. Hearing voices behind me near the servants' walkway between the house and kitchen, I turned to see someone who in the shadows resembled Stuart. But the man argued with a mulatto woman who wore a turban on her head. As I watched, he pressed her against a tree and jerked her face up. She tried to wiggle away, but he pinned her.

"Hiding, are we?"

The sudden voice at my elbow startled me. I turned to see a tall man dressed in a dark evening coat and white cravat and vest, but there his neat appearance ended. His straight black hair had come loose from whatever pomade was supposed to slick it back and brushed the top of straight brows, while his morning shave had already disintegrated into a shadow of whiskers on his jaw. He lifted a brandy glass to his smirking lips and took a sip.

"I—I'm waitin' on Durbin Maxwell to bring me a drink. He's soon to be my brother-in-law."

"I know that, but he won't find you here." Then the man winked. "It's all right, I'm hiding, too."

"Hidin' from what?"

"Hiding from whom is a better question."

"All right, whom?"

The straight dark brows raised. "All of them."

His verbal game already tired me. "You know, Sir, I don't think we've been introduced."

"And we definitely should be, as I, too, will soon be your brother-in-law."

"You're … William? The brother from Atlanta?" What had Silas said of his middle son, that he had a "philanthropic heart?" This man to me merely seemed bitter, and slightly drunk.

My companion bowed in silent acknowledgement.

"Why have I never met you before?"

"I'm seldom here. You see, my time in Philadelphia corrupted me. I came home with certain liberal views I couldn't seem to shake."

"About ... practicin' medicine?" I knew Silas held firmly to his methods.

William shook his head. "The disagreement wasn't a medical one. I just could no longer blend in on a plantation that employed over one hundred slaves. So I turned the management of that over to your other brother-in-law-to-be and made my own way in the world. You can almost pretend I'm not even here, Miss Charlotte Ormond, but for the record, now we've met."

A burst of sound behind us caused us to turn back toward the kitchen, where the man gestured emphatically toward the house. He held a finger under the slave's nose, then pointed it at an upper window.

"He's always had a way with the ladies, whatever color they may be," William muttered.

A sense like a shard of ice stabbed my middle, and with a shifting of the man's form into the light of a lantern, I recognized Stuart. I swallowed and said, "That kitchen maid must have made a big mistake for him to be so angry."

William took a sip of his brandy and eyed me with calm speculation. Without a hint of pity in his gravelly voice, he observed aloud, "He's going to make mincemeat of you."

"What?" I exploded, incensed.

"You don't have a clue, do you? He's poured on the Southern charm, and you fell for it. Take my word while you still can, Miss Ormond. This marriage is not a good idea."

Too taken aback to speak, I jumped and clasped my shaking hands to my bosom as another figure stepped from the shadows to William's side. An old woman, sixty or maybe even seventy years old, evaluated me with small, dark, glittering eyes, her leathery skin an unusual golden shade, her black hair in a chignon. She wore a black, dress, too, which was why I had not noticed her approach. She spoke. "You listen to William, Miss. He gives you a fair warning."

I looked from one to the other, my mouth open.

"Miss Ormond, this is Aunt Selah."

She nodded at me, but I could only stare.

"The boy needed the guiding hand of a mother," Selah continued in a voice that sounded dry and raspy from disuse. "She died too early. Silas is a good man, but one with many responsibilities. Overindulgence spoils one with a weak character and a strong vanity." Selah glanced behind her, then, before disappearing the same way she came, she added with a firm stare into my eyes, "You remember what I told you."

"My love, where have you been?" Stuart approached, smiling, so at ease one would never have guessed he had just been in an altercation. He reached my side and took my arm. "You look shaken. What's the matter?"

I glanced off toward the outline of the cabins near the house. "I just met your aunt."

Stuart's brows rose. "You did? What did she say?"

"I . . . believe she is not in favor of the wedding."

Stuart looked at William as though noticing him for the first time. "Doubtless you did nothing to help the situation," he said to his brother. "I'm sorry, Charlotte. I never should have left you alone. I had to deal with some . . . problems. I can see the most charmin' members of my family made you feel comfortable in my absence. Whatever Aunt Selah said, Charlotte, dismiss it. One should never put any stock by a recluse who reads tea leaves. She's been bitter ever since she realized no one else would have her after her fiancé died. And as for my brother, he's always been a bit of a killjoy." Stuart condescendingly eyed William and his brandy.

In response, William cut a mocking bow. "Then I shall make myself scarce. A pleasure to meet you, Miss Ormond. And my congratulations to you both."

After he had gone, I turned away from Stuart, from the laughing crowd dancing a La Tempete reel, not knowing what to think or feel. He stepped in front of me and took me tenderly into his arms, kissing my forehead. "Charlotte," he whispered. "Don't let him get to you. He's a lush." He tried to get me to look at him. "Every family has a couple black sheep, don't they? And you like the others, don't you? And they like you. And more importantly, I love you. We know we belong together. You make me a better person. I couldn't stand it if what William or my aunt said came between us. It won't, will it?" He kissed my temple, the rounded top of my cheek. "Will it?"

I shook my head.

"What's that?" His lips hovered just above mine.

I felt woozy from his nearness. "No, Stuart."

Stuart never left me after that. And no one registered any more concerns. I soon wrote off the comments made by William and Selah to jealousy and eccentricity. But the words came back in full force, howling down like wolves upon my consciousness, the night of my wedding. There at the hotel in Athens where we were staying before departing for the coast and Europe, shyness and uncertainty overcame me as soon as Stuart made the first marital advances. I begged him to be patient, to explain what I did not understand and communicate his intentions, but my protests only angered him. The more I pulled away, the more aggressive he became. What followed was not what a young girl dreams of her wedding night, of her groom tenderly wooing her into shared marital bliss. Instead, I experienced a nightmare of tearing, groping, humiliating.

"Stop, Stuart, you're hurtin' me!" I cried, trying to scramble off the bed.

"Stop actin' like a fainting maiden," he growled. As he shoved me back, I filled my lungs to scream, but he clamped a hand over my mouth. The other clutched my throat. His face lowered within inches of mine, and he hissed, "Shhh. You will never scream. Not *ever*, or I'll beat you within an inch of your life."

I had no doubt he meant it. That was when I saw the evil burning through his eyes, and my dream of a loving husband died. That was the day I became a widow.

CHAPTER ONE

Cicadas revved up their scratchy evening serenade as Jennifer Rushmore climbed the porch steps of Dunham House. Most people said the sound of the little varmints made them sleepy, embodied the essence of Southern nights or reminded them of home. Jennifer agreed, and therein lay the problem: the trilling did remind her of home. A home in South Georgia she wanted to forget. But myriads of cicadas existed here in Middle Georgia, too, so she might as well associate their song with a new home, and new memories.

Jennifer reminded herself that home would not be here, either, at least not for long. The longer she lived here in Hermon, half an hour outside the city of her alma mater, the University of Georgia in Athens, the more disposed to forget that little fact she became. She came here to do a job, to oversee the restoration of the house, apothecary and log cabin that represented the physical heritage of Michael Johnson's ancestors, the famous Dunham doctors. Once she completed that job at the end of the year, she would have applied for and hopefully been accepted into her dream job on the coast, at the Savannah Heritage Trust, the state's most prestigious historic preservation firm.

But wasn't it natural for a preservationist to grow attached to the buildings she worked on? As the 1840s house unveiled its beauty under proper landscaping, a crisp red metal roof, repaired black shutters and a fresh coat of white paint, the surge of pride Jennifer experienced every morning she crossed the lawn from the double-wide Michael rented for her on the adjoining lot grew stronger. She now found it difficult to visually identify the place as the same one she'd first dubiously eyed back in the winter. Even then, the unique hodgepodge of architectural features and the abandoned air of the residence hiding behind massive magnolias—some of which she'd ordered removed—intrigued her. Due to the fancy Gothic millwork on the front porch and the one-story nature of the structure, at first glance she made the mistake many others had of dating the Dunham place to the 1870s. She'd been wrong about a lot of things, including many of the people in the community. But she was learning … probably more than she'd ever learned in college.

Realizing her employer could be the person she'd been most wrong about, Jennifer rested the burden she carried on the front porch. The ears of the kitten she, Michael, and Michael's father James had rescued out from under the apothecary poked up from her box. Those ears had earned the name, Yoda.

"Don't worry, you're going to your favorite person," Jennifer told the cat with a sigh. The preference of the pet for Michael remained a sore spot with her.

Yes, Michael's initial lack of interest in his heritage had exasperated Jennifer, but she now knew that stemmed from an ongoing struggle with painful events in his past. Their discovery that, through the "outside" family his great grandfather Hampton maintained with his African American housekeeper in the early 1900s, Michael had relations living in the community, had gone a long way toward easing the early loss of both his mother and his wife. For a fleeting moment, Jennifer wondered what they might uncover next in this restoration process! Then anxiety erased all other thoughts. Even though they'd reached a plane of tentative friendship, her handsome, athletic boss still made her nervous.

Jennifer rang the doorbell, trusting that Michael or his father James would already be at work inside the house rather than finishing their coffee and cereal in the camper providing their temporary residence behind the house. The echo of footsteps in an empty hallway rewarded her. The red door flanked by Greek Revival sidelights opened, and she gazed into the blue eyes, studded by dark lashes, of her employer.

"What are you doing at the front door?" Michael asked. His gaze descended to her feet. "And why are you bringing Yoda?"

At the sound of his voice, their jointly owned rescue kitten leapt out of the large cardboard box Jennifer had filled with a stash of food and toys. The feline, but a few weeks old when they'd discovered it, still bounded around with an amusing, loping gait created by slightly bowed legs. At least the legs had filled out some. Now Yoda climbed onto Michael's shoe. Since he wore shorts and not pants which Yoda would have used as a fabric ladder, Jennifer waited for him to pick the kitten up.

Michael did not comply. "Aw, no. No! I've got a lot of work to do! I'm about to start the shop vac!" Michael gestured behind him, to the bare, yet-unfinished floors. They'd just taken the plastic up yesterday from the interior paint job. "You know how the vacuum scares her." Only last week had the vet determined Yoda was indeed a *her*.

"Well, put her in the camper for a while. I'm going to be gone all evening, and all day tomorrow, too, between Montana's bake sale at the Fourth of July Festival and Bryan Holton's tour. I can't leave her alone in the double-wide that long."

She had, in fact, just left Rita Worley's kitchen, where the Hermon hairdresser, floured up to her elbows, assisted her granddaughter's baking efforts. Jennifer's idea that Montana open a booth at the Lexington Fourth of July Festival had come because she had never tasted muffins as heavenly as those the twelve-year-old sold out of a basket in her grandmother's salon. Now the magazine interview arranged by Jennifer's former professor created a major scheduling conflict, since Jennifer had previously promised to help in the booth.

Meow, came a tiny, pitiful cry. Yoda's head turned up.

"Oh, fine." Michael relented and bent to pick the kitten up. It still fit easily in one of his large, long-fingered hands, while he stroked the dark gray head with his other one.

Observing his tenderness, Jennifer shook her head. "I don't know why you pretend you hate cats. I knew you'd give me a hard time today. Your dad is so much more reasonable, yet it's obvious you secretly love her."

"I do hate cats. I'm a dog person."

"Well, where's your dog?"

Michael blinked, then responded, "Any kind of pet is too much of an inconvenience."

"But you got one the minute you decided to take Yoda to the vet, so be a good daddy and help me out. You do want this tour and interview to go well, don't you? *Old Houses* is a nationally distributed magazine."

"Yea, more people driving out here to look at my private home."

Jennifer sighed at his sarcasm. "Then why are you letting the guy come do the article?"

Michael fixed her with a direct look. "I told you. Because it will be helpful to you."

She felt her face go red to the roots of her hair. "Thank you," she managed. "I've got to go meet him and Dr. Shelley in Athens right now."

"I know. You look … nice."

Jennifer glanced down at her white-on-white embroidered peasant top and long rust-colored skirt. She counted on her hand-tooled, brown leather purse to match her sandals and pull the ensemble together. Now that she was out of college, she became increasingly aware that her SoHo look might no longer prove advantageous. But she didn't really know what to do about it. To deflect her discomfort at Michael's assessment, she reverted to her go-to gesture, pushing her dark glasses more firmly up onto the bridge of her nose. "Uh, thank you."

Of course she didn't verbalize her next thought, that Michael's tall, athletic form looked spectacular in everything from Nike Dri-fit to dress slacks and button downs. It wasn't fair. She'd diligently avoided his type in high school and college, and now she had to work right under his nose.

"Well, you'd better get going, then."

"Um, yeah. Thank you. For taking Yoda."

"Well, you give me little choice, but sure. Can you shut the door behind me?" Michael bent to pick up the box with his other hand, the kitten's furry head cradled adorably under his chin.

"Of course." Yoda blinked at her, supremely satisfied with her hand-off. "*Traitor.*"

Michael rolled his eyes. "See you at noon tomorrow, right?"

"Right."

Jennifer nodded and closed the door behind him, then darted across the sodded yard, through the row of Leyland Cypresses, and to her Civic parked in the gravel drive of the double-wide. As she accelerated up the highway toward Crawford and on toward Athens, she thought of all the things she wanted to tell Bryan Holton, from the way they'd used local work crews for all the specialized jobs to the plans they were just now digging into for the apothecary. Her mentor and former professor, Barbara Shelley, had e-mailed Bryan a copy of the HPIF form Jennifer filed for the National Register listing in June, but she wanted the magazine article to capture so many things beyond dates and names. Like the story of Georgia Pearl they'd uncovered just as surely as they'd uncovered the red diaper pattern wallpaper in the dining room.

When Michael first came to Hermon, he'd never seen the house where his great grandmother had been born. His grandmother Gloria's dying wish bequeathed him the property and the money to restore it. Before Gloria died, she told her husband Donald, now living in the VA home in Milledgeville, the reason her mother broke with her family of origin in Oglethorpe County, Georgia, in the 1920s. But only an unexpected admission from Donald, coupled with two strange photographs Jennifer and Michael found in storage and the facts Jennifer dug up at the local library, disclosed the full truth.

Following a frightening brush with the KKK, Georgia Pearl, the youngest, fair-skinned daughter of Dr. Hampton Dunham and his black housekeeper Luella, chose to create a life as a white nurse in Atlanta that did not include her black relations near Athens. They'd gotten the full story from Stella, the talented, local African American painter who, along with her husband Earl, brought fresh color inside Dunham House, from the basic wall paint to historical stencils and now a Hudson River Valley-style parlor mural. Stella was also a distant cousin of Michael's, descended from Georgia Pearl's older sister.

Jennifer jumped when her phone jangled. As she pulled the cell out of her purse and saw "Professor Barb" highlighted on the screen, she navigated past a tangle of cars mobbing the Lexington Road Wal-Mart on her right. Jennifer slid the lock button with one finger. "Hello?"

"Hi, are you in town yet?"

"Just coming in."

"Oh, no. I'm so sorry, Jennifer, but I just got Bryan's message his flight was delayed. He won't be here until the morning."

"Aw, man!" Jennifer wheeled her car off the main road and into a parking spot at a mattress warehouse.

"I was going to call the restaurant and tell them we'll have to come for lunch tomorrow. It won't be as nice, but … hey, why don't you come on out for dinner? You're already here, right?"

"No, that's OK. We'll just be eating there tomorrow anyway."

"Why waste the trip? We can make sure we're on the same page before the interview."

Jennifer chewed her lip. Forget a "page." She felt certain that the string of texts she and her former assistant professor from UGA's historical preservation department exchanged on the topic in the last couple of weeks constituted a full book! And one they should now be at the end of. She wasn't sure which made her more uneasy, the control Barbara seemed determined to continue to exert over the Dunham project, or the awkward transformation the older woman attempted to make from professor to friend.

Barb had been her strongest advocate since the moment she'd recognized Jennifer's potential. The older woman understood her preference for staying in Athens over returning to Stewart County over breaks, opened the door for Jennifer to apply to the Savannah firm, referred her for the Dunham project when the property's former manager requested a graduate for the perfectly timed stop-gap job, and now arranged this interview with a leading magazine in the field. It was hard to say "no" to someone to whom you owed that much. But she really wished Barb would give her a little personal space now. Stella and Michael felt the same, and Jennifer trusted no one's judgment better than Stella's, even after only a few months' friendship.

She drew courage in with a deep breath. "That's an awesome offer, but I think I'm good. I really do have this, Barb. And to be honest, I left a couple of friends in a bad place to drive up here tonight. I should go back and help them out."

"Isn't the house ready for the tour tomorrow?"

"It's not the house. It's—" she took another breath and plunged in, hurrying through her words—"a young girl with a booth at the festival tomorrow in Lexington. I encouraged her to sign up, and she doesn't have enough baked yet. The parade is at ten, and that will mean a big rush for muffins and sweet rolls."

"Muffins and sweet rolls?!" Barbara's voice reflected just the amount of indignation Jennifer expected. She'd made it clear in the past that she thought Oglethorpe County's natives provincial and behind-the-times, especially where matters of religion were concerned. "Jennifer. Sweetheart. You don't have time for baked goods. Did you not hear me? We have to meet Bryan Holton for lunch now instead of dinner. I told him eleven so that he can still get out to Hermon by 12:30 and have plenty of time before his evening flight. You'll have to leave the country by 10:30 at the latest."

Jennifer cringed. When had Barbara started calling her "sweetheart?" And "leave the country?" As though she dwelt in the African bush. Then she sagged. She would have to leave by 10:20, which would pretty much nullify her helpfulness at the festival. Her voice came out small as she watched the traffic ooze by. "Oh, no. I promised her." She almost asked if Barbara could just lunch with the writer and then meet her at Dunham House. But that would give her former professor even more professional ground Jennifer was trying so hard to claim for herself.

Barbara's tone turned warm but firm. "And that was really sweet of you, but we're talking about your career versus a middle schooler's bake sale. Right?"

"I know, I know." Jennifer bumped her head on the steering wheel, picturing Montana's blank, then hurt, look when she told her she could no longer help man the festival booth until noon.

"You need a drink. You're taking too much on yourself. Come on, and I'll meet you at The Last Resort."

"No, this is all the more reason I should get back home. I should tell her tonight and help them finish and clean up. It's only fair." But first, she did need a drink. But not with Barb. And not Barb's yucky tasting old wine. Jennifer turned the car back onto the highway and headed toward town. "Thank you for letting me know. I've gotta go."

"Jennifer—"

"See you tomorrow at eleven, Dr. Shelley." She stabbed the "end" button with a fingernail, and a grin spread across her face. That felt good.

Jennifer knew fighting traffic to Five Points would cost her precious time, but she'd been missing her old roommate, Tilly Edmonds. Tilly always worked Friday nights at Jittery Joe's, and nothing sounded more comforting right now than a tall, foamy latté. She could kill two birds with one stone.

Inside, the familiar but long-lost sounds and smells of a coffee house almost outweighed the disappointment of a five-deep line. Hermon—and even Lexington—lacked such luxuries. Jennifer spied her old friend behind the counter, her long, dark hair up in a spiky pony tail, a headband helping secure any strays. Her orange apron hung loosely on her tall, thin frame. Absorbed in her work, she didn't see Jennifer in line. Finally, waiting until she stood right beside the latté machine and a break in its steamy labors arrived, she called Tilly's name.

The girl jumped and looked up. "Oh, my goodness, Jennifer! What are you doing here?"

"I needed a latté."

Tilly laughed. "Your Keurig and the country getting disappointing?"

"Maybe one of the two."

"It sure is good to see you."

"How's summer semester?"

"Miserable! I'm *so* stressed. And the new roommate doesn't help. She *snores*." Tilly widened her eyes as she hissed the last bit of information. Then she poked her lip out in an effective pout. "Will you come back?" Someone shoved a cup in her hand, and she started pouring in milk.

"I'm sorry, I won't distract you. You're busy tonight."

"Yes, and this old machine doesn't help. It takes forever."

Sliding a cup under a large pump bottle of caramel syrup, a guy also wearing an orange apron said, "Good news, I heard the boss has a new one on order."

"What will they do with the old one?" Jennifer asked.

"Sell it!"

A sudden mental visual of the wooden counter in Mary Ellen McWhorter's Hermon antique store punched into Jennifer's consciousness. Mary Ellen constantly asked people to come in and have a Coke with her out of her old Coke machine. The vision expanded to include the metal and glass case that sat on the counter, filled not with rhinestone earrings and cameo brooches, but with Montana's pastries. A tingle of excitement shot to Jennifer's toes. "Will you call me, Tilly? Call me?"

"I do call you, silly. You just never get reception in Podunkville."

"No, I mean, call me about the machine, when they're ready to sell it. Tell me how much."

"Uh, sure." Tilly shrugged blankly, then steamed the milk in the cup she held. "But it's awful big for just one person, even someone who loves coffee as much as you do."

Jennifer fumbled for cash and her recently little-used rewards card as she stepped up to the counter. "It's not just for me. I have a local business in mind."

Tilly got permission to come around and give her a hug after making her latté. "I miss you!"

"I miss you, too."

"So how is it, working in the real world?"

"I don't know that I would call Hermon the real world. More like a time warp."

Also a preservation major but with an emphasis in nonprofit management, Tilly waggled her eyebrows. "Sounds like a dream," she joked. "And how's the dreamy guy?"

Jennifer sipped in cinnamon dolce and rolled her eyes heavenward before focusing back on her old roommate. "We really shouldn't speak of my boss in such terms."

"Aw, come on. You know he's a hunk. Has he made a move on you yet?"

She almost spewed out her coffee. "Right. Tilly, you know he's the type who went for the cheerleaders."

"I doubt there are many of those around the job site. You just get rid of this." She swished Jennifer's shoulder-length, straight, mouse brown hair. "And this." She poked at Jennifer's glasses. "And it will be like the female Clark Kent."

"Tilly, you are crazy. Come see me some time."

"You, too! When I'm not working."

"Right. And you can come when I *am* working." Jennifer leaned in for another hug. Normally not given to demonstrations of affection, the years had made her comfortable with Tilly's casual but trustworthy friendship. That was more than she could say for most "friends" in her past.

"It must be nice, having a *real* job," Tilly whispered, then waved her out the door.

Her spirits lifted by the brief encounter and the miles seemingly shrunk by the foamy, hot beverage in her hand, Jennifer felt fortified to return to Rita's house with her bad news. When Jennifer left, they'd just mixed red, white and blue icing for the sugar cookie stars Montana had insisted on adding to her normal line-up. Upon her return, Rita looked bemused to see her, but let her in and informed her they were almost done applying the frosting. In penance, Jennifer went straight to the pile of dishes in the sink, rolled her sleeves up, and announced why she had returned to help. She couldn't quite look at Montana as she spoke, so she concentrated on squeezing in plenty of Dawn. But she had to peek over her shoulder when the adolescent cried, "Oh, no!"

Yep, it was bad. The twelve-year-old's round face wreathed in dramatic agony. The poor girl, an outcast of the public school system, invested so much of her worth in her baking. Her very plainness had drawn Jennifer to her, as Montana reminded Jennifer of herself at that age. And now she was letting Montana down in what was to her a debut moment. The noses of ravenous baseball boys and the eyes of skinny, pretty, blonde pony-tailed girls, both groups that had picked on her last year, *must* be drawn to Montana's cutely decorated booth bursting with cookies and cinnamon buns.

"I'll still come out to help you set up, and I'll stay until the very last minute."

"Which is ...?"

"10:20." Jennifer cringed.

"But that's in the middle of the parade! You won't be there to help during the rush afterwards!"

"Montana, this is Jennifer's work," Rita said in a warning tone, tilting her cotton-candy swirl of white hair down to her granddaughter's level.

Montana's face crumpled as she said softly, turning back to scattering sprinkles over her cookies, "It's my work, too."

Jennifer knew from her first meeting with Montana that the girl dreamed of opening a bakery of her own in Hermon. "I'm so sorry, Montana. I can't see any way around it. But I'll make it up to you, I promise." Jennifer came around the counter and tentatively held her arms open. "Forgive me?"

Montana looked up and forced a smile, though her lips wobbled. "Sure. I know it wasn't your fault." She gave Jennifer a hug as Rita nodded approval, then tilted her head back again to gaze into Jennifer's eyes and add in a tone of childlike sincerity, "Thank you for believing in me."

Jennifer's heart melted. Her own history illustrated that nothing good lasted, friends always failed, safety created an illusion ... and family brought the worst pain of all. If only someone had believed in *her* at twelve. Maybe that was why she found it so hard to assert any independence from Dr. Shelley.

But Jennifer had new friends now, Michael, James, Stella, Earl, Mary Ellen, Amy the decorator who owned the local paint shop and whose husband Horace once managed Dunham House as a rental, Rita, Montana ... and more recently, the friend Stella and Michael introduced her to, Jesus. It sounded funny to say it or even think it, but ever since Jennifer prayed with Michael to turn her life over to God, she felt Him near her, inside her, just like she'd felt Him in Stella's church.

There at Harmony Grove the pastor explained that God wanted her, Jennifer Rushmore, straggly stepchild from the South Georgia trailer park, to be part of *His* family. He'd taken her in just like they'd taken in Yoda. And here in Hermon, in what Stella modeled in her marriage to Earl and offered to her in companionship, in the strength of the father-son relationship between James and Michael, and in the admiration of a twelve-year-old, she witnessed what the Good Book Stella had given her said about community and adopted family.

Her old defenses stirred to squash her warm fuzzy moment, and Jennifer found herself wondering if it would all prove too good to be true.

CHAPTER TWO

The next morning, waking to sunshine creeping in past her blinds, Jennifer realized she felt happy. She wanted to lie in bed and examine that, but knowing time was of the essence today, she puttered into her mauve-and-ducks, '80s-themed kitchen and turned on the water for coffee. Even without Yoda's steady gaze focused on her waiting for the human to warm milk, the freshly steamed carpet, overstuffed living room furniture and sunny picture window oozed welcome. Except for various relics of yesteryear, the little old lady who had lived here had scarcely left a mark. Jennifer sent up a grateful prayer that when her surviving relatives decided to rent the place, Michael anticipated what a boon it would be for his employee to live close during the restoration project.

The place might be described as humble, cozy at best. After all, this was a double-wide, yet one so different from the trailer she'd grown up in—more like a glorified tin can than a home—it bore no comparison. The difference had less to do with the size of the place than who lived in it. True, she'd been happy in college. Tilly had been a great roommate, and Jennifer had enjoyed the other girls in the townhouse, like-minded members of the College of Art and Design. For the first time there, she'd had real friends. For the first time here, she was alone, but safe. Safe from the fighting, the drinking, the crushing abandonment of her natural father, the focused interest of her stepfather, and the selfish disinterest of the mother who had failed to protect her from it all. And that safety made her happy now.

After eating a banana and a muffin with her coffee, Jennifer brushed her hair and teeth and peered at her delicate but plain features in the mirror. She should wear her hair up. It was long and out of control. Rita kept begging her to come in for a trim, but she knew the elderly hairdresser envisioned layering and God only knew what else. Jennifer harbored a rather irrational but deep-seated fear of beauty parlors. Her mother, Kelly, had never let her visit one when she was growing up, but Kelly herself always came out with shocking revisions. Most of the time she settled on bleached blonde to compliment her tight jeans.

After a deflating inspection of her closet, Jennifer decided her best option lay in re-wearing yesterday's ensemble. Michael, Rita and Montana had seen her in it, but the festival required something cool and casual, while the lunch and tour called for a semblance of professionalism. She really must go shopping soon.

Outside, Jennifer unlocked the door of her car before she noticed she had company. Between two of the head-high Leyland Cypress trees Michael had planted to block her view of the hideous bungalow next door, complete with a truck on cinder blocks in the yard, stood Calvin Woods, her neighbor everyone described as a grumpy hermit. Jennifer's only encounter with the man so far had been a bizarre, middle-of-the-night near-miss as Calvin fired his .22 at an armadillo his dog chased. She'd met Otis the mutt before that, however, when the lab-boxer mix pretty well stalked her across the back yard the day she investigated the contents of Michael's old storage shed. Now Otis crouched just over the line on her lot, staring at her as he did his most private business. Disgusted, Jennifer raised her gaze to Calvin. In the daylight she could see that his stout form sported dusty pants, the kind automotive workers wore, and a blue cambric, short-sleeved shirt. Lank gray hair encircled a tanned, lined face with bulbous nose. He nodded at her. She didn't know what to do, so she waved back and slid into her car. Why couldn't Calvin make the mutt stay in his own yard? And she still wondered if it had been Calvin who locked her in the shed after she shooed Otis with a big stick.

The memory of the fear that assailed her in merciless waves returned as she backed her car out onto the main road. She might have been there for days had Michael not heard her yelling for help hours later. Another night, she thought she saw lights at the back of Michael's property. Jennifer guessed three possibilities existed to explain the incidents: a combination of accident and imagination, a nosy prankster, or someone who was unhappy about their restoration of the property. She liked the last the least.

Jennifer cleared her mind as she approached Lexington. Aware that certain streets would be blocked off in preparation for the parade, she parked on the outskirts of town and walked to the crafter area. Montana's father had their tent up and now unloaded boxes of baked goods and Lil' Hugs Kool-Aids from the back of his truck. Montana bounded up to hug Jennifer, then Jennifer helped Rita set up two tables with brightly checkered cloths. Around them, the air hummed with the activity of the other crafters and food vendors and the sound check of musicians setting up on a stage in front of the 1887 Romanesque Revival courthouse, red brick with looming bell tower. The scent of funnel cakes sweetened the humid breeze, but Montana's goodies attracted the attention of various children, who ran up to investigate and promised to return with money from their parents. Soon, Montana's penchant for decorating paid off. Moms started strolling by too, admiring the Mason jars full of daisies, donut boxes trimmed with polka dot ribbons and flowers, and individually wrapped cookies tied off with color-coordinated curly string.

Jennifer took charge of the money box. Knowing well what people were accustomed to pay in coffee shops for baked goods, she'd encouraged Montana to raise her rate from the humble dollar per muffin she charged in Rita's shop. As predicted, no one balked at the slight price increase, especially after tasting the samples Rita kept replenished on a plate.

"See? What did I tell you?" she whispered to Montana between customers. Montana grinned, and they did a discreet fist bump under the table. Then Jennifer spied two lovely young girls about Montana's age, clad in Chaco sandals and cute summer shorts and shirts, talking as they walked past and observing the bakery booth with slightly snide faces. Montana dropped her gaze and rounded her shoulders. Loudly, Jennifer added, "You're making so much money, Montana, you should go with me on my next shopping trip. And over lunch we can talk about the ideas I have for getting your business up and running!"

"Really?" Montana squeaked. "You mean it? Like—now? Not when I'm twenty or something?"

"I mean it, now." Jennifer smiled, pleased the girls registered surprise at her announcement and now eyed the merchandise. "It will depend on some other people, so we'll have to see what the future holds, right? But I'm behind you, in favor of bringing some new life to Hermon."

"Would you like to sample the cinnamon rolls?" Rita asked the adolescents, holding the plate out toward them.

Who could refuse? They thanked her, popping the smallest bites available into their mouths, then blinked with pleasure. "Wow, that's good. I don't have any money with me, but I'll send my mom by," one of them said. "See you later, Montana."

Montana colored up and smiled. "Sure, see you."

Jennifer winked at her.

People began to line the sidewalks, and policemen controlled the nearby intersections as the parade time neared. They could hear the *blurp* of ambulance sirens and the warm-up scales of the high school band in the distance. Before long, a police escort proceeded the mayor in a convertible, followed by other dignitaries and pageant winners, floats by the 4H and church youth groups, dance and gymnastics studios displaying their moves to portable boom boxes, and majorettes in flashy uniforms twirling their batons. The band completed the short procession with John Philips Sousa's "Stars and Stripes Forever."

The sales resumed full force. Jennifer took money and made change so fast she lost track of the time. When Rita said, "It's almost 10:30, aren't you supposed to be leaving?" she gasped and looked at her watch.

"Oh, no! I sure am, but I hate to leave you in the midst of such a rush." She handed a dollar in change to a smiling elderly gentleman.

"It's OK, I asked my son to come back and take your job. He'll be here any minute. I can take over until then."

Jennifer took the payment of a mother whose three small children handled everything on the table. "If you're sure," she said, bending to feel for her purse under the tablecloth. At that moment, the tow-headed toddler hovering at the edge of the display dropped his red Kool-Aid. As it hit the pavement, liquid gushed out the open top and all over Jennifer. "Oh, no!"

"Oh, I'm so sorry! Bradley!" the flustered mother exclaimed. She scrambled to pick up the Lil' Hug as the boy burst into tears. "It's OK, we'll get you another one. Is your shirt OK, ma'am?"

Jennifer held out her white blouse. Red already saturated one shoulder.

"Uh oh," Montana muttered.

As Jennifer stood, Rita tried to press a paper towel below her collarbone, clucking in dismay. The young woman fumbled in her diaper bag for baby wipes, which when applied merely smeared the Kool-Aid into a fainter but larger pink splotch. Anxiety rushed over Jennifer like a cold flood when she realized she would have to arrive at her important luncheon not only late but also stained. And at that moment Michael Johnson sidled up to the table, eyebrows raised as he beheld two women trying to clean Jennifer's shirt while Montana frantically conducted her sales.

"*Nice*," he said with that crooked grin that irritated her to no end.

"What are you doing here?"

"Why, I'm here to support our budding young baker, of course." Michael smiled at Montana much more genuinely and selected two packs of cookies, handing her a five.

"Well, this just looks awful," Rita declared with her usual honesty. "You can't go into your meetin' like that."

"I don't have time to change. I'm already late."

"Here." Rita started working loose the knot of the bright red and white starred scarf, shot through with silver threads, around her own neck.

"Oh, no. No."

"Just give it a try, honey."

Michael chuckled as the beautician tied the ends under Jennifer's hair.

"It does match your skirt, sort of," Rita said, fluffing both the scarf and Jennifer's hair. She leaned back to evaluate the look.

"She needs earrings," Montana observed over her shoulder.

"You're right, earrings would tie it all together."

Jennifer grabbed her ears to cover them as Rita reached to remove the silver stars dangling from her own earlobes. "No, please, I can't! I'll feel ridiculous!"

Rita paused and looked offended. "Are you sayin' *I* look ridiculous?"

"Well, no, but I'm not you. I can't pull this off, Rita."

"Of course you can. Now put them on." She shoved the jewelry at Jennifer. "Put them on."

Glaring at the grinning Michael, who now enjoyed his snickerdoodle in addition to her discomfort, Jennifer acquiesced. Hands shaking with embarrassment and hurry, she secured the posts behind the stars. "OK?"

"OK. You look great, Jennifer," Montana told her, sticking a stubby thumb up in the air.

Rita nodded. "You can hardly see the spill. Now go. Go!"

As Jennifer shouldered her purse strap and accepted further futile apologies from the nearby mother, Michael brushed up against her and said, "You look like you need a six shooter with that ensemble, ma'am."

She shoved an elbow in his ribs and whirled around to stalk off to her car. To her dismay, a four-wheel drive diesel truck with a float trailer attached blocked the exit onto the main road. She pulled up behind it and waited, thinking the driver with the idling engine would get the clue, but nothing happened. Finally she put her car in park and dashed up to the man's door. She shouted up into the cab, "Excuse me, but I have to go! I'm late for an appointment!"

With a frown, the guy in his hunting T-shirt rumbled off to another place to wait for whatever he was waiting on, and Jennifer sped out of Lexington. She called Barbara on the road to tell her she'd gotten delayed at the festival. Jennifer knew the professor well enough to pick up on the undertone of displeasure in the polite response she made in front of Bryan. Sighing, Jennifer angled her rear view mirror in quest of her reflection, then growled. She did look like a rodeo performer. But without the scarf, she resembled a child who had spilled her Kool-Aid.

Having fought the Saturday traffic all the way to Clayton Street, she dashed past the mural of root vegetables growing in soil on the side of the restaurant and into the lobby, giving her name and telling the host whom she was meeting. Just then she spied Barbara waving at her from a table against the red brick wall. The professor, clad in dark slacks and a deep blue silk shell which complimented her short, salt-and-pepper hair, retained her seat as Jennifer approached, but the lanky man with her rose. As Barbara did the introductions, Jennifer guessed that he probably hovered between her own and Barbara's ages, blonde and pleasantly but not uncomfortably attractive. He would wash into insignificance beside Michael. Jennifer bit her mental tongue. Bryan Holton was definitely the focus of all their attention today.

Barb pushed a menu at her. "I've taken the liberty of ordering some fried green tomatoes, and we're ready to order whenever you are." Barbara's gaze slid over her, stumbling at the firecracker red scarf, which provoked a disturbed frown.

Jennifer decided to confess. "I'm so sorry I'm late. I promised a little girl from our community that I would help at her bakery booth at the festival this morning, and well, right when I was ready to leave, some kid spilled his Kool-Aid all over me." Looking at Bryan, Jennifer sheepishly lifted her neckerchief to reveal the stain. "I'm not usually this ... scattered."

"No, she is not," Barbara agreed with firm inflection.

"It's all right. I find it quite excusable on the grounds that you were supporting the youth of the community." Bryan winked, grinned and sipped soda through his straw.

"Thank you. I couldn't really back out considering the booth was my idea in the first place." Jennifer opened her menu, then focused on it when Barb widened her eyes in a clear hint. "Uh ... I'll have the quiche." After she'd gazed at Montana's pastries all morning, breakfast remained foremost on her mind.

Barbara gestured to a nearby server and dictated their order, making it clear everything went on her check. She selected a salad while Bryan ordered a chipotle lime pork roll. As soon as the waiter submitted their order, he returned with the appetizer.

Reaching to spear a golden, encrusted tomato with his fork, Bryan said, "I'd like to hear more about the community where this Dunham doctor property is located. Dr. Shelley said it was rural, but it sounds like there's some local enterprise."

"Well, both are true," Jennifer said, and, unwrapping her straw, went on to explain how Hermon, originally a railroad boom town, declined after the 1920s, while Lexington, fifteen minutes away, retained a number of impressive historical structures and small businesses. "I'd like to see Hermon become more like Lexington, especially as it has a chance of becoming a stop on a Rails to Trails project from Athens to Union Point, which is a short drive south of Hermon."

Bryan nodded, craning his neck for tomato bite number two from his bread plate.

"I think the most important thing we need to discuss is the history of the property," Barbara suggested.

Jennifer nodded. "Of course." She started to relate how the original Dunham in the state, Levi, son of a Virginia planter and doctor, came to Oglethorpe County before 1790 to take possession of a tract of land awarded him for Revolutionary War service. Levi's log cabin, she said, remained on that plantation. Levi's son Silas became regionally renowned as a physician who incorporated herbal cures alongside traditional practice, drawing thousands of patients over the course of his lifetime to his sanatorium on Long Creek. Just south along current State Route 77 in Hermon, his sons had branched out with an apothecary and house.

Bryan cut in. "Forgive me for interrupting, but I have a pretty good grasp of the history behind this project from the excellent National Register report you copied me on." He paused to bare his teeth at her. "I will incorporate the necessary facts, of course, but our readers take in so many similar stories of historic preservation and restoration they become numb to a barrage of dates and genealogies. What I'm going for is the personal angle, the heartfelt story that grips their attention. So whatever that is, I want to find it. Why don't you start by telling me about yourself, Jennifer, and I don't mean what's in your bio."

She froze. She could not have experienced greater dismay had Bryan required her to do a table dance in her lingerie. Her gaze skimmed reflexively to Barbara, who read her panic during the brief beat of silence.

"Jennifer is always a little reticent to talk about herself," the professor made excuse, "but she was my best student, which is why I recommended her when this project came up."

"And how did that happen?"

"I sent students to a local gentleman who specializes in the sale and rental of historic structures, Horace Greene, to help with projects. He once acted as the property manager for the Dunham place. He's since passed ownership of Athens Area Property Management to his son and now focuses solely on real estate. But when Michael Johnson inherited the Dunham house and asked about a preservation graduate to oversee the restoration, Horace approached me."

"I see." Bryan jotted notes on his pad while Jennifer played self-consciously with Rita's ridiculous star earrings dangling from her earlobes.

"Another thing Jennifer won't tell you is she's on the short list for hire at Savannah Heritage Trust, so anyone else wanting to attract her attention will have to step up quick." Barbara winked at Jennifer, who flushed. She appreciated her mentor's diverting any potential digging into her less-than-admirable background and its resultant insecurities, but, as usual, Barb went a little too far. She continued, "Even this soon after her graduation, Jennifer has bloomed under my guidance. To make sure things go well, I've been very hands on with this project. I'm sure you'll see for yourself how impressive the results are going to be, Bryan."

Nothing like using a name as a power tool. As always, Barbara's good intentions digressed into their usual channels of self-gratification. A secondary potential embarrassment also loomed. Jennifer feared Bryan would laugh at what a hot commodity she was *not* when he realized just how far off the beaten path her efforts were concentrated.

But to her surprise, Michael angled his shoulder away from Barbara as he focused on Jennifer and said, "I'm sure I will. I'd like to ask you, Jennifer, what has surprised you most about this project?"

She leaned, pondering her response as the waiter slid their entrees onto the table. She hardly registered the savory aroma of her bacon and tomato quiche as she answered, "I'd have to say, the people. At first glance you think Hermon is Podunk, and all the residents must be either rednecks or stuck in another century. But there is such an interesting combination of overflow from the university and old Southern class. Most of the people are educated, talented, and so caring. I've never seen so much community remain when so few of the buildings do. It's clear it isn't about buildings. It's about relationships."

Bryan scribbled, also ignoring his food. Barbara regarded them with her mouth and brows both flat-lined and started dressing and stirring her salad. "What kind of talent?" he prompted.

"Well, there's Amy Greene, Horace's wife, who owns Drapes and Drips in Lexington. At first I thought her an absent-minded ex-cheerleader—don't quote me on that—who played at being an interior decorator, but she did all our paint and will help me with period correct window dressings, and she really has an eye. And Mary Ellen McWhorter, who runs the antique shop right next door. She knows her antiques and all the hole-in-the-wall places to find them. Even Montana Worley, the granddaughter of our hair dresser—" had she just said "our?"—"who makes pastries better than Starbuck's. She wants to open a local bakery one day. And most of all, there's Stella, the wife of the man Michael hired to do most of the painting on the house. I ended up visiting at her place, and I couldn't believe the antiques she had and the paintings of the local area she had done. Bryan, her art is better than most I've seen around here. It has this ... rustic, lonely, bygone feel to it, with this golden light. She helped us paint the walls and hang the wallpaper, but more importantly, she stenciled and will do the faux wood graining on the baseboards if we find under the paint that they were originally that way. And the best thing in the house is Stella's mural. I can't wait for you to see it."

"A mural? What of?"

"The original Dunham plantation, Hudson River Valley style." Jennifer leaned back with a satisfied smile as Bryan glanced at her in surprise.

"I encouraged her to finish it in time for your visit," Barbara added. "I knew it would make the best impression in person rather than in a photograph."

So on a roll now Jennifer forgot to be uncomfortable in her scarf-and-earrings ensemble, she went on, "Yes, there's so much that is not done that I wish was, like the floor refinishing and of course the decorating, but we've only been at it since March. I hope to have everything under wraps here by December, in case I'm selected for the job on the coast. I trust I can send you photos up through your publication date?"

"Mmmm." Bryan sliced his tenderloin. "The drop date is October 1. I could only accept photos through mid-August. Our layout crew gets really crabby when we try to narrow their working window."

"I understand."

"We're just so thankful you decided to feature us," Barbara intoned.

He gave a nod in her direction. "But it sounds, Jennifer, like you've already invested your heart in this project. How hard will it be to leave?"

His question took her off guard. As the faces of those who had already grown so familiar flashed through her mind, she shoved back any sadness and lifted a shoulder. "I mean, it's a job, right?" She picked up her fork and sliced its prongs into the quiche, releasing a puff of steam.

Bryan did not look convinced by her show of disinterest.

CHAPTER THREE

Since Bryan would leave in his rental car straight for the airport, they all drove to Hermon separately. That gave Jennifer more time to think about whether or not to relate the story of Georgia Pearl. Michael had given her permission if it proved helpful. His grandmother Gloria had not known how to fix her mother's mistakes except by leaving Georgia Pearl's childhood home to her grandson upon her own death. Since he'd lost his mother Linda early to cancer and his grandmother quite recently, Michael's maternal past required some deep emotional processing. For reasons Jennifer still did not completely understand, apart from his father, Michael struggled to let people in. He'd now opened up to Stella and Earl and was getting to know their two teenage sons and extended family. Could delving into the still raw past jeopardize that in any way?

By the time Jennifer pulled into the house, she had decided not to raise the story with the reporter. He would have plenty to chew on with what she'd already given him. If he asked if Hampton Dunham had married and had a family, she'd tell the truth, but no more than necessary. She knew what it felt like when people pried in sensitive areas.

He did not. Dunham House's eclectic mix of architectural styles captured all Bryan's attention. He admired the triple-layer baseboard trim and thirteen-foot ceilings, approved of their paint palate and verified possession of usable photographs of the original back three rooms' enclosed gables, verifying 1840s dating. Yes, he agreed that the kitchen had probably been brought up from the rear of the lot and attached to the then-two-room structure before the family added the front part of the house and porch with fancy curlicue millwork.

Jennifer related how, in keeping with a bachelor's residence, they planned to decorate to enhance the earlier, simplified period, rather than the later Victorian. She neglected to mention how she and Michael had fought over the "girly" 1870s carved mantels in the front parlor and bedroom, although she thought she caught a glimpse of humor shining from said bachelor's eyes as he looked at them during the tour, leaning against the doorframe with his arms crossed.

Bryan took a number more photos from artsy rather than educational angles. When he saw Stella's mural, he asked if they could call and ask her to come over. "Tell her to bring a couple of her paintings along if she can," he added.

Jennifer hoped Bryan did not notice Barbara's poorly veiled impatience. While Barbara had indeed suggested Stella put in extra hours in order to finish the mural before the journalist's visit, even mentioning that it could open up future opportunities for Stella, Barb's past comments indicated a disdain for the African American woman based on her conservative Christian faith.

A bemused Stella agreed to an interview. While they waited on her to arrive, Jennifer retrieved Stella's oil-based likeness of Hermon from Michael's walk-in closet. She'd purchased the painting from Mary Ellen's shop unbeknownst to Stella. When the tall, stately woman arrived, garbed as usual in clothing that conveyed bright elegance, she looked both surprised and touched to see her own framed creation leaning against the front porch table. She sent Jennifer a scolding look and leaned the print Jennifer had admired while visiting Stella's home, of unused railroad tracks fading into an autumn sunset, against Jennifer's. Of course, her natural modesty dictated that she bring only one piece of artwork. She shook Bryan's hand.

James and Michael had furnished the porch with wicker rockers, providing more places to sit than just the original swing.

"Can I get you a drink, Stella? Bryan?" James asked the two as they sat on either side of the table. He switched on the ceiling fan to stir the liquid of afternoon humidity.

They both agreed to the drinks.

Jennifer hovered long enough to hear Stella relate her early training at UGA followed by her sporadic teaching of local art lessons while staying home as the mom of Gabe and Jamal. Jennifer gestured to Barb, who rose without hesitation to trail Jennifer and the men down one of the two unusual parallel hallways inside the house. Jennifer wrung her hands in happy nervousness. "This is good, right? His interest in Stella?"

"Sure it is," Michael said, setting out glasses while his dad retrieved a pitcher of lemonade from the fridge. "Barbara?"

"Yes, please."

"Oh, I've got a glass for you. I meant the interview. Do you think it's going well?"

She cleared her throat. "Exceedingly well."

Jennifer glanced from one to the other. The subtle prodding of each other they'd mastered created greater tension than encounters between Barb and Stella, who merely refused to be drawn into innuendo or insult. "It's getting late, and we haven't even shown him the apothecary yet. While they're busy talking, I wonder if I should run up to the store and order dinner at the grill."

"No need, I've got it under control," James said.

"You do? You mean you're going to make dinner?"

The slim but wiry older man smiled mysteriously. "Just leave it to me. You ladies do what you need to for the tour."

Jennifer found James' use of the term "ladies" a bit on the generous side. Anyone could see she was a frump while Barb was a cookie cutter feminist. But for reasons she didn't fully understand, she kind of liked him more for it.

James dismissed Barbara and Jennifer with a tray of full lemonade glasses. She heard him talking to Michael as she and Barbara returned to the porch. Barbara gave her an eyebrows-raised, mouth-down expression that said if the men pulled off any sort of worthy dinner, she'd be impressed.

Post-lemonade, Bryan photographed Stella's artwork before they took him to the apothecary fronting the main road. Stella headed home. Brushing aside yet another new spider web and unlocking the door of the three-room, white frame shop, Jennifer announced, "This is the next big challenge that lies before us."

Bryan scribbled in his notebook. "So you've pretty well got the house in shape, once you get the floors refinished and decorate. Phase two is the apothecary, and phase three ..."

"The log cabin, which we will move into the pecan grove this fall."

The door swung open, and the writer peered into the dim interior, saying, "Wow."

Jennifer had responded almost identically during her initial visit. The curved shelving, now a fading shade of puce green, with the mid-range drawers labeled with various vial sizes, fitted into curved walls of disintegrating plaster. Narrow lathing peeked from beneath. The green compounding desk with mustard yellow inset panels stood slightly to one side. Bryan whisked out his camera. Jennifer explained the middle room had been used for exams, while the rear room, once warmed by a now-removed fireplace, had been used for sleeping quarters and storage. Following the apothecary's operational period, it had also served as a makeshift garage for the 1945 Cadillac of spinster Ettie Mae, a descendant of Anne Dunham Maxwell, the last family member to occupy the house before it became a rental. They discussed their plans to clean the ceilings of kerosene lamp and coal fire soot, replaster, blow in insulation, wire for electricity, refinish and repaint the shelving, and refinish the floors. They would also replace the rotted boards in the middle of the rear room, at the same time they exchanged the tacked-on addition on the back wall for Hardiplank.

"And all this work will be done by local crews?" Bryan asked.

"Yes, just as everything has: the fireplaces, the painting, the replacement of the metal roofs on both buildings, the landscaping. Next week I'm going to the local nursery to purchase heirloom varieties of roses and quince. Then I'll be consulting with a local herbal expert about getting a medicinal herb garden started behind the apothecary. Every person, every crew, has done excellent work. And it's neat to see how people take pride in the place. It's like they know it's giving the community ... not a face lift really... but a focal point."

Bryan nodded and smiled. "I wish I could be here to see it when it's all done."

"Well, you'll just have to come back and visit," Barb said.

"I just might. What will the apothecary be used for?"

Jennifer sobered. "They're not sure yet."

"May I suggest they keep it relevant to the building? A history museum, a tea shop, an herb shop. You just mentioned a local herbalist?" He raised his eyebrows by way of suggestion.

"Yes." Jennifer recalled her conversation with Michael about landscaping, when she'd first highlighted the importance of planting a medicinal herb garden. "Michael likes his privacy, but he did indicate he wouldn't be completely closed to the idea of a shop of some sort ... if we can find someone else to run it."

"Yes, I'd recommend you look into that. Let's walk down to the downtown," Bryan said.

Barbara chortled at his word choice but refrained from commenting in the face of the esteemed writer's burst of enthusiasm.

"Sure," Jennifer agreed as she let them out and locked up. They strolled just off the main road past the antique store and post office. "Do you want to go in?" she offered a little lamely as they passed Mary Ellen's.

"No, just looking."

"That's Rita Worley's beauty shop across the street, and up the road a piece toward Crawford, they have a grill inside the convenience store. Then there's city hall."

Bryan shaded his eyes to gaze at the unimpressive, tiny cement block building with the impressive title. "That's it?"

"Yep. And the depot next to it."

"What's the depot used for?"

"I hear the local historical organizations are raising funds to restore it."

"It would make a great museum, and more town meeting space."

"Agreed."

He paused in front of the only other building on the Hermon strip, a two-story brick building with boarded-up front windows and remains of glass on the sidewalk. "What's this?"

"This was the Gillen's Department Store. It had the first elevator in the county, believe it or not."

"You ever been in there?"

Jennifer shook her head, surprised her curious nature had not yet lured her here on an evening walk, despite her busy schedule.

Barbara tried the door. In amazement, she pulled and said, "It's unlocked."

The three adults grinned like explorers discovering remains of a lost civilization. For a moment no one moved because they couldn't decide who should go through the portal first. In respect for authority, Jennifer stood back while Barbara held the door for Bryan. Inside, Jennifer gasped and Bryan removed the cap on his camera lens.

"This is great," he said as he began to photograph a rusted iron staircase that ascended partway to the second story before splitting into two directions, leading to balconies on either side. "Gutted, but great."

They moved carefully through glass and remains of old boards. In the absence of partitions or other rooms on the bottom story, they studied the floor above and speculated as to its sturdiness.

"It almost looks like a hotel. I wish we could see upstairs," Jennifer said.

"I wouldn't chance that stairway until someone evaluated it," Barb told her.

Bryan wanted to know why no one had purchased the building.

"Stella said the owners are asking an arm and a leg for it."

"A shame. The structure is sound and possesses such character. Imagine all the uses," Bryan speculated. "Event facility, dance studio, art gallery, specialty boutique, tea room."

Jennifer agreed with all of those, but two in particular reverberated in her head as they closed up and headed back to the house. She asked Bryan some questions, and he and Barb provided suggestions and estimates regarding renovation cost. Finally, as they crossed the yard of Dunham House, she told the writer that James was counting on him to stay for dinner before he hit the road. "Do you have time before your flight?"

Bryan glanced at his watch as they entered the front door. "Uh …" He sniffed, and at the wonderful aroma wafting from the kitchen, perked up. "Sure!"

They found paper goods stacked on the counter and Michael closing up the grill on the back porch and entering with a tray of grilled corn on the cob, while James uncovered BBQ ribs, garden green beans and rolls. "We're still not fully stocked in here, but with smart use of the grill, I hope this is presentable," James told them.

"Oh, my goodness, yes!" Jennifer exclaimed.

"This looks like my second great Southern meal of the day," Bryan murmured.

Barbara just looked surprised.

James chuckled. "Well, don't thank me, I'm not the grill master. And wait until you see what's for dessert. Montana dropped by one of her pineapple upside down cakes while you were gone, said it was left over from the sale and she wanted to say thank you to Jennifer."

"Aw, did she say how it went?"

"The pineapple cake was *all* that was left, and she has orders for two events next week."

Jennifer clasped her hands together. "Oh, that's so wonderful!"

Michael smiled at her and gave a nod. The approval she thought she saw in his eyes made her joy skyrocket past the white bead board ceiling, the one he'd finally agreed not to refinish and caulk at her bequest.

"Well, why don't I bless this food?" James suggested. "This man has a plane to catch."

Barbara looked uncomfortable but bowed her head as James launched into a hearty prayer. Jennifer peeked, afraid James' assumption about her newfound shared faith might offend the visitor. Bryan peeked, too, but smiled in an indulgent manner. He gave her a nod to show that all was well. Barbara, however, frowned with her eyes closed.

"Well? How do you think it went?" Michael asked after they had waved both the professor and the writer off from the driveway, refueled for their respective journeys with the fresh, simple and good.

Jennifer released all her lingering tensions and expressed her heartfelt gratefulness in a big sigh. "Wonderful. It was like it was ... blessed."

Michael smiled at her. "'Blessed' is exactly how I would expect your first weeks as God's child to feel."

She glanced at him as a sudden chill purled through her. "Are you telling me to batten down the hatches, because it won't last?" She hoped not, but that was exactly what she had expected.

He shifted his weight. "I'm telling you that I think God would be in agreement that you're overdue for some blessing."

"And you?"

"Maybe me, too." Michael looked thoughtful, like a battle waged in his head. "But He's relentless, you know."

Why did he persist in making vague statements that fomented her unease? "What do you mean?"

"I mean that unless you totally shut Him down and shut Him out, He doesn't stop until He gets you where He wants you." He paused. The troubled expression clouding her face caused him to do something uncharacteristic, reach out and touch her arm. He shook his head. "Never mind. I'm glad your day went well, and you should enjoy it. Go get some rest. You've got another early morning tomorrow if you're going to church with Stella and Earl."

Jennifer nodded, but remained standing where she was.

"Is there something else?"

She smiled. "Can I have the cat back now?"

CHAPTER FOUR

The early 1870s apothecary listed slightly to one side. In a previous walk-through, Jennifer had discussed with the men what they would repair versus replace. Of course, after they leveled the foundation, task number one was to remove the messy addition tacked on in Ettie Mae's day. They would install Hardiplank for the rear wall, then replace the rotted boards of that back room. On the other end of the building, the full-length green shutters needed to be removed, mended and repainted by experts. Michael and James felt capable of using their table and skill saws to recreate missing sections of the curlicue millwork on the front porch. After that, Stella would paint the trim according to Jennifer's diagram of which sections original paint flecks revealed to be white or green. The cords and weights in the double-hung, sash-weighted front windows needed to be replaced. And the worn down condition of the side window's muntins demanded that they locate a substitute, no easy task. Once they took the outside details in hand, they could begin work on the interior of the apothecary.

Now James prepared to jack up the building and add stones to the pilings as needed, but first it made sense to empty the place of leftover paraphernalia. Since Michael would run the sander on the floors of the house before Stella completed her work on the baseboards, creating an atmosphere akin to a mini-dust bowl, the chosen location to stash the medical items was Jennifer's spare bedroom. Before being stored, the dusty bric-a-brac required a good cleaning. Taking advantage of the day's clear, hot weather, she and James decided to carry everything to the side of the house next to the water hose, where Jennifer had piled soap, sponges and quilts.

First they removed the vials and small jars from the drawers in the front room. "Some of these look pretty cool with the old medicines dried in the bottom," Jennifer remarked. "I believe this is mercury. I think I'll just clean around the outsides and tops of these." Next came the few larger jars, then the rough canes and walking sticks they'd found. While they were at it, they pulled a spring bird nest out from the front wall behind the plaster.

Together they carried the antique reclining examining chair out the rear door, avoiding the caved-in center of the room. Jennifer intended great care in wiping it down, removing years of dust and spider webs. Little else remained in the small middle chamber.

The rear room contained a rough cabinet with glass doors on the top, drawers in the middle and cupboards on the bottom. To Jennifer's disappointment, with the exception of a few legs-up roaches and winged insects, she opened each to reveal … nothing. Jennifer remarked when she peered into the bottom component, "Look, James, at these wooden pegs attached to the wall where they must have hung up clothing."

The older man bent over next to her. "Interesting."

"Do you want to try to move this out, too?"

"No, since it's open to the back I think it will be easy to move around the room as needed when we're working in here. But I'm afraid we must have a go at that crate." He turned to face a large Victrola box sitting on the floor across the room, a picture of a dog with a cocked head listening to the device on the side along with the wording, "From Bernstein Bros, Athens, GA," and "Value $125."

If Jennifer remembered right from her first tour of the apothecary, bamboo runners wrapped inside the crate cradled a mouse nest. She approached and wrinkled her nose. "And I'm afraid these are in no condition for anything but the trash heap."

"Agreed."

"I'd like to keep the crate, though. It has character and could be used for other things."

"Also agreed. I'll do the honors in case any friends remain within that we haven't run off yet." James pulled on his work gloves and lifted out a roll of the runners, trash and dust flying. Holding the mess at arms' length, he made two trips to the burn pile without any appearance of varmints. Jennifer lugged the crate to the side of the house. Standing over the water hose, a thought struck her, and she bolted back to the apothecary looking for James.

"I can't believe I didn't think of this sooner," she told him, breathless and sweating, "especially after we learned with Georgia Pearl's story how we shouldn't take things at initial appearance. And because it's a cardinal rule of restoration."

"What?" James demanded, a little exasperated with her roundabout manner of speech.

"Leave no corner unexplored. The attic!"

James' face brightened. "Of course. They may have stored things up there! Maybe even valuable medical supplies."

"And another huge consideration is that if the main floor is dirty, the attic must be filthy. It would do us little good to clean down here only to have silt and dust filtering down forever through the ceiling!"

"I'll need to fetch my ladder. The only access is a latched opening in the back room."

Minutes later, James thrust his upper torso through said aperture, wielding an industrial-sized flash light. Jennifer could hardly tolerate the suspense. She bounced on her toes. "What do you see?"

"Tons and tons of the blackest dirt possible."

Oh, disappointment. Jennifer said, "My guess is that the smoke from coal fires settled through the original wooden shakes on the roof. Between that and the soot from the lamps on the ceilings, a lot of cleaning awaits us. Is that really all you see up there?"

"Uh, sadly. Wait, something is in the back corner." James put down his light in preparation to continue his climb.

"You should let me go. I'm lighter."

"It's OK, I'm already up, and by my assessment the boards are quite sound."

As soon as his body cleared, Jennifer climbed the rungs herself until she could see. She needed a mental image of the space if only to assure herself James did not overlook any hidden treasures. He was right about the dirt, and the heat waves assailed her like a sauna. The arch of light from his flashlight sluiced over a metal child's bed in the front corner. And for a second, Jennifer thought she saw the shadowy form of a little girl with coffee-colored skin seated on the filthy ticking, her hair in nubs and a finger in her mouth.

"Oh, my stars!" She blinked hard and looked again.

James froze in front of the bed, which was most definitely empty. "What?" he asked in a strained voice.

"It's—nothing. I just—thought I saw …"

"Saw what?"

"I could almost imagine a little girl sitting there on that bed. I imagined it so well, it almost looked real."

James turned back to her, and by the expression on his face, Jennifer could bet the hair on the back of his neck stood up just like hers. "Imagined? Or *saw*?"

"Imagined. Of course. I'm sorry, I'm not usually given to fanciful impulses like that. Why, you didn't see anything, did you?"

"No, but right when you spoke, I felt this intense, cold chill." He glanced back at the bed. "I don't know whether to leave it or bring it down now."

"Bring it down, of course. It might be useful in a display. It's just being wasted up here."

After they shifted and tugged the tiny bed out of the attic, James closed up the opening with an expression that bordered on relief.

"Well, we definitely have to clean the attic first," Jennifer said with dismay.

James wiped his sweaty face with the back of his arm. "You know what I'm thinking? Let's see if Stella's boys want to make a little above their normal wage."

Given the hallucination she'd just suffered, Jennifer was in no mood to argue. She helped James carry the bed out into the bright sunshine. After taking the smallest items from the apothecary to the kitchen sink to clean, she ran the hose on a gentle spray setting over everything else, then wiped the relics with a soft sponge sudsy with gentle, organic liquid soap. The mattress she sprayed, soaped, then sprayed again, rivers of dirt running out onto the pine straw. She was completing her rinse cycle, enjoying the cool water dripping down her hot, bare legs, when a shadow fell over her. She jumped, surprised to see a tall, slender woman with a similar casual retro sense of fashion to Jennifer's, her long, gray hair drawn back into a pony tail.

The fifty-something woman stuck her hand out. "Hi, I'm Allison Winters. You must be Jennifer."

Jennifer responded with ease to Allison's confident but earthy, humble manner. "Yes, I am. Oh, Allison, I must apologize, I quite forgot Michael told me you were coming today." Jennifer paused to shake the newcomer's hand, realizing this was the local herbal expert she had asked Michael to contact. "But I'm so happy to meet you!"

"You, too! Are these things all out of the apothecary?"

"Yes, aren't they cool?"

Allison knelt to pick up a bottle. "They sure are."

"We just discovered the little bed up in the attic. James is getting ready to jack up the foundation, so we're moving this stuff into my double-wide for the time being. It's actually great timing to walk over to the apothecary and see the place, once I get everything spread out to dry in the sun."

"Oh, let me help you. When we're done, I can lend a hand to take things to your house."

"That would be great, thanks!"

A few minutes later, they paused on the way to the apothecary to admire the antique climbing roses freshly planted by Jennifer on the trellis archway. Inside the shop, James, having traded his ladder for a broom, knocked down the latest infestation of spider webs. Jennifer made introductions.

"I've never been in here. This is awesome," Allison declared. James filled her in on their renovation plans, and she added, "It will be a one-of-a-kind place, that's for sure. Will you be looking for more items to stock this room? Kind of create a museum in here?"

James leaned on the handle of the broom. "Well, I hate to say it, Ms. Winters, but we haven't really decided yet. I do know my son doesn't care to maintain a museum."

"Well, it would be a shame to just let it set empty."

"I agree."

"I wanted to ask if *you* had any ideas, Allison," Jennifer put in tentatively. "I know you're an expert on herbs, and you both write about them and grow them to sell, but have you ever considered opening a shop?"

The make-up-free brown eyes in Allison's tanned face opened wide. "Here?"

Jennifer cut a glance at James. "Well, I haven't spoken to James and Michael about it yet, because there would be no need to unless you had an interest." She decided this was as good a time as any to float her ideas, since James normally proved more civic-minded than his son. When it came to being a loner, Michael shared more in common with Calvin Woods than, say, Rita Worley or Mary Ellen McWhorter. "Bryan Holton, the magazine writer who just visited, suggested the building retain its original purpose, or as close to it as possible. Couldn't you see this place as a museum-slash-herb shop? I mean, there's this huge demand for organic and natural remedies now, right?"

"For sure," Allison agreed.

"I could keep my eye out for a few period pieces, like scales, a mortar and pestle, a surgeon's blade set, old thermometers ... just to recreate the atmosphere. But wouldn't it be neat if someone stocked modern herbals here, along with stuff like organic hand creams and scented soaps and even teas? And maybe some books on related subjects and local history? Another idea is to have a live herb and flower sale once a month under a tent on the grounds. So much could be done. And it would be a perfect complement to the antique store, not competition." In the ecstasy of her vision, Jennifer rubbed her hands together, and she couldn't help beaming.

"You, my dear, are an entrepreneur at heart," James declared.

"Then you don't hate it?"

"No, I don't hate it at all. And I think if someone else had run of the place, Michael might be open to the idea as well."

Jennifer turned back to Allison, who looked pensive. "Well? Will you think about it? Maybe if it's not something you'd like to do, you'd know of someone else to run a business along those lines?"

Allison laughed and smoothed her hands down the front of her multi-pocketed gray capris. "It's funny, but what you described is exactly what I've always dreamed of, only it's never seemed practical. You know I even make my own soaps and teas. I've set up booths before at festivals, farmer's markets and plant sales. But I live out in the country in the Wolfskin area, no place for a shop, and rent in town is always so high. I guess it depends what you gentlemen would charge."

James pursed his lips. "I'll talk it over with Michael, but I'd think the amount would be very reasonable, just enough to help with maintenance. Seems to me such a venture would be a great community asset and would allow the public access to a building that needs to be appreciated."

Allison bit her lip, which Jennifer took as a sign of repressed enthusiasm. Practicality would come first with her pragmatic nature. "It's not something I could consider full-time. I'm quite busy with my writing and lecturing, not to mention my own nursery at home."

"I would think Thursdays through Saturdays would be adequate, don't you?"

Allison nodded, allowing her pleasure to break through with a smile. "I could do that."

"Now if Michael will just agree," Jennifer murmured.

"Best time to approach him would not be now, but first thing in the morning after he's had his coffee." James grinned. "We can do it together."

"Then we'll put this discussion on hold until we've spoken with Michael," Jennifer told Allison, "and for now we'll get around to the reason you came, which is the herb garden."

They excused themselves from James and walked around to the back of the house, where they discussed how a garden set farther back from the apothecary would leave an area free to gravel for parking. Allison used stones to mark off a plot that suited her, part sun and part shade, and went on about which plants would need which. She whipped out a pocket notebook and drew a sketch with numbers representing plants and a key where she wrote in the species, including yarrow, thyme, garlic, pennyroyal, fennel, peppermint, rosemary, comfrey, and medicinal flowers such as foxglove, peonies and poppy.

"In the woods, if we don't find local specimens like Joe Pye weed and butterfly root, I can bring some native species to transplant. A short trail with the plants marked would be quite educational."

"That's a great idea!"

"In fact, why don't we just take a little trek right now so I'll know what to add to my list. You don't mind a few weeds, do you?"

"Uh, of course not," Jennifer said, although she eyed the full-blown summer underbrush with skepticism. She had not forgotten her encounter with the huge rattler in the ramshackle outhouse now scheduled for demolition, not to mention ticks, spiders, poison oak and ivy, all waiting to rub on her lower extremities currently exposed by shorts and sandals. But Allison, who wore tennis shoes and out-of-style, long socks even with her capris—*were they men's socks?*—forged into the wilderness, not looking back. With caution, Jennifer followed, thankful that at least here near the apothecary and house the woods remained relatively open.

"Aha, see this clover-looking stuff?" Allison called, pointing to the ground. "Oxalis, very common in this area. Dr. Dunham called it common wood sorrel."

"Wait, you're familiar with the Dunham doctors? Which one are you referring to?"

"Why, yes, I put together a book of his receipts. *The* Dr. Dunham would be Silas, of course, although the doctor who practiced in the 1870s here in Hermon would have been William. He's the one who built the apothecary."

Jennifer scrambled to keep up. "But how do you know that? Is that documented somewhere? Everything I saw was very vague as to what the Dunham sons did and when."

"Yes, there was some overlap with where the sons practiced. Most of what I know is by word of mouth. I talked to a lot of the old natives about the history and receipts from this area."

The way Allison said "receipts" made it sound like she'd compared sales tickets at the counter of the local food mart with these people, but Jennifer realized the modern word would be "recipes," or medically speaking, "prescriptions."

"Look here." Allison bent to pluck something from near her feet and extended two types of leaves for Jennifer to appreciate. "These make a great salad, or 'salat' as they called it in colonial times. The wild lettuce has jagged leaves. The smoother one is sow thistle. The early settlers knew how to search these woods and creek beds for what would help sustain them. They learned more from the Creek Indians. It was a starvation existence at times. They took nothing for granted. Everything had more than one use."

Jennifer felt hopelessly lost. Despite her education on ornamental landscaping, if she were tossed out in the wilderness and forced to survive on her own, she'd have little idea what to eat or not to eat, besides the most obvious nuts and berries. Her ignorance on the topic proved sobering.

Allison went on, further animated by the discovery of rabbit tobacco or "life everlasting," a biennial plant called white plantain by the colonists and used as an infusion or tea for lung troubles. Jennifer wondered if this was how she sounded to normal people, even Michael, when she spouted about American Empire scroll legs, Gothic spindles and Italianate cornices. She resolved to speak plain English to him as much possible.

Later that day, apothecary treasures stored safely away in her spare room and Yoda playing with a ball at her feet, that intention remained uppermost in her mind as she printed out a collage of pictures representing three decorating styles in keeping with the period of his house: American Empire, Rococo Revival and Gothic Revival. She felt almost a hundred percent sure what he would go for, although she hoped he might prove open to incorporating touches of a secondary choice authentic to the eclectic spirit of Dunham House. Her collages of each style included pictures of whole rooms as well as individual pieces of furniture, decorations and artwork. She took extra time hand-labeling features typical of each style so that he would know what to look for in selecting pieces.

Jennifer planned to do most of the shopping but hoped detailed knowledge would increase Michael's sense of ownership. Maybe she could even convince him to embrace antique hunting with her occasionally. The idea of shopping for anything with Michael generated an uncomfortable tingle of awareness, maybe because that was something couples did. Still, it could be fun, if they could get past the awkward. Pleasantly contemplating the idea, she fed Yoda, put her in her cat carrier with the door open, and was about to settle down for a good night's rest preparatory to her morning presentation when her phone dinged.

She went to retrieve it, half afraid it would be Barbara again. To her delight, it was Mary Ellen, issuing an official invitation for a Coke and peanuts break at her shop the following afternoon. She included Stella in the text. Jennifer smiled. Perfect timing. First, following her meeting with Michael, Jennifer would know exactly what type of furnishings to seek, and Mary Ellen could provide her starting point. Second, since her attention must now be focused on the apothecary, Jennifer missed the visits she used to enjoy while painting alongside Stella inside the house. Besides those practical reasons, Jennifer found it refreshing to have someone else initiate something, just for the pleasure of her company. Even in college, most of her social outings had occurred because she tagged along on other people's plans.

Jennifer fell asleep with a smile but jerked awake to a horrible howling in her back yard. She sat bolt upright and spied Yoda's little eyes gleaming at her from inside the open cat crate. Otis again. She waited. Otis bayed. And she stomped over to her dresser to put on a bra under her tank top. Shoving her feet into slippers, Jennifer let herself out the back door. Someone shouted over at Michael's house. She jogged through the Leyland Cypress trees to behold three male figures congregated on and around the front porch.

"What in heaven's name is your stupid dog doing?" Michael's disembodied voice demanded from near the swing. Beside him, James handed him a flashlight, which he shined below him on a bathrobe-bedecked, balding Calvin, who attempted to get a leash around Otis' thick neck. This proved impossible, as the dog bobbed and lunged in frantic digging.

"My quince bush!" Jennifer wailed, darting forward. "He's ruined it!"

Indeed, the rare and expensive bush listed precariously, but Calvin took exception to her blame. "It wasn't him that did it, it was the — armadillo," he cursed. "It's done tunneled under there, and Otis is just tryin' to dig him out."

"Oh, no! No, no, no! The whole bed is destroyed!" Jennifer cried as she noticed pine straw strewn everywhere.

"These armadillos have been here forever. They don't care if you make pretty beds and buy expensive bushes," Calvin told her. "I saw babies in the spring. Four from a single egg. They multiply like rabbits. If you want to get rid of 'em, you're gonna have to hunt 'em. Trap 'em."

Michael came down from the porch and aided Mr. Woods in seizing the digging dog by the upper body, dragging his nose out of the dirt long enough to leash him. "Well, your dog is not helping. If you would keep him tied, we might not all be out here right now."

Woods fumed and huffed, "He stays inside with me, and I gotta let him out to the bathroom some time, now don't I? I can't help it if them varmints happen to be carryin' on when he goes out. And he pulls right off any stake or run line when armadillos are near. I don't want him sick on their account, so I don't want him over here anymore than you do. I been killin' 'em off with my .22 on my land. You're gonna have to take care of 'em on yours."

"Well, what do the local folk do to get rid of them?" James inquired.

The hermit repeated his previous advice to Jennifer. "Put a bullet between their beady eyes."

"But how can we know when they're coming?" Jennifer asked.

"You don't. You sit up and wait to hear 'em rooting about, generally between midnight and three."

"The witching hour," Michael reflected grimly.

James laughed, but Calvin just grunted and said, "Yes, Sir, they are straight from hell, I can tell you that. You don't want to tangle with 'em. They carry all sorts of disease, including leprosy, although most generally they just run away. They can run fast, too, and jump head-high straight up in the air."

A snort escaped from Jennifer. She covered her face.

Calvin turned to her. "You don't believe me? You'll see. You want help taking 'em out, I can call my nephews from down south in the county. They got experience."

"Surely that's a little extreme," Jennifer said. "Isn't there just some way to keep them out of the landscaping?"

Calvin tugged Otis back to his feet, where the dog finally crouched, exhausted, heaving deep breaths through his clay-encrusted snout. The owner scratched his head. "Some tries moth balls, but I can't say as I've seen that work. You can buy traps at the local hardware store. You hang earthworms in a pair of ladies' hose to lure 'em in, then the door shuts on 'em. But I've seen 'em get outta those, too."

"According to you, these creatures are almost magical, Mr. Woods," Michael observed.

"Laugh all you want, they're a curse like the foxes in the vineyard in the Good Book," Calvin retorted, tugging his dog away with him. He threw over his shoulder, "Come see me when you want them boys to come out."

CHAPTER FIVE

"The nine-banded armadillo," Michael announced the next morning when she found him in his camper. His laptop sat on the table in front of him, his router winking a reassuring rhythm attesting to nearby civilization. He lifted weary eyes to gaze at her as she entered and closed the spring-loaded door. "Calvin wasn't lying, about the quadruplets, or the jumping, or the leprosy."

"Yea," Jennifer responded in a flat tone. "I saw the damage. It wasn't just that one section. They tore through the ivy and the azaleas in that back bed as well."

"I know. I'll go out and fix it when I finish this cup of coffee. Want some?"

She sat down opposite him, sliding her folder onto the table. "Just had some." Annoying how being unshaven and bleary-eyed in no way decreased the appeal of the man's dark good looks. With a gold hoop earring and a few more inches of hair he could pose as a pirate on the cover of a Harlequin romance. By contrast, the tender skin under Jennifer's eyes puffed from lack of a single night's sleep, something even her thick glasses could not hide. "I can help you in the yard."

"It's no problem."

"I can help."

He glared at her. "Fine then, tough girl."

She shrugged that off. She'd heard a lot worse and would prefer to be thought tough than weak any day. "Actually I'm glad to find you here. I wanted to talk with you about a couple of things."

"Uh-oh."

Jennifer eyed his almost-empty coffee cup. And James was not present to support her. On a whim, she grabbed the coffee pot for a refill and decided to launch into a summary of her meeting with Allison Winters. She concluded by introducing the notion of an herbal shop. "Your father kind of liked the idea," she said as Michael finished stirring in sugar and cream and took a sip of the fresh brew.

"He did, did he? Imagine that."

"You can see how advantageous it would be to the community to have the apothecary open and something available there people actually want to buy. It would require almost no oversight from you, and Allison would only be open at the end of the week."

"I like Allison. She's low key."

Jennifer twined her fingers on the table before her and smiled hopefully. "So you'll consider it?"

"I suppose I'd be footing the cost of graveling a drive and parking lot over there."

She bit her lip, raised her brows and looked pleading.

"I'll think about it. What was the other thing?"

Deciding to leave the first topic percolating, she went on to the next subject at hand. "I wanted to talk to you about the interior theme of your house."

"The interior theme of my house," he repeated in the same tone she'd used to cheer about the armadillos. "Meaning what?"

"Meaning there are three influences on the furniture and décor from the 1840s, and I need to know which one you prefer before I look for furnishings. First of all, do you intend on moving a lot of furniture in that you already own?" She tried not to make it obvious that she held her breath.

Michael's mouth tightened. "I've sold the furnishings of my apartment, all but a few favorite pieces in storage. I'd like to bring those up, but it shouldn't be anything too upsetting to your plans. The sofa, recliner, TV and electronics can all go in the sunroom. Dad will bring a few family pieces, mostly end tables and occasional arm chairs, but he is renting his house in Lawrenceville partially furnished. Then there are the pieces you approved from Grandma's storage, pretty much more of the same, and that one four-poster bed."

"Ah, yes. That would probably go best in the front bedroom. I'd like to find a whole suite for the master." She paused, deciding whether to ask the question that formed on her tongue. It pressed its way out. "Did you and your dad rent the house out instead of selling it, thinking you might go back?"

To his credit, Michael smiled rather than clammed up. "The situation turned out perfect, actually. A missionary friend of dad's returned home on furlough and owned only a little furniture in storage here in the states. We had a big yard sale, reserving whatever that friend would need. Whatever didn't sell and he didn't want in the house, we donated. So yes, I guess we could go back to that house in the future if need be, but our plan was always to make a permanent change."

But they had retained a fail safe. Jennifer wasn't sure why that made her uncomfortable, since her job did not hinge on whether Michael stayed or not after the restoration was complete. "And if you stay, will you sell the house there?"

Michael nodded, one arched eyebrow the only sign of possible impatience with her line of questioning. "That's the plan, when that family returns to their assigned country."

What Michael and James did with their other property did not concern her, she reminded herself. Only the furniture did. "Very well. Let's look at some options." Jennifer opened her folder and laid page one in front of him. "Rococo Revival."

Michael looked down, and his eyes bugged out. "Good Lord."

"Since I'm a Christian now, I would appreciate it if you wouldn't toss that name around like that," Jennifer said. "And you shouldn't want to, either, if you also believe in Him like you say."

He glanced up, half-contrite and half-joking. "Yes, Mother."

Jennifer pursed her lips. "Anyway, some laminated rosewood and gilded mirrors should hardly evoke such a strong reaction."

"Oh, yes, they should. It looks like this furniture threw up on itself."

"Michael!"

"Sorry, but it does."

"You don't have to be so crass."

"Why are you getting onto me when you just showed me a picture of a mirror with a woman's bare bust at the top? It looked like it came from Belle Watling's establishment in 'Gone With the Wind.'"

Jennifer's mouth fell open. "You've watched 'Gone With the Wind'?"

He scowled at her. "It was an eighth grade history class assignment. Seriously, did you think for two minutes that I'd like any of this? After all I've said about not wanting to live in a doll house? After our fight over the mantels?"

"No." Jennifer snatched the page away and put another in its place. "But in the interest of historical accuracy, I wouldn't sleep well at night if I didn't present you with all the options. Gothic Revival."

Michael dragged the paper closer with a thumb. "Now you're trying to move me into a church!"

Jennifer sighed. "Yes, some of the influences are high church, but consider how reflective this style is of your house. Think about the stenciling Stella did in the office. The trefoil pattern was Gothic Revival, and you liked it. It was masculine, right? See the spindles on this mint julep cabinet? They're like those on the gables of your house. And this chair, it has the Gothic arches, the high points like your roof line, so common to the movement."

"And that chair looks like I couldn't sit in it for five minutes. It's got a perfectly straight wooden back, for crying out loud! Everyone who came over would think me some kind of self-righteous, wanna-be priest. They would expect to discover a penance closet with an altar and a whip."

"Don't be ridiculous."

In his trademark gesture of frustration, Michael ruffled his hair. Then he sighed and said, "Jennifer, I've told you I want you to mix antiques with easy living. Nothing fusty or unapproachable, either one. If you can't do better than this, I'm going to limit you to the apothecary and do the decorating myself."

Her eyebrows shot up in genuine alarm. "And fill the place with leather sofas and glass coffee tables?"

"Honestly? That's sounding better by the minute."

"How about this?" Jennifer placed her final suggestion sheet on top of the other one. She waited while Michael surveyed the leaf-carved arms of Girandole lighting fixtures, burl mahogany table tops with scrolled legs, beds with fluted canopy columns and heavy, masculine wardrobes in clean lines.

He leaned back. "I think your method of getting your way is kind of like a siege, leading with the big guns, then peppering me with infantry, and finally sending in a convoy under a white flag."

Jennifer laughed out loud. "These pieces come from a slightly earlier period whose influence lingered into the 1840s. So you can see American Empire mixing with your leather sofas and coffee tables?"

"Is that what this is called? Yeah, maybe, if you rein it in some. Any piece that makes a person do a double take is out of contention, understood?"

"Understood. But I don't have my way quite yet." Pressing her lips together, Jennifer reached over to slide the top paper slightly to one side so that a Gothic occasional table peeked out. "I won't rest at night if a house that would have been furnished in Gothic Revival doesn't have a least a few touches here and there. One or maybe two carefully meditated pieces per room would make an incredible statement."

"You and your sleeping at night. It's either the furniture or the armadillos."

"Let it be the armadillos, then." Sparkling, her eyes met his.

"Your size really throws people off, you know."

"Really? That's good. But you can see it, can't you? Admit it."

Michael sighed again. "Maybe." He pointed to a couple of the more exaggerated pieces. "Nothing like this. But I might accept a hint of Gothic influence, under the condition that you text me photos of anything of this nature you consider buying first."

"Done."

"I feel like I should pour you a drink."

"Maybe we need something stronger than coffee to get this day started," Jennifer joked.

She left her design notes in the camper while they went out to repair the beds. Stella stood by the front porch, eyeing Jennifer's quince with concern. "Heavens to Betsy, what went on here?" she asked, hands on the hips of fitted black jeans worn under a typically blousy shirt. Jennifer had never seen her wear shorts, even in the hottest weather. Stella said jeans were best for dragging around on the floor of a dirty house. When Stella dressed up, she wore long, flowing skirts or tailored church suits in solid, primary colors. Today, she carried a satchel Jennifer had not seen before.

"A midnight armadillo attack," Michael told her.

"That's what I was afraid of. Once you get 'em, they're mighty hard to get rid of. What's your battle plan?"

"Well, Calvin Woods was out here last night with his dog and told us we could try moth balls or traps. I figured I'd go for both. I'll run to the hardware store later today."

"You can try, honey. What you need to do is find where they've burrowed in under a house or building. Set the trap up right against the entrance."

Jennifer nodded. "What's in the satchel?"

Stella's features transformed from concern to delight. "I had a dinner last night, and y'all were busy at the apothecary, so I didn't get to tell you what I found before I left yesterday."

"What?" Jennifer's voice sounded breathless as she anticipated the next surprise the house yielded.

"I used a little stripper on a corner of the parlor baseboard. Modern paint comes off so much easier than the old kind. I was able to see without damagin' what was underneath that the trim was indeed faux grained, heart pine to look like walnut, just like you thought!"

Jennifer clasped her hands to her chest and bounced on her toes. "Oh, I knew it!"

Michael's response was a patient smile.

"Gettin' the paint off will take some time. Hopefully I can just repair nicks and go from there. But if bigger sections are damaged, you choose a base coat from the brightest hue in the wood. I have a brown-black glaze already, and I brought my tools to keep here just in case." Stella showed them the tin can she wrapped her graining tool around, along with her flogging brush. "You apply the pattern with a rockin' motion, then pat with the flat of the brush to give the grain follicles. I practiced at home to get back in the saddle."

"Oh, Stella, it's going to look great! I'll pop in to keep track of your progress."

After Stella went in to "see what the wood revealed today," Jennifer and Michael located a spot against the foundation of the last remaining slave cabin, which Barbara had called the cook's cabin in front of Stella. They replanted all the damaged bushes in hopes they would re-root and smoothed the pine straw before Michael headed to Lexington in his truck.

After sticking her head into the parlor to admire the wall of faux grained baseboard Stella had uncovered, Jennifer made sandwiches for herself, James and Stella, and kept one covered for Michael. He still had not returned when she went out to water the plants. She didn't trust the sprinkler system to saturate the newly replanted bushes and flowers. While dragging out the hose, she heard the rumble of an engine and assumed it to be Michael's F150. But when she looked up, an Explorer bumped to a stop next to the apothecary shop. Barbara? She was not expected today! Sure enough, her former professor stepped out, opened the back of the vehicle, and pulled on something large and heavy. Jennifer dropped the hose and jogged toward the front of the lot.

"Barbara? What are you doing?"

The older woman turned to her with an expression of joy. "Bringing you a huge surprise."

"What ...?" Jennifer walked around Barbara to behold a perfectly sized, nine-over-nine, circa 1870 window in the back of the Explorer, with muntins that stuck out just like they were supposed to. "Oh, my goodness, where did you get this?"

Barbara smirked. "I have a friend who works at the Hardeman-Tipps House in Athens. They recently renovated the schoolhouse that sits on the property and closed part of it off for special events. I recalled seeing some extra materials on site and remembered noticing what poor shape your apothecary's side window was in, so wa-*lah*!" She waved a hand.

"Uh, wow! How much do they want for it?"

Barb shook her head. "It's my gift."

"Barb, I can't let you do that."

"It's not up to you, now, is it?"

Jennifer put her hands on her hips. "*Michael* won't let you do that."

"Are you speaking for him now? There's been some progress if that's the case."

"No, but it's too much. I know they'll want to pay you."

"A 'thank you' will suffice."

"Thank you." Jennifer smiled and, with a vague sense of discomfort, leaned into the arms that Barbara held out. "I just don't understand why you would go to so much trouble."

"Then you really do need to get some new friends."

Jennifer stepped back and said, "I am."

Barbara didn't seem to appreciate that comment, but at just that moment, the F150 pulled into the driveway. When he saw them by the apothecary, Michael stopped the truck not far from the main road. Another truck that followed him barely had room to edge onto the driveway. Michael jumped out, trailed by Horace from the other truck, right as James headed across the yard from the house.

"This is really the happenin' place in town, hm?" Barb joked.

"Yeah, I guess. It's always like this. People stop by unannounced all the time," Jennifer told her. "I told you I haven't been lonely."

Barb eyed her. "No, I guess not."

"What do we have here?" James called out.

As Barb warmly greeted Horace, Jennifer explained about the window and said, "A surprise to see you today, Horace."

"Yeah, well, Amy knew I was coming out this way and sent me by with those swatches. You're to look them over and tell her which ones you prefer for the drapes in Michael's bedroom." So saying, the rotund, middle-aged man handed her a fabric booklet bound with a rubber band.

"Sure, the gold damask like we talked about."

"To coordinate with the golden-brown paint," Barbara supplied. She'd been on hand for the paint walk-through when Michael insisted on a plain palate rather than her period, room-by-room colors suggestion.

"Right." Michael winked at her. "So good to see you again, Barb."

Jennifer suppressed a chuckle at Barb's reaction to the wink—it bore a slight resemblance to the bowing up of an irritated cat—but as usual, James came to the rescue. "It's really thoughtful of you to bring the window. What can we pay you for that, and for your gas and time out here?"

Barbara waved a dismissive hand. "Oh, nothing, I told Jennifer. Just consider it my lasting mark on the project. Anyway, I have to have an excuse to drive out every now and then to see how things are coming." No one mentioned her recent visit with Bryan Holton. She glanced at Jennifer. "So what's next on your agenda?"

"Tomorrow I plan to wash down everything in that apothecary with soap and water," she said. "James swept, but it's just so filthy I can't imagine starting on anything in that condition. Care to come back for that?"

"Sure, if you need me."

"I was just kidding. It's not a job I'd wish on anyone else. I'll get started bright and early and have it all done by nightfall."

"Yes, you always did like everything neat and clean," Barb observed.

Jennifer paused. What did she mean by that? And whether she intended to reference the mental or physical, why advertise inside knowledge in front of these men? Was she put out that Jennifer hadn't accepted her offer to help? Regardless, the comment just didn't fit.

"Well, it sure was nice of you, and we thank you very much, don't we, Michael?" James said.

Michael hung his thumbs from the loops of his jeans and agreed, "Sure do."

"This will save us a boat load of looking around for a fit replacement."

"For sure." Barb chuckled. "These nine-over-nines are almost impossible to find. I can't imagine how much you'd have to pay to have one shipped here."

Jennifer shifted in embarrassed silence, then noted Stella approaching across the yard. The arrival of anyone else would have broken the awkwardness of the moment, but given the situation, the best they could hope for was Stella diverting Barb's negativity. Smelling like chemicals and sporting flecks of white on her shirt, the painter smiled as she joined them. "Hi there, everyone. Dr. Shelley. What an awesome window you've brought."

"Is something wrong, Stella?" James asked, surprised to see her.

"Not at all. Jennifer and I are supposed to meet Mary Ellen next door now."

"Oh!" Having completely forgotten the time, Jennifer glanced at the watch hugging her petite wrist. "So we are, but Barb's just arrived."

"Well, I'll just have to go with you. I've been wanting to see the antique store for quite some time." Barbara smiled at them.

Horace took that as his dismissal, waving his hands as he backed toward his truck. "Well, don't let me keep you ladies. Good to see you again, Professor Barbara. You just give Amy a ring about those drapes, you hear, Jennifer? She'll get that fabric ordered pronto."

"I sure will. Thank you, Horace." She waved back as the real estate agent hobbled over to his truck as fast as a bad knee allowed, hoisted his weight into the cab, and reversed onto the main road.

"Well, Michael, let's unload this window into the apothecary until I can get it installed," James suggested.

"See you later," Jennifer told them as she led her two unlikely companions toward Hermon's antique store.

As the customer bell jangled their arrival, Mary Ellen hopped off her stool and came forward to be introduced to her unexpected guest. To her credit, she showed no surprise or displeasure, only welcome. But then again, as far as Mary Ellen was concerned, the more company or customers, the better. Today the antique store owner had drawn her thin brown hair back on each side with metal clips, and she wore a floral print shirt with brown slacks. Jennifer explained Barbara's visit as the professor tugged a Sprite from the squat, humming, old-fashioned vending machine on the wall. After popping off the cap, Barb made an assessing revolution through the crowded aisles before joining them at the tall counter.

"So I'm seein' more activity at the apothecary," Mary Ellen observed, popping a peanut into her mouth. She winked at Jennifer. "And I do mean *activity*."

Despite the curious gazes of Stella and Barb, Jennifer determined she would not allow embarrassment over the woman's implied double meaning to register on her face as she said, "Yes, that's the focus now." She went on to tell the women about her meeting with Allison Winters.

The last thing she needed was for Mary Ellen to launch into an account of the day she'd watched Michael and Jennifer talk, then hug, behind the apothecary. While Jennifer had called Stella that very night to relate what happened, Mary Ellen did not yet know the reason for the hug. Michael had led Jennifer in a prayer surrendering her life to Christ. At the moment, Jennifer couldn't guess which would solicit more contempt from her liberal professor, the fact that she had embraced Christianity or Michael! Barbara had warned her not to become romantically involved with her boss, but even more importantly, she provided frequent reminders that Jennifer did not need a man to complete her life. She would not take the hug as it had been intended.

"So Michael is considering the idea of Allison opening an herbal shop in the apothecary," she concluded. "What do y'all think?"

"I think it's an amazing idea," Stella agreed. "For a long time I've said how much this town needs a business in every building, especially when that Firefly Trail goes through."

"Oh, we checked out the old department store when Bryan Holton was here," Barbara put in, brushing a peanut skin off her slacks. "It holds a great deal of potential as well."

Jennifer nodded. "Yes, when Bryan said what he did about an art gallery, I thought of you, Stella. Wouldn't that be a fabulous place to host art shows and classes?"

Stella laughed deprecatingly. "Aw, honey, that's sweet, and yes, it would be beautiful, but I sure ain't got the money to buy and renovate the place."

"Well, you never know what the future holds," Mary Ellen said. "For now, I love the idea of the apothecary as an herb shop. Not to mention, it will bring more business in here as well!"

"What about you, Mary Ellen?" Jennifer asked. "Have you thought of ways you might lure more people in if the trail comes to town? Like ... maybe a coffee counter instead of just Cokes? And some pastries?"

"Well, that's a great idea, but how could I afford to set all that up? And learn to run it?"

"But if you could, would you?"

"I'd certainly give it a try."

Pleased, Jennifer nodded, not yet ready to say more.

Mary Ellen shook her head. "It's all fanciful thinkin', anyway, to imagine Hermon could be any place of interest. But if you can get that young man to agree to the notion of an herb shop, that would be a step in the right direction, and you'll have even more hold over him than I think you do."

Jennifer smiled and brought her shoulders up to her ears in an embarrassed shrug. "I kind of hoped you all could help convince him. I really don't have any extra influence. I already pushed my luck this morning with him."

"How so?" Barbara asked.

Jennifer glanced at her. "You know how opinionated he is. I had to talk with him not only about the apothecary but about the style in which we're to furnish his home."

"Ooh, right. Men can be stubborn and must be led gently sometimes."

Ignoring Stella's crooked eyebrow, which Jennifer feared could precede a question on Barb's romantic qualifications, she continued, "Well, he hated Rococo and wasn't much more fond of Gothic. We settled on American Empire to complement his more modern furniture, most of which I plan to try to contain in the sunroom. And he's agreed to a few Gothic pieces as well, provided he approves them before purchase. So I'm at a point now of readiness to locate the antiques, with your help, Mary Ellen."

Mary Ellen brightened. "Sure, Jennifer. I tell you what, I got a real tip for you. I got wind that Harmon Stone, who lives down 77 on his family's old Bartram Trail Plantation, has some pieces in his barn he might be willing to part with. The auction at Union Point is this Saturday, and his place is right on the way. How 'bout I call and see if he'll meet with us early that morning? Then we could skedaddle to the auction for the rest of the day, except for a lunch break, of course."

"That sounds fabulous, Mary Ellen! Thank you!"

Barb rubbed her hands together, either showing anticipation or shedding salt. "It does sound intriguing!"

If that comment dangled bait, Mary Ellen didn't bite. The shop owner cast her a glance but asked instead, "You wanna go, Stella?"

"I would love to, honey."

"Stella's the best at auctions," Mary Ellen told them.

"I have Saturday free," Barb said, plain out now.

Jennifer bit her lip, which didn't escape Stella. The artist said, "Mmm, I'm a little afraid too many visitors could put old Mr. Stone in a bad mood. I don't mean to be rude, but it's well known he doesn't open his home to anyone he doesn't know. He has some very valuable pieces, and I guess he's had some break-ins out there in the country. We'll already be pushin' him by bringin' Jennifer."

"*You're* going," Barb pointed out.

"Oh, he loves Stella," Mary Ellen hastened to clarify. "He's been the main collector of her paintings. He gives them to his family as Christmas presents."

Barb gave a slow nod. "Right. We wouldn't want to scare a defenseless old man by showing up with a professor of historic preservation from UGA, would we?"

The awkward pall descending with her words caused the other three women to squirm.

"You could call and ask him in advance, Mary Ellen," Stella suggested.

"Or you could meet us in Union Point," Jennifer offered. "Either way, we could work something out, Barb." As much as she didn't want Barb to go, she knew all too well what it felt like to be unwanted.

Barbara stood up and stretched. "No, it's OK. It sounds like it will go better without an outsider. I would never want to jeopardize a good opportunity for Jennifer. Listen, ladies, I'm going to head back to Athens, but Mary Ellen, it was a pleasure to see your shop."

"And it was great to meet you."

Jennifer slid off her stool. "I'll walk you out."

"It's not necessary." Barb waved a hand. "No need to interrupt your visit."

"No, I'm going out with you." Jennifer spoke firmly, somewhat alarmed at the professor's retreat. She'd never seen Barbara back down, and she feared they'd truly offended her this time. The weight of all she owed her mentor suddenly hung heavy, and she remembered that it wasn't until August 15 that the application window for Savannah Heritage Trust opened. That is, if a word from Barb didn't close it first. Jennifer didn't think her former professor would be that petty, but neither was she fully sure of the nature of the understanding between Barb and her friend on staff there.

Sure enough, Barbara maintained complete silence on the way to her truck.

"I'm sorry about the Harmon Stone thing," Jennifer ventured. "I really don't think Stella would say anything unless it's true that he's quite private and eccentric. She's not that kind of person."

Barb's lip twisted. "Of course she's not."

Jennifer didn't know what to say. "Thank you so much again for the window."

"You're welcome." Barb reached out and squeezed her hand. "I really do want this project to go well for you, Jennifer. It's my pleasure to help you. I just don't want to see you get lost out here. You know what I mean. You've worked so hard for your success and come so far. This was meant to be a temporary assignment, not a place you'd get stuck. Just keep that in mind." She got up in the cab and pulled the door shut, lowering the window.

"But how would I get stuck? I'm still planning to apply for the Savannah job. It's not like there's a permanent place for me here. I know that."

"Do you?"

When Jennifer didn't reply, Barb waved and circled the vehicle around to the main road. The flattened line of the professor's mouth and stiff posture underlined her lack of effort to reconnect and smooth things over. Jennifer watched a minute as the Explorer vanished toward Athens. She went back into the antique store with a heavier heart.

"What's wrong?" Stella asked.

Jennifer shook her head as she resumed her seat. "Nothing really. I just think Barb felt excluded from the Union Point outing."

"Honey, there's no reason for her to *go* on the Union Point outing. Can't you see that? You done graduated from her class. She needs to let you go about your life now. And if she makes you feel bad about that, then that's manipulating you, and that's not healthy."

"I think she's afraid I'm making unreasonable assumptions about how long I'll be here in Hermon and doesn't want me to get hurt."

"Who's gonna hurt you?"

"*Leaving* might hurt."

Stella reached for her hands and said, "Honey, don't you listen to her. We'd love for you to stay forever."

"But there's no work for me here after this project is done!"

"You don't know that!" Mary Ellen burst out, sympathetic tears springing into her eyes at the sight of Jennifer's distress. "What did you just say about the Gillen store? And there are all kinds of old houses and buildings in Lexington and all around the county! Why, who knows what God might have planned?"

Jennifer glanced from her back to Stella, who nodded. "She's right. Why don't you just wait and let God show you the direction *He* has for you? Remember when you committed your life to Him, you agreed to let Him be the pilot."

"Yes." Jennifer pulled a hand away to swipe an embarrassing tear from the corner of her eye.

"Why you cryin'?" Stella asked.

"I don't know. I guess I just never had anyone want me to stick around before."

"Well, honey, you do now," Stella said, reaching out to hug her. Mary Ellen also came around the counter, and Jennifer found herself engulfed in an awkward but very sweet group huddle.

"Do you know where Jennifer needs to go?" Mary Ellen exclaimed when they started to pull back. Stella asked her where, and she said, "The Mid-Summer Gala at Cloverleaf Historic Oglethorpe is hostin' in early August!"

Stella said, "Yes!" while Jennifer said, "No!"

"Why are you sayin' 'no' before you even know what it is?" Mary Ellen demanded, hands on her rounded hips.

"Because the word 'gala' was spoken, and I assume that means dressing up and talking with a bunch of important people."

"That's exactly right, but they are exactly the people you need to talk to," Stella told her.

"Oh, you'll love it, Jennifer," Mary Ellen went on, eyes sparkling. "This year we get to go inside the Edward-Byrd Plantation, which is now called Cloverleaf Farm on Wolfskin Road and is used as an events facility. Mordecai Edwards built the house in 1859. It's Italianate and full of lovely antiques. You know I'm a member of *all* the historical committees in the county, and I can introduce you to everyone, so you won't be alone. You should hear what is happenin' and share your ideas. The chair of the Firefly Trail Fund will be there!"

"Maybe Michael can go as your escort!" Stella exclaimed. "As the new owner of Dunham House, he needs to meet all those people, too!"

"Oh, my stars!" Jennifer covered her face with her hands, mortified at the idea of becoming some modern-day "historyella." "OK, OK, I'll answer the e-mails from the woman at the library, that Grace Stevenson lady who is a member of UDC, and I'll speak to every club in the county, but please, please, don't suggest I attend this gala! And especially not with Michael!"

Mary Ellen pried a hand loose and leaned in. "But Jennifer, you can kill all those birds with one stone. Just make an appearance."

"They're all people like you who care about the same things," Stella urged.

"Think how you could encourage the culture and industry in our flaggin' little community," Mary Ellen hissed seductively. Her eyebrows even leapt up onto her forehead, then fell with a sly smile.

Jennifer's wide eyes darted from one to the other. She squeaked, "Do I have to buy a formal dress?"

"Cocktail," Mary Ellen replied.

"I can help you," Stella offered. "And I happen to know Rita will, too."

Jennifer let out a full-fledged moan.

Mary Ellen clasped her hands joyously before her ample bosom. "So can I tell the president you'll be coming?"

"Will you leave me alone about it if I don't?"

Mary Ellen shook her head.

"Fine. But no Michael. We don't need to add to my embarrassment."

"Uh-uh-uh." Stella did her typical finger wag. Then she winked at Mary Ellen. "Just you leave Michael Johnson to me."

A few days later, Jennifer wondered what she had gotten herself into. She found herself avoiding Michael in case Stella had already cornered him. He would think she'd put Stella up to arranging a date. He hadn't wanted to take her down to Milledgeville to meet his grandfather and buy tomato plants for the VA home, for crying out loud! He sure wouldn't want to be stuck with her at some formal function with a bunch of strangers. Michael liked his personal space maybe even more than she liked hers, which was saying something. They'd be a mess trying to navigate Oglethorpe's upper crust together!

Gabe and Jamal proved very good-natured about cleaning the apothecary attic. Working tirelessly in the heat, sweeping, shop-vaccing and then wiping, they knocked out the job in impressive time. Surely she could clean the main floor herself. She didn't want Michael and James to think they had to either do all the messy, manual work themselves or hire the teenage boys.

She grabbed her buckets, sponges, cloths and liquid soap and snuck up to the house to drag the garden hose as far as it would reach toward the apothecary with the extension. Rather than walking back and forth a bazillion times, the best plan she could muster was to leave the hose dripping into her second bucket while she cleaned from the first one, then exchange them. If the bucket overflowed in her absence, the new knock-out roses in the bed would only thank her.

Jennifer entered through the front and surveyed the dim, already stuffy interior with hands on her hips. She glared at the ceilings, noting the extra darkness above sections sporting hooks where kerosene lamps must have hung. Two hooks dotted the ceiling to the right in the middle room, above where the exam table had stood. After today's cleaning, a good ceiling scrubbing using TSP, trisodium phosphate, would be in order. As much as she hated to admit it, that soot would surrender to Gabe's and Jamal's athletic muscles much faster than her own limp arms.

Sighing, she decided to open the back door in hopes of capturing a cross breeze. She marched to the rear of the shop, having already committed to memory the path across the floor necessary to avoid the hole in the middle of the windowless room. Before she knew what happened, her foot slipped on something slick, and she traveled in a downward and inward trajectory that landed her on her bottom. Her first foot came down on the floor and slid right into the hole, twisting as the rough edges of a board stabbed the back of her ankle.

"Ow! Ow, ow, ow!" she yelled, grabbing the offending part. She pulled her leg up from dangling below the foundation and flexed. Her foot would not move to one side.

Feeling behind her, Jennifer's fingers sought purchase, only to be denied. Something thick and slippery covered the floors. Had someone been in here painting? But that would be ridiculous! She wiggled her way backward on her rear end, pushing with her uninjured foot, until her back almost touched the wall, then raised herself onto one leg. Hobbling to the rear exit, she fumbled with the lock and latch. Finally the wide door swung open, and morning light flooded the chamber. She gazed at the floor. And gasped. Then she raised her fingers to examine them. Oil. Just like the liquid had oozed right out of the past and back onto the boards where Ettie Mae's 1945 Cadillac had sat.

CHAPTER SIX

"Ta-da!"

Balancing on her crutches at the back of the F150, Jennifer tugged the tarp off the prize yielded by Harmon Stone's barn and looked expectantly over her shoulder at Michael. Even with the truck parked near the kitchen door floodlight, the giant mahogany sideboard on the bed blended into the shadows of the cricket-chirping July night. Michael drew closer to inspect the piece.

"I felt it was awfully plain for that fancy red dining room," Mary Ellen put in, "but Jennifer insisted you liked plain."

To Jennifer's delight, Michael said, "She was right." He ran a hand over the wood.

"1830s furniture often featured a lack of hardware, as well as these heavy legs. American Empire just as we discussed. Granted, we have some work ahead of us, but it's not like I don't have time to do it now, with this hurt ankle. We'll have to strip and restain it with a number of coats, and tighten some loose pieces, but the best part is, Harmon said this was made right here in Oglethorpe County! His great-great-grandfather hired an itinerant cabinet maker to construct it right on the Bartram Trail Plantation!"

"Really?" Michael cocked an eye at her. "Why did he want to part with this? And second question, how much did you pay?"

"He has so many valuable pieces, I think Mr. Stone agreed with Mary Ellen," Stella said.

"And since it requires a lot of work, it was within budget," Jennifer assured him.

"Do I see that you bought more?" Michael wanted to know, noticing Mary Ellen's truck which they had also driven to Union Point that afternoon in case they had a lot of luck. They had.

"Yes, against the cab of your truck is a gentleman's dresser with shaving mirror. It's a little early for the period, but it's open between the top and bottom, which will give you some storage. And the lines were so clean, I knew you'd love it. It also came from Harmon's barn. In Mary Ellen's truck, we brought back a couple of pieces from the auction, an arched, four-poster bed and an early American Empire wardrobe with a really exaggerated cornice that will fill in your tall bedroom walls great. We also found an Oushak!"

"A what?" Michael asked.

"A carpet, from Iran, near Turkey," Jennifer supplied with excitement. "Very prized in the 1840s, and with perfect period colors for your bedroom, gold, brown, blue and apricot."

"Apricot," he repeated in a low, skeptical tone.

Jennifer grinned. "Just touches."

"But what perfect timing, Michael," Mary Ellen suggested. "Who wants to move in that heavy furniture only to be forced to move it again to put down a rug?"

Michael nodded, while James said, "That's definitely true. Well, you ladies had a productive day."

"Oh, you should have seen Stella bidding at the auction. She was the one who got the furniture," Jennifer said. "She waited until two other bidders thought they'd duked it out before slipping her hand up all sly. It was all over before the other two knew what happened."

"Thanks, Stella. We can be properly appreciative of your finds in the morning, when we can actually see them, but I guess we'd better unload Mary Ellen's truck now so she can leave, Dad."

James nodded, but Mary Ellen said, "Oh, no need to bother. I'm comfortable leavin' it right here until morning. I'll give you the keys, and you can just park it behind my shop when you're done."

"If you're sure," James said, "I can just drive Stella home."

"That would be great," Stella said. She reached out to give Jennifer a hug. "I had a good time, honey."

"Me, too." Jennifer couldn't remember when she had laughed so much. Like a bunch of teenagers, they'd almost embarrassed themselves in front of the waiter in the Union Point restaurant. She turned and hugged the yawning Mary Ellen as well before the antique store owner said goodnight and headed out across the yard to the shop she lived above.

"Now remember what I said!" Stella wagged her finger at Jennifer.

"What was that?"

"About you callin' Rita, or I'll do it for you. This ankle will be better enough for the gala. You just get that appointment made."

"What's this?" Michael wanted to know.

"I'll fill you in soon enough, young man," Stella told him before turning back to Jennifer. "You wanna go into Athens tomorrow afternoon to shop?"

"Thank you, but I'm worn out. These stupid crutches make my underarms hurt. I could use an afternoon of sitting with my feet propped up."

Stella pursed her lips. "Well, you probably can, just so long as that isn't an excuse to put it off indefinitely."

"I promise I'll go, but I already have a commitment to Montana. I promised her I'd take her shopping with me and out to lunch."

"You don't have to take her with you to look for a cocktail dress."

"I do if it's the only shopping I intend to do until the very remote future."

Still looking disapproving, Stella finally conceded. "Well, OK. That was awfully sweet of you. You can arrange that the same time you arrange your hair appointment. Just be sure you want to trust a twelve-year-old's sense of fashion. The look you are going for is elegant and *tailored*."

As Jennifer assured Stella she would choose accordingly, she was glad Michael, who listened with an expression of amused disbelief, could not see her blushing in the dark. After James left with Stella, she turned to him and asked, "Is that wood smoke I smell?"

"It sure is. We got the outhouse torn down today and added that mess to the pile from the apothecary." They had sealed the back of the shop with Hardiplank the day before. "Wanna come sit by the fire a minute before walking home?"

"Sure! I can't resist a bonfire." Jennifer followed Michael's lead around the side of the house, carefully watching her step.

In honor of Barb's request to build any fire on a different spot than the hole the outhouse left so that an archeology class could excavate the area in the fall, Michael had used a sandy clearing, where he and James had placed a large metal burn barrel. Jennifer could see the indentation remaining where the outhouse once stood. She shuddered.

"Did you encounter any more snakes?"

Michael pulled up a folding chair for her, taking her crutches as she eased herself down with a sigh. "Thankfully, no. But we did encounter something else really strange."

She glanced up at him, mystified. "What?"

"A layer of concrete only slightly sunk in the soil."

"You're kidding."

"Nope. It seems fairly thick, like a standard slab. We couldn't bust through it easily with a sledgehammer. Your professor will have to bring her jackhammer."

"Assuming she still wants to come," Jennifer muttered under her breath. Ever since Barbara's exclusion from plans to attend the auction, the sudden airwave silence felt downright eerie. When Jennifer broke down and texted to ask if she was OK, the brief reply indicated that Barbara got the message that Jennifer needed personal and professional space, and she was not into forcing her presence or expertise on anyone. That kept Jennifer up all night, struggling with whether to respond or not. On one hand, she still needed Barbara's support for the upcoming job in Savannah. On the other, Stella would say that was what Barb counted on. Finally the next morning, Jennifer settled on texting that she would send updates with anything new to share. Barb said, "OK." Did the older woman realize the extra power she wielded now by virtue of how rarely Jennifer had experienced past kindness?

Trying not to feel punished all over again as she recalled the brevity of the professor's answer, Jennifer redirected her thoughts to the present and asked, "When do you think it was poured?"

"I don't know. Not really recently. Maybe during the house's rental period? We figured someone else might have feared a nest of snakes and lifted the seat to dump wet cement into the hole. You know that seat did lift and could be easily removed."

"Yeah. That is so bizarre. I don't know what to think about that."

"We didn't, either. Would you like something to drink?"

"Oh, no, thank you. We had a drink on the way home."

Michael nodded and took a seat next to her, taking up a stick on the ground and leaning forward to poke the contents of the burn barrel. Behind the profusion of sparks that created, Jennifer noticed the remaining pile of boards they must have gradually fed the fire from all afternoon. She leaned back, stretching her legs in front of her and taking a deep breath of the deliciously smoky air.

"How's the ankle, anyway?"

"A little swollen after our adventures today, but overall I'm seeing progress. The doctor said I should expect to feel almost normal by the end of next week. I'm so thankful the sprain wasn't worse. It's getting in the way of my work."

"Don't worry about that. I'm more concerned that you got hurt, and about the fact that Stan had no more idea than we did who would have done something so strange as to pick the back lock on the apothecary and pour oil all over the floor." Stella's brother Stan served as Oglethorpe County sheriff. After learning someone might have locked Jennifer in Michael's storage shed that spring, he'd made her promise to report any further strange incidents.

"Well, two good things come to mind now."

"What's that?"

Jennifer held up one finger, then a second one as she explained. "Stan also said he'd send patrols by on a regular basis to monitor the area, and you and James got that rear entrance sealed off today, so as long as we keep the bolt on the front door in place, it should never happen again."

"Yeah, but the police can't hover around all the time. What if this prankster goes for something more serious next time? I haven't forgotten the incident where you got shut in the shed. But oil? What kind of point were they trying to make? Did they think that was funny? Were they trying to scare us? Hurt us?"

"Maybe it was an apothecary spirit from the past, rejecting the renovations," she joked.

"That's not funny."

"Do you believe in spirits, too, like Stella does?"

Michael rose to retrieve a couple more boards. Giving her a grumpy glare, he shoved them into the fire. "Yes, frankly, I do."

"Did ... your dad tell you about what happened when we got the child's bed from the attic in the apothecary?" Jennifer ventured. The skin on her arms prickled even as she said it, despite the warmth of the nearby fire.

He nodded.

"I'm sure it was just a weird moment in the heat," she made excuse, embarrassed when he did not respond to the opportunity to discuss the apparition. "I mean, what else could it be?"

The fire popped suddenly, but Michael didn't move. "I think dark times can leave dark shadows, some more real than others."

"What does that mean?"

"Evil spirits. They can remain where bad things happened."

In that case, several spirits hung around the trailer park where she grew up. Unsettled, and clued into Michael's reluctance to elaborate by his terse response, Jennifer decided to redirect the conversation. "We still need a lot more furniture if we're going to fill a house with such large rooms. I paid for a couple of pieces from Mary Ellen. Now that you've got the floors done, you can pick those up tomorrow when you return her truck." She paused until Michael nodded. "But that still won't be enough. I went up to Lexington to order the drapes from Amy yesterday, you know, and she volunteered to go with me to the warehouse in Augusta where she and Mary Ellen said they have such good antiques. It will probably be next month. It's only open every other weekend."

Michael nodded. "That will be fine as long as you keep in mind that I—"

"Don't want things overdone, I know."

"And—"

"Don't go crazy with the checkbook."

"Right." He smiled. "You're finally getting to know me."

Jennifer didn't know about that. He still discussed so little of his past, not to mention his views of many things, as just evidenced. She wanted to ask questions, but when she looked into his eyes, he shifted uncomfortably and sat up in his lawn chair.

"So, it's almost time for my armadillo watch. Can I help you get home?"

She wanted to say no, she'd get there herself, but she knew all too well that the ground between here and her double-wide contained many pitfalls. She reached for her crutches. "Sure." As she hefted herself to standing position, she added, "Maybe the fire will keep them away tonight."

"I sure hope so. I could stand some decent rest."

Jennifer had stuffed too much irritation inside over the situation to chuckle. Undeterred by the mothballs she liberally scattered among the flower beds, the pests caused further damage several nights during the past week. Jennifer's invalid state forced her to leave the repair work to the men. The traps remained empty, although James thought he dinged one of the critters the night before. He described it grunting, running a few yards, then falling over with its feet sticking straight up in the air.

Yet this morning, it was nowhere to be found. "I think they have nine lives like cats," he declared.

She followed directly behind Michael, trusting him to warn her of any holes or large clumps of grass. The Leyland Cypress trees that separated the properties had gotten so full she had to turn sideways, hold the crutches in one hand, and hop through on her good foot. On the other side, she scarcely knew what happened when she heard Michael mutter, "Good heavens," and grab her beneath the arms and legs. She scrambled to hold onto the crutches as he pulled her tight against his body.

"Stop it! Put me down!" Jennifer protested.

"Oh, just hush. You already got injured on my property. I can't have you breaking your neck on my account now, too."

"Well, I'm hardly going to sue you!"

"Maybe not, but your loving professor might!"

A laugh escaped Jennifer before she could stop it, and she acquiesced, the side of her face squished against Michael's chest. She heard his heartbeat. And he smelled ... like him. Very male. A wave of unease washed over her. To get up the steps to her porch, she needed to wrap her arm around his neck. As soon as she pressed closer, however, a half-formed memory jangled into her brain, flooding her entire body with intense panic.

"Put me down! Right now. Put me down!" Jennifer scrambled to get away from him, dropping a crutch on the porch and almost falling in her lunge for the handle of the storm door.

"Jeesh, don't have a fit." Michael bent to retrieve the fallen crutch, holding it out to her. "You know, when feminism crosses a certain line, it becomes very unappealing. I was just trying to help."

Jennifer snatched the crutch and leaned them both against the side of the house, fumbling in her pocket for her keys. The sense that danger waited right behind her so overpowered her that her head swam. She paused, dizzy, momentarily covering her eyes with her shaking hand. Her breath came fast, audible.

Michael leaned in behind her. No longer accusing, his voice sounded concerned as he asked, "Jennifer? Are you all right?"

Her behavior totally lacked logic. During her teen and adult years, she learned how to keep men who might hurt her at arm's length. What she didn't know was how to interact with one close to her who meant her no harm.

"I'm fine. It's not you. I just—have to go." She finally fit the key in the lock and pushed her way inside. She only felt better once she turned the bolt and stood alone in the darkness of her living room. Then she remembered the child's bed stored in her guest room and wished she had left it in the attic like James had suggested.

Following a night filled with dreams of creatures tunneling beneath her double-wide and spirits hovering in her spare room, Jennifer dressed in a zombie-like state for church. She still attended Harmony Grove with Stella and Earl. Mary Ellen's family and James had both invited her to go to Hermon Baptist with them, and she visited once and appreciated it, but Jennifer supposed she had already adjusted to the African American style of worship. Having attended a Baptist church in Stewart County as a little girl, she would have expected the quieter Caucasian service to better match both her background and personality. But something about the soul-felt, minor-key song rhythms and Pastor Simms' stirring sermons tapped something deep inside her. Besides, Stella's—and now Michael's—extended family had so immediately welcomed her.

She and Stella wanted Michael to attend, too, but so far the closest they had gotten was that BBQ where Michael first met Luella Wright's branch of the family which her daughter Georgia Pearl had pruned from her life. The day Jennifer accepted the Lord, Michael confirmed that he had indeed suffered more heartaches in his life than the early death of his mother Linda to a rare and aggressive form of cancer, he just wasn't ready to square with God over them—or tell her about them. But then, why should he ever?

Due to Jennifer's full weekend schedule, Michael had custody of Yoda, freeing Jennifer to hobble her way outside before the Stella, Earl and their boys arrived. The sight of Dunham House's flower beds verified the uneasy sensation in her gut. Michael stood in front of the Seven Sisters rose bushes Jennifer had recently planted, now prostrate on the ground.

He turned without comment to survey her shapeless dress and Mary Janes. Doubtless she looked about as droopy to him as the bush did.

"Did you even get to fire a shot last night?" she asked.

"I sat up tending the fire until one, then thought it safe to sleep. And I wake to this. And come around here." Jennifer followed him to the cook's cabin behind his house, where a mangled trap lay beside the burrow entrance. He held it up, shaking the door which hung by one squeaky hinge. "Apparently the creature from hell butted it until it broke open."

Jennifer let out a disgusted huff of air. "I hope you're going to take that contraption back. You deserve a refund. And I've had enough. I'm going to talk to Calvin Woods right now." She started to turn when Michael laid a hand on her arm. Expecting him to argue, she pulled away, not bothering to hide the blaze of protest in her eyes.

Michael raised his hand in the air. "I'm sorry," he said. "I didn't mean to grab you … again. I just wanted you to know before you leave that I shouldn't have picked you up without asking like that last night. I was just … too impatient, and I thought you could fall. I was actually on my way over to apologize."

"You were?"

"Yes. I was."

"Thanks." She stood there dumbly, unnerved by the sincerity in his eyes. While yes, he could have communicated better, his intentions had been honorable. So considering how ridiculous her hysterical reaction must have appeared, if he owed her an apology, she probably owed him an explanation. She shifted her weight onto one crutch. "Sorry I freaked. Too many obnoxious college guys with the wrong ideas, you know. I learned how to keep them at arm's length."

"Yeah. I guess you did."

Jennifer colored, fearing his tone might mean he found it surprising any would *want* to get that close. But if she kept stalking off so frequently he'd realize just how sensitive she really was. She eyed his running shorts and T-shirt. "So you're not going to church?"

Michael shook his head.

"There's still time to change if you want to come with us."

"Thanks, but I don't think so today."

Exactly the answer she'd expected. Funny, but the armadillos served as something of a foil for their relationship; just as soon as they made a little progress with communication and trust, one of them went back and tore it up. They were both too guarded and defensive. "You know you're going to have to give in to Stella one of these days."

He smiled. "I know."

"OK."

"Do you ... want me to come talk to Calvin with you?"

"Really? You won't take it as an insult to your manliness to hire his nephews?"

"Are you kidding? I'm not a bad shot for a city boy, but hunting armadillos is like hunting phantoms. If these kids have skills I don't, I'll gladly surrender my .22 for a chance at a peaceful night!"

"And a chance to avoid spending more money at the nursery, too, no doubt," Jennifer chuckled as he fell into step beside her.

"Right." As they approached Calvin's ramshackle dwelling and heard Otis bark from inside, Michael raised a brow at her. "I'll feel better if you won't come over here alone."

"Agreed," Jennifer said as Michael raised his knuckles to knock.

After a moment, they heard grumbling and bumping and a few choice curse words as Calvin made his way to the door. Just before it opened, Michael joked, "Not sure you're gonna want to see this."

Jennifer stifled a laugh. Calvin had belted a bathrobe about his rotund middle, but his hairy chest was still visible above and wiry legs below. She winced and focused on her neighbor's sleep-encrusted eyes. "Mr. Woods, we're sorry to wake you, but we're fed up and ready to hire your nephews."

A laugh belched out of the man. "Ha. Come to eat humble pie, have you?"

Michael frowned. "It's in all our best interest to get rid of the varmints, so if your boys can do that, please call them for us. They can come tonight."

"They won't do it for free, mind you."

"I'm willing to pay a reasonable amount."

Calvin nodded. "They'll be there."

"Do you want to call us if they have a conflict, Mr. Woods?" Jennifer offered.

"They won't have a conflict. There's nothin' they like better than hunting, and no hunting's more satisfying than 'dillos." So saying, Calvin shut the door in their faces.

CHAPTER SEVEN

Before church Sunday morning, Jennifer sent several texts. She checked in on Tilly, inquired with Barbara what to do about the concrete layer found in the outhouse, and invited Montana on a shopping expedition. The positive responses Jennifer received helped smooth the edges off her disappointment over her up-and-down relationship with Michael. Tilly missed her and suggested some days to meet for lunch. As Jennifer had hoped, the professional question broke the ice with her professor. Barb encouraged them to leave the outhouse site as it was. The concrete could prove fortuitous, helping preserve the layers below. And Montana's eagerness to shop that very day became impossible to deny. Montana's family required her presence at the family Sunday dinner table, but Montana could have dinner out. That turned out to be a good thing, since the lengthy Harmony Grove service and Stella's list of qualifications for Jennifer's cocktail dress barely left Jennifer time to heat a Lean Cuisine.

Stella's directions replayed in Jennifer's mind as she made her way to the Worley house. She hadn't needed to get the address, because she already knew Montana lived on the large dairy farm on the outskirts of Hermon. Nothing too long. Nothing too short. Nothing too loose. Nothing too tight. And most of all, nothing too black.

Jennifer pulled into Montana's driveway, completely at a loss as to where to find such a specific creation. When Montana bounded out to the car with her brown hair in a low ponytail and plopped into the passenger seat with a cheery "hi," Jennifer looked askance at her. "So where are we going?"

"Really? I thought you'd already have a favorite place."

"No clothing store on earth is my favorite place. And in case you can't tell, I spent most of my college life in Athens frequenting second hand stores."

"Uh. Yeah." Montana gave her a critical eye as her mother, Jean, a petite, sandy-haired woman in her late 30s, trailed her daughter out to the car for introductions. Dressed in walking shorts and a sage green, embroidered top, Jean wore her hair in a simple, shoulder-length bob, and brown eye shadow highlighted her hazel eyes. Jennifer had never learned the trick of applying makeup without feeling like a clown, or worse, like a Kelly. Trusting her mother-in-law's judgement of Jennifer's character, Jean seemed at ease with the outing, merely confirming a return time.

When Jean waved them off as Jennifer backed down the drive, Montana stepped with delight into her role as leader. "So big bucks or little bucks?"

"How about Starbuck's?" Jennifer jested.

"Seriously."

Jennifer stopped the car before pulling onto the main road. One of the reasons she hadn't wanted to shop with Stella was because Jennifer hadn't wanted her friend to know what a limited budget she was on. Michael paid her plenty for this job, but she still had expenses and a substantial amount of college debt not covered by scholarship. "Definitely little bucks."

"OK, so not all second hand stores are a bad thing, if you know the look you're going for, and that would definitely be a different look than your current one."

"Thanks."

Montana pointed a stubby finger. "Just drive. There's a place in Watkinsville with a lot less overhead than downtown Athens, but it's fancy, like Oconee County. All the rich people there go in to sell their castoffs."

"Great. I can hardly wait. Rich people castoffs."

Montana ignored that and directed her on a cut-through past Crawford that spared them of Athens traffic.

"Wolfskin," Jennifer said aloud upon seeing the road sign. "I've heard of that before. Oh, yeah, Allison Winters lives out this way. Wonder how the area got that name."

"I've heard two stories," Montana told her with a grown-up air of wisdom that Jennifer loved. "According to one, a pack of especially aggressive wolves prowled the community during Colonial times. The other says the name came about from a bunch of brothers out here known for their drinking, womanizing and gambling."

Jennifer arched a teasing brow at her youthful companion. "Maybe the boys were the wolves. Like *Twilight*."

According to her satisfied smirk, Montana liked that idea. "Right, although I wasn't allowed to watch or read that series."

"Probably just as well." Glancing over, Jennifer winked.

Montana crossed her arms. "I'm not a child, you know."

"I know that. But listen." Jennifer reached out to briefly touch the defensive arm. "Your parents and grandparents are wise to protect you and guard your innocence as long as possible. I wish I'd had family like that. The world isn't as nice as Hermon."

"You don't have a great family?" Montana asked, lowering her guard and her stance.

"No. I don't have a great family." Jennifer pressed her lips together, not about to elaborate no matter how rabid Montana's curiosity proved, but the girl delivered her next statement in her unpredictable, endearing manner.

"You can stay here. Hermon is like a family."

Jennifer smiled. "I'd like that." She tapped a finger on the steering wheel and bit her lip, deciding whether to divulge more about her future plans. "You know I'm applying next month for an important job in Savannah, but we'll just have to see what God wants."

Thankfully, Montana accepted Jennifer's statement without further argument. "Yes," she repeated. "We'll just see what God wants." Jennifer thought she glimpsed a faint, sneaky smile dance over the girl's face. No doubt she'd be praying against Savannah starting tonight!

The rest of the drive passed with conversation about the scenery, which included several historic homes Jennifer admired, including post-Civil War Hawk's Nest and 1856 Farm Hill, whose plantation plain façade peeked between trees far off the road. Both had been built by the Dillard family, Montana told her. The girl asked her to slow down as they approached a white antebellum Italianate proclaimed by a wooden sign to be Cloverleaf Farm—the site of the upcoming gala. Further enchanted by the grape arbor and clustered outbuildings, Jennifer craned her neck as long as the narrow, curvy road allowed, her enthusiasm for their outing considerably perked.

Now in full tour guide mode, Montana revealed that during the 1870 smallpox epidemic, five miles of homes and outbuildings were burned in this area to help prevent spread of the dread disease. Then, as they crossed the Oconee River and began the climb to the adjacent county, Montana reverted to the modern world with talk of how much fun a local kayaking trip on the Middle Oconee or Broad River would be with Jennifer. Jennifer agreed.

"Ooh, a Jittery Joe's," Jennifer cried as they came into the little town of Watkinsville.

"No," Montana said firmly, pointing to the strip of quaint brick buildings beside a more modern courthouse. "Focus. You can park there on the street."

"Yes, my bossy little friend."

"You're goin' to have to trust me today if this is going to work, Jennifer. Even though I'm only twelve, I do know more about current fashion."

Jennifer turned around in the tiny front lot of the courthouse, casting the younger girl a pointed look.

"I know, I know, I don't exactly dress like it, but I do look at fashion magazines."

"Why don't you dress like it?" Jennifer asked as she maneuvered her Civic easily into a parallel spot.

"Have you made note of my *girth*?"

"Oh, Montana, you're adorable."

"Adorable. Just what I want to be. Grandma calls me adorable. Boys don't think adorable."

"Well, you don't want any of them yet, anyway."

"Maybe not, but I do want them to think I'm pretty."

Jennifer put the car in park and gave Montana her full attention. "You *are* pretty. And you're in a time of great change. Everything goes where it's supposed to within a year, I promise. But for now, I'm sure we can find fashionable things that look good on you."

"We're not lookin' for me today, we're lookin' for you."

"Still, you never know what we'll find." Jennifer's tantalizing tone faded as her gaze slipped past her companion to the store front. A frothy red prom dress hung on a wicker mannequin in the window, not a good initial impression. "It looks kind of dark inside. Maybe it's closed on Sundays."

"Read the sign, Sherlock." Montana reached for her door handle, but Jennifer put a hand on her arm.

"Listen, we have some ground rules. *These* are mine: no tulle, no sequins, no lace, no puffy skirts. Got it?"

"Mmm-hmm."

"And apparently Stella has some, too." She went on to elaborate.

"The field is gettin' really small," Montana said with concern. "Shrinking and shrinking. Because ..." She reached into her bag and plopped a strange card that looked a lot like a paint sample strip on Jennifer's lap.

"If you're making a bid for Amy Greene's job, I'm sorry to say she's already completed her work at Michael's."

Montana shook her head. "No, silly, these are the colors an autumn should wear."

"A what?"

"A person with an autumn color palate. My mom is a Mary Kay consultant. Grandma knows that stuff, too, and she says you're an autumn. See, you wear the colors of fall. She says you've had it all wrong. You keep tryin' to wear spring colors. Lots of people with brown hair instead of red hair make that mistake, but it doesn't go by hair color, it goes by skin tone. You're a secret autumn."

"That sounds like the new seasonal scent from Bath 'n' Body," Jennifer murmured with a shudder. Montana, who looked like a tomboy and had sounded perfectly coherent while describing the history and scenery of the area, had now morphed into a girly girl. Tweens were supposed to be changeable, but really?

Montana laughed and hopped onto the sidewalk. Jennifer made her way more carefully out of passing traffic. "Don't worry," Montana encouraged her. "We have Mom to help. She said I'm to text a photo of anything you consider before you buy it. She's goin' to share with Stella, so you might as well just text Stella directly as well."

"What? This is not cool!"

Montana tugged her hand, pulling her through the glass door into a surprisingly long boutique. "Just think of us like your personal makeover team. We're goin' to have you looking fabulous for this gala. You have to meet important people. And go with Michael Johnson."

"He hasn't said yes yet."

"He will. Today."

Jennifer moaned. At the sound, the two perfectly put-together sorority girls behind the counter greeted them with expressions of concern. When they asked if they could be of assistance, Jennifer quickly declined, stifling her urge to flee in favor of Montana leading her past silky summer tank tops and lace-trimmed shorts to the formalwear section, or in Jennifer's opinion, out of the frying pan and into the fire.

"What size are you?" Montana wanted to know.

Jennifer told her the number she normally sought when pressed beyond small, medium or large.

"No, you're not. There's no way. You wear your clothes way too big, but considering that fancy dresses usually run small, we'll start with just one size down."

Montana attacked the rack, reaching up to shift the hangers while Jennifer watched, perfectly content to let the child wrestle through the bouffant dresses in their full-length plastic bags without assistance. She started holding out possibilities. After Jennifer rejected three, Montana declared, "You've got to try something! Just take them. You don't know until you try."

Jennifer sighed as her arms filled. Finally she made it into the dressing room with six creations of the less formal variety.

"Lose the socks," Montana commanded before she snapped shut the curtain. "And come out no matter what you think."

"I am really regretting my offer to take you shopping. I had the mall and the cookie store in mind, anyway."

"I don't need any cookies."

Jennifer slid on the first dress, a sage green with thick straps and flat horizontal folds. She stared at herself in the mirror before cracking open the fabric that shielded her from mortification. "I feel like a weed on the side of the road," she told Montana, who rolled her eyes but gave her a dismissive hand wave on the grounds the gown was not stunning enough. *Jennifer* felt stunned. She had not showed this much skin since skipping with her brother Rab to the public pool in her bathing suit back in elementary school. She also felt like she was putting on airs. Who was she trying to kid?

Dress after dress she rejected despite any positive comments from the Hermon audience and Mini Miss What Not to Wear. Finally, only one remained on the hook, a dark brick red iridescent taffeta shot with black, a shade that Jennifer would have considered suitable for the curtains in an 1890s Bordeaux but maybe even more alarming than swimwear to put on her own body.

"Come on, let me see my favorite. I've been waiting," Montana called from outside the curtain. With that tone, she was definitely tapping a toe.

With another sigh, Jennifer complied. She didn't even look in the mirror, just snatched the fabric aside with a disgusted expression. Montana gasped. Jennifer said, "I know, right?" and started to close it back.

"Wait, stop! No, I meant it's fabulous." She popped up from her chair and ran over to stand by Jennifer in the mirror, reaching up to pull Jennifer's shaggy mane back into a pony tail. "Imagine different hair, and the right shoes. See how it flatters your skin tone. It looks flawless."

Jennifer blinked. On her frame and out of the sun, the black threads in the material toned the red down to the shade of … an autumn leaf. And her skin did look milky. The classic, fitted shape of the dress dropped off the shoulder with a tiny, flat band of a sleeve edged in matching tatting, the lower half hugging her in the right places to suggest but not flaunt curves. Still, she resisted.

"It's not good to look this provocative. I'd be setting a bad example for you."

"Oh, please. It almost goes to your knees, and no bosom is even showing. Come back out so we can send photos, but I already know it's the one."

Stella and Jean almost blew up their phones with praise, emojis and exclamation points.

Jennifer just wanted it to be over, and in her heart she knew she would not find a dress that looked better on her even though the appealing cut made her uncomfortable. "OK, fine," Jennifer relented as she wiggled out of the dress. "We can be done with this and go eat."

"Oh, no, we're not done. We have to look at shoes and accessories now."

Jennifer groaned but did not argue. However, while Montana poured over heels with the help of one of the sales girls, Jennifer snuck over to the teen and petite racks, scooping out several items she thought might flatter Montana's in-between frame. Wobbling up with her feet slid down in a pair of black stilettos, the tween froze in trepidation at the sight of Jennifer's finds. Jennifer gave her a wicked grin. "Your turn."

In the end, Jennifer only persuaded the girl into a dressing room by agreeing to try on more clothing herself, this time two casual outfits and one Sunday dress Montana selected. Her sacrifice proved worth her trouble when she saw how cute Montana looked in a loose, silky romper in a small blue floral print, and a pair of denim shorts with geometric print blouse. The girl couldn't stop looking at herself in the mirror. When Jennifer told her to hand over the clothes for check-out, Montana underwent yet another change, this one to winsome child.

"Oh, Jennifer, are you really goin' to buy these for me?"

"I most definitely am."

"Mom will pay you back."

"No need. It's my thank you gift for your ... ahem ... excellent help today."

"Done." Montana raised a hand to high-five her. Then she announced, "Let's get outta here. I'm starving!"

Jennifer and Montana enjoyed a great dinner at one of Jennifer's favorite places downtown Athens. For dessert, she took Montana by Jittery Joe's to introduce her to Tilly. There, she received some great news about the retiring latté machine, and she treated her young charge to a caramel-drizzled decaf frappé for their drive home.

Finally, at dusk, Jennifer sat on her front porch, allowing the mindless swoosh of occasional passing traffic and the trilling of cicadas to lull her into a near-hypnotic state, which was a relief after her day. The encounter with Michael and the shopping had tunneled beneath her carefully balanced state of self-assurance, leaving her off-kilter. Sleep would help. Tomorrow Earl would prime the apothecary's exterior while Michael and James replaced the rotted boards in the back room, and she would start stripping the fabulous sideboard for the dining room. Her work in the house would give her a good excuse to avoid Michael after Stella persuaded him to escort Jennifer to the Mid-Summer Gala.

Of course, the refinished floors of the house now beckoned the eager men to abandon the camper. They planned a trip to Lawrenceville this week as well, to load Michael's F150 and a small U-Haul with belongings stored in the unit there. It would be a little harder to ignore her handsome employer as he manhandled heavy furniture in and out of the historic residence.

A bark from Otis alerted her that a beat-up pick-up rumbled into Calvin's yard next door. She watched as two young men clad in camouflage climbed out and approached the door. Calvin appeared, but rather than invite them in, the three of them started walking her way. Wait. Clad in camouflage.

As they drew closer, Jennifer saw the guys carried rifles and had smeared some sort of dark paint under their eyes. Really? Since she was still dressed and they had already seen her, she could hardly justify making a run for it. She remained on the porch, pulling her legs down from their folded position on her chair and standing.

"Jennifer, these here are my nephews, Tom and Mike," Calvin said by way of introduction. "They're here to take care of your armadillo problem."

She nodded at the nephews, who nodded back. Both Tom and Mike were heavyset like their uncle. "Thank you, but you'll have to walk on over to Michael's."

"You take 'em. Tell 'em what you've got in mind. I'm right in the middle of the season finale of 'Mountain Men.'" Calvin didn't give her time for argument. He turned around and headed home, leaving Jennifer gazing upon the two hulking teenagers with the sinking realization that she'd have to face Michael already.

"Let me get my shoes on."

The boys trailed silently behind her to the front door of Dunham House, where Jennifer rang the doorbell. Michael answered with his own .22 loosely clasped in hand. He clearly expected the night hunt to occur, although the face paint took him aback a little, too. He gave directions for where he wanted to post the boys and detailed his own lookout point.

"OK, well, have fun, y'all," Jennifer said, waving a hand as she tried to sidle away.

"Hold on a minute, Jennifer. Boys, why don't you go on inside and see my dad for some coffee while I speak to Jennifer a minute? He's got some brewed up for our night. I'm thinking we'll be needing it."

"Sure thing," Tom said. He and his brother provided a pleasant surprise when they wiped their feet before entering the house, slamming the heavy, sticking door loudly behind them.

Michael came down from the porch and stood before her. She couldn't meet his eyes. This was when he was going to tell her she had no need of his escort to the Historic Oglethorpe event.

"Jennifer, Stella filled me in today on why you and Montana went shopping. She also talked about the importance of the Mid-Summer Gala, about both of us being able to meet important business people and homeowners in the area. I rarely attend social events like this, but believe it or not, I do see the value of your ideas for Hermon. So I will support Allison opening her herb shop, and I wanted to know if I could accompany you this Saturday."

Her lips parted, and her eyes drifted up to his in silent astonishment.

His crooked smile appeared. "I think we can help each other through the evening, don't you?"

Actually, she thought his presence would throw her off a lot more than going alone would, but she was not about to tell him that. The part of her that had missed out on attending the prom begged to arrive somewhere special, just once, on the arm of a man like Michael. And she liked him enough that this time she wouldn't let her pragmatic, self-protective nature deny that part. "Yes. Yes, I do."

What was it exactly that one did with a gentleman? To figure that out, Jennifer realized she'd need to begin to feel like a lady.

Oglethorpe County, Georgia
1861-1864

In a season of darkness when we think we can die no more, life is often born. So it was for me in 1861. To anyone viewing my affairs from the outside, I was the privileged young wife of the handsomest man in the county, perhaps the whole state of Georgia. The Dunham name was respected throughout the Southeast. I presided over my own home with a maid who attended my every need. But no one knew I had been plunged into the depths of a slavery no less binding, but far subtler, than hers.

On the surface, Stuart acted gallant, attentive and respectful. No one questioned why I rarely visited in the county or invited guests, why Stuart always accompanied me on my brief and rare sojourns to Athens. Everyone assumed we preferred to remain in the privacy of newlywed bliss. No one imagined his jealousy even of my female friends, much less the belittling accusations he hurled should I be so unfortunate as to capture the attention of another man over dinner. I attempted to avoid such suspicions by focusing all my efforts at home, yet no matter how hard I tried to make everything perfect, I was a young girl doomed to many failures socially and within my household.

Stuart told me he had married me in hopes that I was not narrow-minded, selfish and demanding like other girls. His sarcasm, criticism and insinuations eroded me from the inside out. The outside did not escape, either. He was not above raising his hand to me on the rare occasions I found courage to "talk back." Should I ever attempt to evade his rough demands in the bedroom, he made sure I heard his pleasure fulfilled from the cabin right behind the house, that of my maid and cook, the mulatto he'd taken from the kitchen of his father's plantation. The fact that I also heard sounds of struggle only added nausea to my irrational combination of relief and jealousy.

In 1859, Lettie gave birth to a daughter with coppery curls and tawny skin. Lettie named her Sally. The next year another daughter, Beulah, followed, also light-skinned. The babies slept on ticking in a little metal bed with side rails that Stuart provided for her cabin, while an old slave woman tended them during the day.

And then, two things happened. I discovered I, too, carried a child. My status earned me something of a hiatus from Stuart's impatience. And that spring of 1861, the Southern states seceded and went to war with the North. People talked about how the North did not allow us adequate representation in Congress and impeded industrialization in their greed for cotton. The established national precedent of secession traced back to our war for independence from Britain and had found expression in Texas and Mexico. Northern politicians recently supported the concept. But when the Confederacy formed below the Mason-Dixon, suddenly the Union was inviolate. States had no rights outside the Union.

Yes, these reasons to support the South rang true. And had I remained in my father's home in Athens, I'm sure I would have embraced the concept of states' rights. But from my new viewpoint as a captive in Hermon, I just wished they'd call a spade a spade and admit that one of the main rights they wanted to preserve was slavery. And I saw now the unspeakableness of it.

Ironically, the war sprung open the door of my prison. Stuart offered his services as assistant surgeon with the Oglethorpe Rifles, Hermon men who drilled right in our home town. With George Lumpkin as their captain, they attached to the 8th Georgia Infantry alongside notable companies from Rome and Savannah. The days before Stuart left for Virginia felt almost like the days of our engagement. All the prominent families represented Oglethorpe, including Phinizy, Brightwell, Maxey and Gilham. So did colorful characters like William Butler, said to never be too tired to sing, and Jesse Dalton, so old Colonel Bartow said he'd have to get him a chair to sit down in so he could fight.

Poor Dalton was horribly wounded at the 8th's first fight at Bull Run. Stuart's letter home told us Union shells bowled into the regiment as they fought near a pine thicket in an exposed position. Under regimental surgeon Homer Virgil Milton Miller, Stuart operated all night in a willow grove near a stream, amputating and digging out bullets while Miller hollered "next" like a barber snipping haircuts.

The heaviest fighting of the whole battlefield centered on that pine thicket. Well after that hot July afternoon, the men of Company K, Oglethorpe Rifles, realized why they had suffered no casualties. Back home, at that exact hour, citizens in a county-wide prayer meeting at Atkinson's Church beseeched the Lord's protection on their men. No one doubted the power of prayer after that.

What would they all have thought if only they knew Dr. Dunham's wife never once offered up a plea for the surgeon laboring behind the lines? Not then, and not once throughout the war.

As my confinement approached, Stuart's family agreed I should close up house and come stay on the plantation. Silas oversaw my care, but told me the delicate needs of women in such a condition would necessarily dispose me to feel more comfortable in the hands of Aunt Selah. I was too afraid to tell him how afraid I was! Anne befriended me, but I learned early in my marriage she would not be receptive to anything negative said about her little brother, whom she preferred to see as high-spirited but harmless. To Selah I did not have to say anything. She already knew her prediction about my marriage to Stuart had come true. Her respectful and compassionate manner lent me a dignity sorely lacking, and, lubricated by a couple of quarts of witch hazel tea, she brought Hampton Dunham into the world without incident. Afterwards, she rubbed bitter herbs on the bottom of my belly and had me drink garden thyme tea.

After that, I rarely saw Aunt Selah, and I never sought her out. Despite her gentle manner, something about her made me uncomfortable. Anne became my closest companion as we shared the challenges and rewards of motherhood.

As Hampton grew into a rosy-faced, sandy-haired toddler, headstrong outbursts occasionally punctuated his normally easy-going temperament. I comforted myself that he was not like his father because he responded quickly to discipline. Or maybe Stuart had just been lacking in it like Aunt Selah said. I had been forced to bring Lettie with me to the plantation, where she returned to the kitchen and her offspring were accepted without comment or question. Anne's maid took her place in serving me. While in Oglethorpe, I encouraged Hampton to play with his cousins, but he preferred Lettie's Sally and Beulah. They doted on him like they were much older. He found them even when I tried to keep them separate, like some invisible magnet drew the secret half-siblings together.

As early as 1862 the blockade of Southern ports created shortages. Army demands caused meat, flour and coffee to run low. Local residents' pleas for food besieged a colonel who moved to Oglethorpe from Athens and supplied the Confederate Army corn at a dollar a bushel. We kept fairly well supplied on the plantation, but my parents agitated to see Hampton once we were strong enough to travel.

In the home of my father, with my healthy, happy baby in my arms, I could almost pretend the wasteland of the past three years a bad dream. But the alteration in my personality revealed the truth. I who had once laughed and chatted freely now preferred solace to company. I tiptoed and groveled in my efforts to placate. And I flinched when anyone made a sudden move.

I feared my parents would excuse Stuart's behavior as the prerogative of a husband, but when my mother finally heckled the truth out of me, and told my father, I could hear him roaring and breaking things all the way upstairs. He declared that except for visits to the Dunham plantation in Stuart's absence, for Stuart's relatives to see Hampton, I now resided again in Cobbham. My father would deal with Stuart when he returned from Virginia.

But something happened in autumn 1864 to change all that. The North's greater numbers and industrialization, coupled with our inability to feed the troops and repair our railroads due to blockade, wore the superior Confederate fighting machine down to its last leg. Union General Sherman advanced from Northwest Georgia to the supply city of Atlanta. In Athens, the pine knot gas had long been turned off, the doors of Franklin College bolted, and a solemn stillness filled the town, interrupted only by warning bells alerting citizens to nearby Yankee cavalry. Once, Captain Lumpkin's local battery lobbed shells in the direction of raiders as close as Barber Creek, sending them fleeing back toward Monroe. Federal prisoners taken in the countryside were quartered on campus en route to Andersonville Prison, and in September around 1400 Confederates flooded our town as General Wheeler's cavalry rendezvoused in Athens. Even so, this seemed preferable to life in Oglethorpe, as we heard tales of soldiers pillaging and stealing in the country. After the siege of Atlanta, we also heard that the Yankees tore up tracks of the Georgia Railroad as far from Atlanta as the Oconee River crossing.

Another siege, however, most impacted my life, one happening not a day's journey away but all the way up in Richmond, Virginia, where the 8th Georgia defended the Confederate capitol. Cut off from communications, we did not know until much later that many Oglethorpe Rifles paid in that endeavor with their limbs and lives. My husband had been assigned to a field hospital closer to their ranks than the municipal hospital. I first learned of the shell that exploded over that field hospital when a servant came to fetch me from Dunham Plantation. We were preparing for a paltry Thanksgiving. The man came to our back door and soon placed Anne's note, written crosswise over a recipe for apple turnovers, in my hand.

"Stuart has been gravely wounded by a shell which exploded over the field hospital where he labored. The shell fragment lodged in his head was removed, but he is greatly affected. According to the latest news, he is alive and convalescing in Richmond. You know William served with the faculty of Atlanta Medical College. The evacuation of wounded and civilians from that city prior to the application of Sherman's torch freed him from duty in the surgical hospital there. He left by way of South Carolina to fetch Stuart home. We must pray they make this hazardous journey safely and return to us by Christmas. We know you will want to be here."

"She's not goin'," my father announced.

"George, she must," Mother disagreed. "Do you want to make public her private shame? Stuart will be perceived as a war hero. What wife would not be there to welcome such a husband home?"

"One who does not deserve further abuse!"

Mother shook her head, the tails of her lace day cap floating over her silvery chignon. "It would be different were he returning home well in body at the end of the war. But you heard what Anne said. He is 'greatly affected.' There's no way he can hurt her now."

I found the household in Oglethorpe in great agitation. Silas battled an outbreak of measles among the slaves. Lettie's Sally fell prey to the deadly childhood illness at but five years old, while Anne's older son contracted the sickness but escaped. No one could console Lettie. I kept Hampton in a separate part of the house, allowing no contact with the other children.

William did not come back with Stuart by Christmas. Finally, on a gray, sleeting day in January when meager fires in the main rooms of the house kept the penetrating chill at bay, we heard the rattle of carriage wheels on the drive. Standing frozen in my twice-turned wool day dress, I could not bring myself to even look out the window, while Silas hurried from the house with as much speed as he could muster at sixty-six.

Before following him out onto the porch, Anne clasped my hand and said, "Pray William treated him as his father would want. The last thing we need is a rift in the family now."

I knew of Silas' displeasure that William had attached himself to Atlanta Medical College instead of the Georgia Eclectic Medical College, which Silas himself helped found. Anne said this was due to William's skill as a surgeon, but Silas said it was due to rebellion. Silas had taught his sons to rely more on herbs than on potent and often toxic drugs and venesection, or blood-letting.

"Come," she added, tugging at my hand.

I hung back.

"Charlotte, what is the matter? Yours is the face he will most want to see. Are you afraid of how he might look?"

"I think … I'm more afraid of what he might be like inside."

"I understand." She squeezed my fingers. "Should Durbin walk through the door right now, I'd probably faint. I'm sure we will find them altered by the war, but underneath they will still be the same men we fell in love with."

That was exactly what I feared.

Anne changed her mind. "You do look pale. Go wait in the bedroom you've prepared."

I did as she said, seating myself by the bed in the chamber at the top of the stairs, from where I could hear the grandfather clock on the landing ticking, marking the minutes until I also heard sounds of struggle. Stuart's manservant helped William carry Stuart up. When they entered with Stuart's long length distributed between them, William holding under his brother's shoulders and Charlie moving backwards with his legs, Stuart looked more mummy than man. He wore a heavy, dark gray overcoat, and clean bandages swathed his head. I stood back so that they could settle him against the pillows. Charlie pulled off Stuart's boots, then assisted with the coat.

William straightened and looked at me. "Charlotte."

A moment of surprise made me silent. William was so much leaner than I remembered, his eyes shadowed from lack of sleep and his straight dark hair shot through with silver.

"He will recognize you, but is unable to speak except for certain slurred words and sounds. Come to his left side. He is more sensible there." As I began to move, he added, "Don't let the bandages alarm you. The wound is closing up nicely, I just wrapped it well for travel."

As shocking as I found William's loss of weight, Stuart I could have termed emaciated. His green eyes in a face someone had shaved sought me out as

I took his left hand. He tried to smile, but the right side of his face only responded slightly, making the attempt look more like a grimace.

"Cha … char … lll …"

I bent close to hear the name Stuart could not complete.

Anne, standing in the doorway, snuffled into her handkerchief.

"Welcome home, Stuart." I kissed his hand. Everyone waited. I leaned forward and also kissed his cheek near his lips, then, embarrassed, I glanced at William. "Thank you for bringing him home. Was it a terrible journey?"

"Our rail system is in deplorable condition, and with Sherman in Savannah, let's just say I had to be creative in the routes we traveled."

"I'll not even ask how you came by a carriage and horses," Silas said. The hint of pride underlying his tone brought a brief smile to his son's lips.

"Should I bring in Hampton?" I asked, looking over my shoulder.

"I think that can wait until he's rested," William replied, beginning to rifle through the black medical bag he'd set on a table.

Stuart gripped my hand. "Brrrr," he growled.

"I think he wants to see him." As ambiguous as my personal feelings were, I could only imagine how much a father would want to see the son he'd only remember as an infant. I didn't want to frighten Hampton by introducing this strange, wounded soldier as his father, but my internal training to avoid Stuart's displeasure had already returned to active duty.

William fixed his brother with a stern eye. "Later." When to my alarm Stuart began to push his left leg toward the edge of the bed, William stepped close and gently but firmly pushed him back. He hissed in his ear, "Whist, man, do you want to scare the boy to death? Give it time."

That idea seemed to sink in. Thankfully, at that moment, a maid entered with some broth and bread.

"Can he eat that?" Anne wondered.

"If you tear out the soft center part," William said.

"My poor little brother," Anne said. "Let me feed him."

"I would think that would be a job his wife would want," Silas told her.

I took the tray from the maid with trembling hands. Pity and repulsion warred within me, and also something else I could not yet identify.

William said, "After Charlotte is finished, I'll show you how to replace the bandage. We'll all have to take turns assisting Stuart in the coming months."

As I spooned the thin liquid into Stuart's mouth, I attempted to reconcile the wasted man in front of me with the virile doctor of four years ago.

Silas asked William about Stuart's medication.

"While in Richmond, we applied yarrow to the wound to slow the bleeding and aid healing. It still is not fully closed, so I recommend we continue to cleanse it with plantain and witch hazel or, better yet, make a yarrow ointment like the Highlanders did," the younger man said.

I felt Anne perch beside me on the bed. She reached for the bread and began tearing small chunks which I could then place between my husband's lips.

"Originally, of course, they treated him with opium, but I advocated for King's remedy as set forth in his 1858 manual of the use of spirits of lavender."

"Thank God you retained some of your early training," Silas commented.

William went on without response, "We did as he recommended, adding lobelia and capsicum and giving it every twenty minutes to stop convulsions."

"Convulsions?" Anne gasped in horror.

"Yes, he had them often after the surgery, less so now, but they still occur when he becomes agitated. So long as I keep him somewhat sedated, he is manageable."

Stuart glared at him.

"And now?" Silas prodded. "Shall I help you prepare the follow-up mixture King recommended? Let's see, skunk cabbage roots, scull cap, ladies' slipper, lobelia, alcohol. What am I missing?"

"Ether, ammonia, and the spirit of lavender. Medical supplies were scarce, but I tried to procure what I could to bring back with me." William shot his father a quick grin. "I even got my hands on some real coffee."

"I also believe my own recipe for hysteria would be advantageous, the one with calimus root, fennel seed and common ash bark simmered in new milk."

"Agreed. Let's see what we can come up with once we've rebandaged his head."

Silas looked satisfied, and Anne gave me a discreet nod.

When Silas admitted growing fatigue after the day's excitement, directions to prepare a yarrow poultice were sent to the slave who assisted him with prescriptions. Stuart moved his left hand over mine to show me he had enough to eat. Anne cupped her hand under her brother's chin while he drank water from a glass. Meanwhile the two men consulted over William's medical bag and poured a liquid medicine into a spoon, passing it between Stuart's lips. The servant took the tray, and not knowing what else to do, I sat holding his hand just looking at him, trying until they began to drift closed to see into those green eyes if he had changed and was sorry. I wanted to hope, but I also hated holding that hand.

I became aware William called my name, and Stuart's grasp had gone completely slack. "Charlotte, I'm going to remove the bandage now. Are you prepared to stay?"

I nodded, but Anne and I went to stand at the foot of the bed. Anne wrapped her hand through the crook of my elbow.

"The shell fragment struck him October fifth," William said, mainly to his father, who leaned in close to watch William work, but also to us. "It entered just outside of the left front protuberance, passing back and up, and removing a piece of the squamous portion of the temporal bone along with brain substance and membrane."

I clutched my stomach as a moan escaped, and Anne tightened her grip.

"Do you ladies need to leave?" Silas asked.

"I think we'd rather know what we're dealin' with. As William said, we may be called on to help at some point," Anne replied.

William unwrapped as he talked. "Before the surgery, brain matter oozed out, and the wound bled a great deal. He had no sensibility on his right side. He came to consciousness after the surgery and has regained some mobility from that initial paralysis."

"Will he regain more?" Anne ventured.

"It's possible. We know so little of brain injuries, and, with this war, the repair of head wounds is a field for pioneers. Unfortunately, the operations are conducted under both privation and time constraint. I imagine the Northern men wounded in such a manner fare better."

From where I stood, the jagged opening in Stuart's temple became visible.

Silas squinted as though having trouble focusing. "There's a little pus," he murmured, turning for a bottle of witch hazel and a sterilized cloth from William's bag. As he uncorked the bottle, he shrugged, then tilted his head from side to side.

"Are you all right?" William asked his father.

"Yes, fine. Just a stiff neck and headache."

William didn't respond to his father's comment, instead gesturing him closer again. "Place your finger here. This is something you'll probably never witness again. The pulsations of his brain can be felt."

I bolted. Anne didn't even try to hold me. I ran outside to the back of the house, where I lost my lunch under a holly tree. My nausea originated from far more than the pulsations of a brain, although I noted the irony that Stuart's outer appearance finally mirrored what I knew to be on the inside. The man who had shattered my dreams and self-respect had returned to me an invalid requiring my tender care for an untold amount of time. Bitterness, that was the emotion I had not been able to name earlier. I tasted it on my tongue now, as I felt the shackles around my soul tighten. My freedom had been an illusion.

CHAPTER EIGHT

"Four dead armadillos, that's how many were lined up the next morning," Jennifer told Rita Worley at the end of that next week as Montana's grandma's wedge heel sure-footedly pumped her higher and higher. She could see herself in the mirror, towel on head, and, like a spread-eagled victim on a Medieval rack, her compromised position had already loosened her tongue. She fairly babbled. Her audience, which also included Montana and Jean, listened with an intent interest that probably had more to do with the project at hand than the midnight hunting adventures of Tom and Mike.

"So was that all of them?" Rita asked, whisking the towel away. She rifled her fingers briskly through Jennifer's wet locks.

"Nope, they had to come back Tuesday night to take out two more, but I think that's finally it."

"What drama," Jean said. "You know, we've had our battles, too. Just about everybody in the neighborhood has. Those armadillos are real pests. Every time you think you get ahead ..."

Reaching for a comb, Rita changed the subject. "We saw the U-Haul this week. What did Michael bring in?"

"Some things from storage in Lawrenceville."

Rita's brows shot up. "If they tried to fill that house with a manly selection of modern furniture, I can't imagine that went over well." She sliced a neat part at the top of Jennifer's head.

Jennifer laughed and held steady as the hairdresser combed. "It wasn't as bad as I'd feared, actually. They sold or donated most of the furnishings not being used by the family renting James' house. Then there were some things from Michael's grandmother. We put all the occasional tables and chairs in one room, from where we can disperse them as needed. They set up the bed we got from Gloria's estate for James and the suite I found on my trip to Union Point for Michael. It's already looking so different. You'll have to come over to see. Last night was their first in the house."

"Oh, I bet they were excited," Jean said.

"Did they see any ghosts?" Montana wanted to know.

"Yes, and no." Having enjoyed a full-sized bed, shower, and an absence of armadillo, Michael had indeed seemed happier and better rested this morning.

Jean asked, "They going to sell that camper?"

"I think so."

A temporary silence fell as Rita shifted Jennifer's wet bangs, then the sides of the hair at her shoulders, back and forth, measuring different potential lengths. Eyes wide and fearful, Jennifer watched the wrinkled lips purse, then thin, the eyebrows raise, then draw tight. Apparently a small change made a big difference in Rita's estimation.

During the moment of contemplation, Jennifer thought she heard the shrill of the table saw from across the street. Michael was cutting replacements for the damaged "X"s on the apothecary porch. She ought to be over there, not because she didn't trust him, but the opposite ... his skill with the machinery impressed her. She had to admit it gave her no pain to watch him. And it would spare her from being over here. But he'd practically run her off with a two by four when she'd dawdled near his work station right up to her appointment time. Was she really that badly in need of physical restoration herself?

Rita's silence continued too long. "Talk to me," Jennifer pled in a tone that hinted at openness to negotiation.

"I'm just thinkin' you really need your length. What do you think, girls?" Rita turned to appeal to the two generations seated behind her. Jennifer still wasn't sure they had a valid excuse to be present.

"Mmm," Jean agreed with an amazing amount of inflection for a non-word.

"But I want to layer your bangs into the back, add some texture all over. That way when you take to it with the blow dryer and a round brush, you get some body."

Body. Jennifer peeked with unease at Rita's own perfect swirl.

Rita seemed to read her mind. "Not that much. I've got a lot more to compensate for than you do, young lady. But right now your cut is draggin' your face down. We want to make a frame, not a dead weight. But first, if you'll let me, I'd like to mix up some color."

"What ... color?"

"Just a little dark auburn. See these highlights in your crown?" Rita held up some strands. "The sun has done its work and showed us exactly what shade to enhance."

Jennifer gulped. "You want to make me a redhead?" Frightful memories of a stranger rather than her mother coming home, crowned with hues so brilliant strangers turned to stare in the grocery store, stirred in the recesses of her mind.

"Nothing over the top," Rita hastened to assure her, "and not all over. Just highlights. You'll be amazed at the depth and richness they will bring to your shade of brown."

"Depth and richness, huh?" Where negotiations failed, she stalled.

"Oh, come on, Jennifer, *please*?" Montana clasped her hands at her chin and batted her lashes, which her mother had allowed her to paint with dark brown mascara today. She looked, yes, *adorable*, in her new romper. "You've got to set a good example for me, right?"

Jennifer had to laugh. "How is getting highlights setting a good example?"

Montana flung her arms open wide. "It would be teachin' me that we should embrace all that we can be, inside and out!"

As Jennifer rolled her eyes, Rita said, "You know, Montana does have a point. No one would say that apothecary over there looked better stripped down to bare boards than it does now that Earl's got two coats of paint on it, would they?" Hands on her hips, Rita cocked her head and waited, her fancy little shoe tapping lightly. What a firecracker she must have been at twenty.

"Rita, that was a low blow, using restoration lingo against me," Jennifer accused, but she conceded with a sigh, "Fine. Do what you want." If she just employed her old technique of mentally putting herself outside this situation, it could be gratifying to see how happy this little assignment made this makeover trio.

As the older lady clapped her hands and burst into motion, seeking some strange solution to mix in a pot, as if on cue, Jean grabbed a nearby chair and drug it up close to Jennifer. She sat down, pulling a satchel onto her lap. Jennifer eyed her with a new level of suspicion.

"Speaking of adding fresh paint," she said with a mysterious lilt to her voice, "I brought a little of my own."

Jennifer's gaze darted to Montana. The girl reminded her with joy, "Mama's a Mary Kay consultant!"

"Oh, no. You don't drive a pink car, too, do you?"

"Nope, I drive a Jeep. Far more practical for the farm. I work hard, and I don't always spend much time getting ready in the mornings, but when I go out to town, sometimes I like to do something special for myself. It's worth it." Jean smiled and laid in Jennifer's cape-clad lap a palate of eye shadows in the same shades Montana had brought dress shopping. "Have you ever had a make-up consultation before?"

"Uh, no. Most definitely not."

Jean nodded. "Well, I wondered if you might be open to a few suggestions for your event while Mama is mixing. I could apply some foundation now and do finishing touches while your color is setting."

"I think you have a captive audience, all but the shackles."

"Oh, Jennifer, you are so silly," Montana giggled. "It's *fun*!"

"Why don't you come over here and take my place, miss smarty?"

"I get a Mary Kay party with my friends when I turn thirteen, but now it's *your* turn! You've got to look *fabuloso* for *Michael*!" Again with the batting lashes and clasped hands, accompanied by a dramatic, dreamy sigh.

Jennifer wished for something to throw at her.

Jean just smiled patiently. "These are the colors a fall person would wear. Montana explained that to you already." She placed a small assortment of bottles, pots and brushes on the counter. "I've taken the liberty of selecting what I think might work best for you, Jennifer, but if you'll hold out your wrist, I'll test a couple shades of foundation on you. Now this will just even out your skin tone ..."

For the next hour, for all but the cucumber application, Jennifer felt like the Sandra Bulloch character in "Miss Congeniality." Rita, Jean and Montana kept her turned away from the mirror, a position that generated both gratefulness and fear. Jean explained how to apply a five-minute face and a fifteen-minute face. Apparently she would need the fifteen-minute face tomorrow night. Jean went over her instructions twice so Jennifer would know how to duplicate the proper look, then gave her a total for the minimum supply order. Oh, gee, she was supposed to *pay* for this? Montana graciously pointed out that the consultation had been complimentary. Jennifer felt pretty sure Montana was there to make sure she followed through with everything. The adults knew she could hardly refuse in the face of the child's enthusiasm. So she wrote check number one just before Rita rinsed.

Rita's silver shears snipped exciting layers from sheer style boredom, then the hairdresser gave Jennifer instructions on the blow dry process, still without swiveling the chair. Jennifer frowned, accustomed to allowing her naturally straight tresses to air dry, then simply running a brush through them. Thankfully, Rita could tell that if she said the words "curling iron," Jennifer would bolt, so she simply explained that with a good root pump and a lift and spray after the blow dry, Jennifer's hair would possess a natural-looking body that would softly frame her face. Both women heartily recommended that she wear contacts for her "town" look, and certainly to the gala. They stood admiring her and murmuring over how amazing she looked before finally getting around to the big reveal.

They were right. Jennifer had to put her glasses on to see, but when she did, she didn't even know what to say. Amazingly, she still looked like herself, just enhanced. Her outlined eyes popped even under the thick corrective lenses. The floating layers of her hair made her cheekbones appear higher, the lip pencil and gloss lent new fullness to her lips, and the new auburn highlights caused her skin to glow. No one could deny that a bit of a veneer made her much more attractive. But at the same time, something bothered her, something she couldn't quite put her finger on.

Montana clapped and jumped up and down. "Do you love it, Jennifer? Do you love it?"

"I have to say … I do." In the mirror, Jennifer saw smiles of relief spread across Rita's and Jean's faces. For their sakes, she shouldn't have been such a grump. She shoved aside the deeply buried unease. "I guess I just never thought I could look like this."

"Well, don't feel bad. We all have to call in the experts sometimes, just like Michael did." Rita winked and reached around to hug her. She whispered, "We all knew it was in there, honey. It didn't surprise us a bit. Thank you for trustin' us."

"Thank you for wanting to help, Miss Rita."

"Just imagine how it will look with that gorgeous dress on," Jean said.

And therein lay the problem. Saturday night Yoda had a lot of fun rolling a lipstick tube at her feet while Jennifer painstakingly recreated the look the beauty shop mirror had reflected. She opened two pods of contact lenses, inserting them over her shocked eyeballs, which threatened to revolt and ruin her makeup by watering. She dabbed with a tissue. Then she went into the closet and brought out the dress. Twisting into unnatural contortions, Jennifer got the zipper up. She clasped the wide, bronzed gold bracelet that Montana had picked out around her wrist and fastened a necklace with the same metallic hue and drips of small, dangling ruby beads. Then, bracing herself on the door frame of her closet, she slid her feet into the low, back-strap black heels she'd reluctantly agreed to and wobbled to her full-length mirror. The butterflies in her stomach exploded into full-fledged nausea.

She saw too much color, too much curve, which led to too much attention. She'd spent ten years learning how to hide, but this ensemble along with the hair and make-up announced overt female presence.

Just one time Jennifer had mustered the courage to verbally hint disapproval of her mother's cheapness of appearance and behavior. She had probably been about thirteen at the time. Kelly's automatic reply had struck like a viper then, and its memory stirred poison in her system even now: "At least I know how to take what I ask for."

Jennifer kicked off the heels and ran to the bathroom, grabbing her washcloth, soaking it, and scrubbing her face free of Mary Kay. She glanced up into the mirror ... and discovered that puffy hair looked ridiculous without make-up. Never ask again for any sort of attention. Be good and keep to yourself and you might be safe. She pulled her hair back into a pony tail. Stupid. Stupid, stupid, stupid. A bun. Yes, a bun at the back of her neck was better, but the color was still too vibrant, and soft little seductive strands kept escaping. Plucking the contacts out of her eyes and tossing them in the nearby trash, she stuck her head under the faucet. She had to wear the dress because she had nothing else appropriate, but everything else could be toned down and brought under control.

The glasses provided both much-needed barrier and magnification. Her hair looked darker wet and slicked neatly back into a simple twist. Jennifer placed gold stud earrings in her earlobes and slid her feet into her Mary Janes at one minute 'til Michael's scheduled arrival. Upon hearing his knock, she situated Yoda in the carrier in the laundry room and grabbed the clutch purse Montana had selected on her way to the door.

When she opened it, she froze, a moment of uncertainty washing over her. Michael looked so incredibly suave in a dress shirt and narrow, striped tie, but his slicked back, dark hair bore way too much similarity to hers. "Hi. Uh …" Michael's gaze slid slowly from tip to toe. "You look … nice." But his voice fell flat.

"Thank you, so do you." And it would be best to look at him as little as possible. Jennifer locked her door. "Let's go."

"OK …"

She set out at too fast a pace for someone who had just gotten off crutches, although she still favored the one ankle. She couldn't have worn those heels anyway. No one would blame her for that. And if she got lucky, Rita and Jean wouldn't hear of the destruction she'd unleashed on their selfless efforts.

Michael trailed silently behind her. When they got to his truck, he unlocked the door, but she scrambled up in before he had time to offer her a hand. As she tucked her dress under her, he stood looking at her from below.

"What?"

He shook his head. "It's nothing. I just thought …"

"You thought what?"

"Nothing." Michael closed her door and walked around to the driver's side.

But she couldn't let it go. If he harbored some droll observation about her appearance, or some reservation about taking her, better to have it out now. "I hate it when people do that. Just say what you're thinking."

"Fine. I'd heard that you were getting some big makeover. Don't get me wrong, the dress is beautiful, but I guess I just expected the rest of you to look really different or something."

"The last I checked, a bun was considered an elegant hairstyle for a formal gathering," Jennifer snapped. "But if you keep looking at my hair, we're going to be late. Can we go now?"

Michael blinked his long lashes and readjusted his attention to the windshield, turning the key over in the ignition. "Sure."

They drove in silence until they were almost there, when Michael must have felt the need to go over their game plan. "So I need to mingle and meet the other homeowners, especially those from Hermon I haven't met yet. I also hear the mayor of Lexington will be here. I should probably shake his hand in case Dad and I start a business in the county. But you have a whole list of folks. Right?"

"Right. Mary Ellen is supposed to look for us and introduce me to the mayors of Lexington and Hermon, the chamber director, the president of Historic Oglethorpe, and the chair of the Athens-Clarke Rails to Trails."

Michael pulled his F150 in the field adjoining the grounds of the historic house, which were illuminated with spotlights and tiny white lights, a magical vision that turned Jennifer's stomach to mush. Now that they were here, the concept of a supportive companion at her side as she approached the big gathering of influential strangers seemed comforting. They bumped to a stop, he put the truck in park, then he turned to her. "But do you want me to stay with you?"

Jennifer felt even more scared, much more of what he was asking than of the social challenges before her. Another thing one didn't do was admit need. "You don't have to. I'll have Mary Ellen to help me navigate."

"But do you want me to?" Michael's eyes bored into hers, demanding a deeper honesty.

She already sensed she had somehow disappointed him. Had he taken the simplicity of her appearance as a snub of his company? She certainly didn't want to make him think she purposefully tried to be insulting. In light of the importance of pleasing her employer, of course, her own feelings weren't really important. That they complied with what she needed to answer anyway definitely did not bear further examination! Jennifer pulled on the door handle. "Yes," she said, "I think that would be a good idea."

"Wait!" Michael's hand shot out. "Would you just ... wait?"

It wasn't the exasperation in his voice that made Jennifer freeze obediently as her escort jumped out and jogged around the vehicle. It was more the overtone of something else ... pleading? Sympathy? When he pulled her door open, she looked askance at him.

He raised his eyebrows. "Are you not wearing a dress? Did you not sprain your ankle recently? Are we not at a formal event? And ... Lord help us, Jennifer, did you never go to prom?"

"Yes, yes, yes and no."

Michael shook his head. "Well, for once, can you just allow the guy to do his job?" He held out his hand.

Reluctantly, she took it, mostly because it would leave hers free to jerk her skirt down if it slid up too much as she descended from the leather seat. "I guess Rob and the other husbands all had other employment, because I never saw any of them treat Mom like this," she joked.

"Well, that's a shame."

The sincerity of Michael's tone kept her from further comment. His mother had lived long enough that Michael, in his impressionable, growing-up years, had certainly seen James hold open Linda's doors, pull out her chairs and compliment her in a million ways, expressions of respect and protection that Jennifer only glimpsed in old movies. She couldn't imagine being the recipient of that kind of attention. In fact, right now, walking into the party as he hovered a hand near the small of her back in case she should stumble, and checking the road before they stepped out, that attention was so opposite of what Jennifer was accustomed to that it made her intensely aware of how undeserving she felt. Whether in employment or personal relations, she'd taught herself and been further trained at the university by people like Professor Shelley to avoid putting herself under others, especially men. Yet did a putting under exist that was not domination, but shelter?

The confusing thoughts churned in Jennifer's head. Exploring deep personal issues often led to mental shutdown, and she could not do that now, with a whole list of people to meet. Projecting past professional to charming would require all her inner reserves, so she'd have to think about the Michael thing later. For now, she needed to compartmentalize this as a business occasion. She and Michael were both here on a job.

CHAPTER NINE

Balancing her chiffon-wrapped solidness on chunky, sparkly heels, Mary Ellen waved and minced over the minute she spied Jennifer and Michael. She led them to a buffet of elegant finger foods and offered champagne. They both declined. She first introduced them to the president of Historic Oglethorpe, an older gentleman in a suit. While they provided a summary of their restoration efforts, Alton Wilson, the Lexington mayor, his wife and the chamber president walked up, sparing them a repeat.

"We're all so impressed watching the changes from the outside," the mayor said, "and it sounds like you have it looking just as nice inside."

"Come by any time, any of you," Michael offered, most generously for him, Jennifer thought. "We'll be happy to give you the full tour."

"We just might take you up on it. What type of work do you do, Michael?"

"Well, my father and I own an Atlanta construction company," Michael replied.

As the two of them angled off to discuss the merits of opening a branch of the business in the county, Marian Dukes, the tall, dark-haired, fiftyish chamber president, inquired further about Jennifer. "You graduated this past May from the program at UGA?"

Sipping her punch, Jennifer affirmed it was so.

"You know we have a number of buildings in our town needing an expert's attention, and we'd really like to put Lexington back on the map. I realize you're probably looking for something much higher profile, but would you ever consider a Main Street directorship?"

Jennifer stepped back in a moment of complete surprise. She had never thought of anything other than working in a larger city's preservation firm. Non-profit management had been Tilly's area of study, not hers. "Um, I don't know."

"Well, think about it. And can I call you when we're hiring?"

"Do you think it would be soon?"

"If you'd be interested, it could be." Marian gave her a confidential smile, winked and slipped a business card into Jennifer's hand.

While Jennifer noticed Michael's gaze follow the gesture, Mary Ellen's mouth formed a small 'O.' When she recovered, Mary Ellen blurted, "Oh, Mrs. Dukes, you ought to hear the ideas Jennifer has for Hermon. She'd be such an asset to the whole county. Why, this is perfect. I'm so excited when I consider the big picture." She waved a hand, then reached out to snag a passing, silver-haired man in a pink-striped, Ralph Lauren shirt. "Jim Cohen, do come here, you really must join this conversation. Jim, this is Jennifer, the restoration graduate who's been workin' on Michael's house. Jennifer, this is Jim Cohen, the local Rails to Trails chair. I think the rest of you are acquainted. Jennifer was just about to share some of her ideas for makin' Hermon an appealing little stop on Highway 77."

Responding to her cue, Jennifer nodded and took a breath. "Well for starters, Michael has agreed to lease the apothecary once it's restored to Allison Winters, to open an herb shop ..." She went on to detail the type of things Allison might carry and local events she might host. That spilled into the concept of Mary Ellen carrying coffee and treats—

"If I could ever afford to upgrade," Mary Ellen put in with a deprecating smile.

Jennifer continued, "And the visualization of the old general store as an art gallery where Stella could provide lessons and arrange showings.

"There's enough room there for event space as well," she added.

"You should speak with Hermon's mayor, Reggie Brown," Alton Wilson said, having also listened to Jennifer's spiel. "I believe he's here tonight. That building's pretty pricey, which is why no private buyers have come forward. But if a lease with Mrs. James could be arranged, plus the income from event rentals, he might be willing to bring it before the town council."

"I'd really appreciate that, Mayor Wilson," Jennifer agreed, "and I'd be happy to provide a cost-free consult on renovation as long as I'm here. Coming in from the outside, I see so much local talent and opportunity as yet untapped. The right publicity could really draw folks out from Athens and make a great stop on the biking trail, don't you think, Mr. Cohen?"

Jim nodded. "I do. Hermon lies about mid-way between Crawford or Lexington and Union Point. I've thought for quite some time that it could prosper if it offered some trendy amenities. Please keep me informed of any progress you make. I can pass along your media files and announcements to our webmaster, which could help generate funding for that leg of the project."

"So that's what you're waitin' for? Funding?" Mary Ellen wanted to know.

"That, and the cooperation of a few local landowners."

"Who would be disturbed by a few passing bicyclists?"

"You'd be surprised."

Jennifer's first guess would have been Calvin Woods, but the trail would lay across the main road from his property. He must have a twin.

"Anyone we can help influence?" Mary Ellen asked.

The Rails to Trails chairman gave a brief laugh and sipped from his wine glass. "The roadblock owns land between your two properties," he said, glancing from the antique shop owner to Michael. "But his current home sits down the street and across the road."

"Bryce Stevenson," Mary Ellen intoned in the flat voice of immediate recognition.

Jennifer asked, "Does he just not want people on his property?"

"There're some folks who don't want to see any kind of change," Mayor Wilson said. "I think Mayor Brown will tell you Councilman Stevenson must be handled with kid gloves. Those kind of people can't be moved by a frontal assault. One must find more creative ways."

"The good news is, we have a secret weapon who's a master at that very thing." Mary Ellen winked at Jennifer.

Jennifer smiled and shifted her weight from her tired ankle.

"Well, you folks can have her in Hermon so long as she's on Michael's project, but I've got dibs on her after that. That is, if I can entice her to stay." Marian smirked.

Having missed the earlier hint of a job offer, Michael raised his eyebrows.

"We'd love Miss Rushmore to put her name in the hat for Main Street director," Alton explained.

"Oh, wow. That's ... a fabulous idea." Michael smiled at Jennifer as the idea sunk in. All the attention so overwhelmed Jennifer that she couldn't tell if the surprise on his face came from positive or negative feelings.

Mary Ellen swayed forward and encircled Jennifer's forearm with her hand. "Well, we still have her," she said teasingly, "so if you don't mind, I'll take her to meet our mayor. I promised I'd introduce her around."

Jennifer cast a glance at Michael, checking on his comfort level, but he just gave a brief nod. "Go ahead. I'd like to speak to Mayor Wilson about the local medical services."

Confused, Jennifer allowed that unexpected inquiry to pass, instead thanking the chamber director and Lexington mayor. Then she followed Mary Ellen past a delightful string trio enveloping a group of well-dressed guests in a soft pocket of historical tunes. Nearby, in the white-lit grape arbor, she put her ideas to Reggie Brown, who invited her to speak before the next session of the town council regarding the potential long-term benefits of the old general store's repurposing. Reggie's warm and comfortable air, enhanced by his Southern drawl, put her at ease, and she found herself expressing her ideas with enthusiasm. As he asked what she thought might become of the current city hall should the offices relocate, Jennifer noticed Michael approaching. Smiling, he placed a drink on the table beside her as she replied that the cinder block building offered just the right amount of space for a local pottery or other artisan shop. They went on to discuss the current state of the depot and Brown's plans to solicit donations for a museum. At the end of the conversation, Jennifer thanked the mayor for his time.

"Why, young lady, it's I who should be thanking you," Reggie murmured, pumping her hand. "After all, you have no investment in all this, yet it's clear your ideas come from the heart. I really hope you'll stick around for a while."

They excused themselves with promises to be in touch.

"He's right, you know," Michael said low in her ear. "That was very impressive. And very altruistic."

Jennifer shrugged. "I can't seem to help it. I'd always pictured myself working for a preservation firm in a big city, but since I came here, the ideas just don't seem to stop. I'm surprised myself at how into the resurrection of a small town I'm getting."

"Maybe you should pay attention to that," Michael suggested, "because when something comes so naturally, it's often because it's meant to be." Before she could respond, he prompted as they passed the stage, "Dance with me."

Jennifer's eyes popped open wide despite the fact that a few couples gently swayed to the music.

"Oh, no one cares. Don't tell me you've never danced."

"Actually, I helped teach historic dances at Westville on more than one occasion, and this happens to be a waltz." How did she explain it wasn't the dancing, it was the partner?

"Then teach *me*."

"All right ..."

Michael responded instantly to the hesitation he heard in her voice. "What? You think I'm too dense to be taught?"

"No, I'm just surprised you want to learn." *And terrified of being that close to you.* But she decided the only graceful thing to do was put a brave face on it and pretend he was an eleven-year-old summer camper. "So basically the man's moves and the lady's moves mirror each other in two sets of three steps. The gentleman always starts on his left foot, the lady on her right. A lot of people teach the box step, but that's really more 1900s, and I think, kind of clunky. I favor the elegant American turning waltz, much like the Viennese waltz of a slightly later period, but with a different hand position."

"Enough with the history lesson, how do I hold you?"

She gulped. Did he have to put it that way? Jennifer explained how to create a low curve of the joined arms and the manner in which the lady clasped the gentleman's thumb, which felt far too intimate with Michael. She hurried on to the three-fourths rhythm and the manner of stepping out and between the partner's feet. Convinced the music would end before Michael grasped the really rather advanced steps, she hardly knew what to think when one of the band members noticed her instruction efforts and signaled to his friends to bridge into "Come Dearest, the Daylight is Gone," a waltz popularized around the time of the American Civil War ... and one of Jennifer's favorites.

Michael proved an amazingly quick study. Before the concluding bars, they slowly circled around each other, laughing when their feet brushed too close or extended too far, throwing them off balance and forcing them to cling with the hand attached to each other's shoulder and waist.

When the music ended, they smiled at each other, Jennifer dropping a curtsy.

"Man, I think you were born in the wrong era," Michael observed. "You're a really good teacher."

She blushed, and they turned to thank the band with their applause. Jennifer paused to get a business card. Good historical musicians could come in handy for special events.

"Have you covered all your social ground for tonight?" Michael asked as they walked away. To her consternation, he allowed his shoulder to brush against hers.

"Amazingly, I think I have. And amazingly, I'm not worn out."

"What else would you like to do before you go, then? Would you like to sit and listen to the music a while?"

Jennifer's eyes sparkled. "I'd like to tour the house."

"Well, come on then."

Grace Stevenson, the genealogical expert from the library whom Jennifer met when she had researched Hampton Dunham, awaited tour groups on the front porch. Her obvious delight over seeing Jennifer again translated to an in-depth verbal history which Jennifer loved and Michael politely endured. Jennifer admired the unusual, delicate cloverleaf columns on the front porch, like those of the Cobb-Treanor House in Athens which when viewed in cross-section created the quatrefoil, or variation of the Christian cross, as Jennifer pointed out to Michael. The renovation of the finest home in the county built by Mordecai Edwards for his young bride Martha into an event facility proved top notch, retaining the original pine flooring, fireplaces and ballroom, but adding mood touches like Baroque wooden crystal chandeliers.

At the end of the tour, since Grace hinted again that she was in charge of recruiting speakers, Jennifer agreed to visit Historic Oglethorpe that fall. She even promised to prepare a photo slide show of her Dunham House work.

"What have I gotten myself into?" she wailed, putting her hands up to her head as they walked toward Michael's truck. "I have to present before the Hermon town council *and* Historic Oglethorpe. I don't do public speaking. I shoulda stayed home."

"No, you should have been right where you are. You're breathing new life into this community. Did I hear you saying something about Stella opening an art studio in the old general store? Is she even on board with the idea yet?"

Jennifer nodded. "If the right agreement can be reached. The mayor of Hermon just agreed to discuss it with the council at the next meeting."

Releasing a huff of surprise, Michael gazed sideways at her. "Admirable."

"We're thinking lessons, showings and special events."

"That could work. And did I really hear the chamber president offering you a job?" Michael opened her door and waited while she climbed up.

Jennifer gave a disbelieving laugh. "Well, it wasn't official, more like a declaration of interest." She took a moment to absorb that truth as her escort walked around to the driver's side.

"Still," Michael said once his truck's headlights illuminated the faded, curving gray pavement of Wolfskin Road. "That's something. What do you think?"

"I don't know. She kind of took me off guard. What do *you* think?" She glanced sideways at him.

"Again, these things usually don't happen by chance. You did start praying God would lead and direct your life, right?"

She appreciated where he was going with this even though her question had really attempted to measure his personal reaction to the idea of her working permanently nearby. "Right, but does that mean everything unexpected that happens is Him at work?"

"No, but when a good opportunity comes, apparently out of the blue, it's a good signal to start praying about it."

Jennifer nodded thoughtfully, then decided on some subtle bait. "It would allow me to keep the friends I'm making here, which would be really nice."

"And to see some of your ideas come to completion."

"It's something to think about."

"Pray about."

Jennifer smiled. "Right. I guess it will take some time before faith becomes my standard mode of operation." And since Michael wasn't giving up his own preference on the matter, she guessed she'd have to trust God with that, too. But she could ask him one more thing. "But can you see me in that sort of position? You know, as a historical preservationist in a firm, you focus on one client at a time, and you spend a lot of time with, besides work crews, well, building materials." She grinned ruefully. "A main street director would constantly interact with all sorts of people. There would be a lot of publicity and fund generating as well. I always pictured a main street director as ... well as ... Tilly."

"Tilly?"

"My roommate. An outgoing and confident person."

When they pulled into her driveway, Michael cut the engine and looked over at her, resting a forearm on the steering wheel. "Remember what you told me about how you felt tonight. I think when your heart's in something, your enthusiasm makes what's otherwise hard easy. You did good tonight," he said. "So good, in fact, that you challenged me to step outside my own comfort zone. That is, if you'll agree to a deal."

She blinked to cover the rapid defense mechanism trepidation triggered in her mind, like a road crew throwing up a barrier. "What kind of deal?"

"You get ready tomorrow for church, do your hair and make-up like you were supposed to for tonight, and I'll go with you."

Jennifer stared at him in shock. "How do you know what I'm supposed to do with my hair and make-up, and how do you know this isn't it?"

"Come on, I know more about women's stuff than you think. And I know they didn't have you in that beauty shop for almost three hours so you could learn how to make a wet bun." The gentle smile that his teasing grin faded into softened his jibe.

She let out a gusty breath. "OK, maybe that's true."

His voice gentled, too. "So why didn't you? Do things like they showed you?"

Jennifer shook her head. "Maybe I'm just not that kind of person." She didn't know why Michael cared if she fixed herself up. She pictured Ashley, the girl Michael's grandfather hinted had broken Michael's heart, as tall, self-assured, blonde and beautiful, everything opposite of Jennifer, and impossible to compare.

"What are you so afraid of?" It was almost a whisper. It raised the goose flesh on her arms.

Jennifer grabbed the door handle.

And he grabbed her arm. "Uh-uh." His teasingly chiding tone and look faded as he intercepted her scorching glance. Michael raised his hand and added, "I'm just trying to complete my gentlemanly duties, remember?"

"You don't have any duties, except to pay me as specified in my contract." Her social graces were expiring about as rapidly as the coach turning back into a pumpkin at midnight. Jennifer opened the door and put her foot on the running board. By the time she slid to the ground, he stood in front of her, blocking her path, but respecting her personal space. He held out his hands.

"I forgot how easy you scare. But Jennifer, I'm not going to hurt you."

She sighed. He'd probably never had a girl run from him before. No doubt it confused him. Jennifer's emotional batteries were too drained by the evening's socializing to explain even if she had the inclination to do so. "I know. And I do appreciate you taking me tonight. It was a very thoughtful thing for an employer to do."

"It wasn't just an employer thing. I think well of you as a person, and I want to see you find all the Lord has for you, but I realize I can hardly keep talking about that when I'm living like a heathen."

"Oh, yes, you're a veritable wild man." He didn't even laugh at her sarcasm. She tried directness. "You really should not put your faith on the same par as my make-over."

Michael shrugged. "That's probably true, but I'm willing to stoop a little bit low since I think this will be to everyone's benefit. Pick you up at 10:30?"

"You don't have to do this."

"I want to do this."

Simple honesty void of manipulation could melt her heart. She wavered. "I'd have to text Stella since I normally ride with her family, but …" Jennifer chewed her lip. She thought of Stella and how happy she would be at the news that Michael would finally set foot inside a church again, after all her invitations. She thought of her reflection in the mirror earlier. With a church dress, the five-minute face shouldn't prove too shocking. The women at Stella's church did go all out for Sunday services, after all. She would fit in, and she would hardly be flaunting anything in church, would she? At last she said, "Fine, but I warn you, if you end up thinking it's worth it, it will be because of God, not me."

His chuckle followed her in the door, and he left her musing over his strange comment: "I'm good with that. Right now, I think I'd take either one."

CHAPTER TEN

The warm, settled feeling Jennifer experienced while seated in the James family pew with Stella, Earl, Gabe and Jamal still embraced her like an unexpectedly friendly stranger. They accepted, wanted, her presence. Never mind her lack of blood kin, or even the same skin color. Their position as children of God joined them on a deeper level, in spirit.

At first, Michael seemed to share her sense of peace, and for plenty of reasons. Stella had explained to everyone at the BBQ that her family's complicated tree included Michael. Today, the relatives present expressed great enthusiasm at his appearance in church. Then there was the fact that Michael also belonged to the family of God. Even when Pastor Simms introduced his sermon topic, "Take Off the Mask," Michael's placid expression remained in place.

Simms explained that believers should strive for truth because God was truth, Hebrews Six taught that it was impossible for God to lie, and according to Proverbs 12:22, "Lying lips are an abomination to the Lord, but those who deal truthfully are His delight." He then went on to point out that the passage just before that verse revealed that deceit led to devising evil, then to being filled with evil, whereas truth led to peace and joy. Falseness only lasted for a moment while truth endured.

"Dishonesty is like wearing a mask," the preacher told them. "No one gets to know your true heart. After a while, other people can't believe anything you say! And you don't have to say it, do you? We can lie with our lives. We can pretend to be someone we aren't. Look at your neighbor and say, 'Are you pretending to be someone you aren't?'"

That was when Michael, and a number of others seated in the pews that hot August day, stared straight ahead and began to sweat despite the blasting air conditioning. She felt for him. She'd wished the floor would swallow her up when Pastor Simms had them tell each other God loved them and they should soften their hearts of stone the first time she'd visited.

She pressed her lips together to stifle a smirk. On the other hand, given his typical composure and confidence, she rather enjoyed seeing him squirm for once. And the sermon had put a stop to those amazed smiles he'd sent her way ever since she'd walked out onto her porch that morning in the knee-length, rayon, floral-printed dress with slitted elbow-length sleeves and a narrow black belt, her soft, smoky eyeshadow not hidden by any glasses, and her auburn-highlighted, layered hair softly framing her face. Nope, he gave full attention to the good reverend now!

"We can lie by concealing things. We can lie by exaggerating things. We can lie by acting one way on Sunday and another during the week. We can lie by acting like one person in front of Christians and another in front of those we work with. You know what that is?"

"What, Pastor?" someone called.

Pastor Simms pointed at the church member. "That's hypocrisy! That's selfishness, thinking more of yourself than the other person. That cheapens that relationship. You want a strong family, strong friendships? Take off the mask!"

"Amen!" several agreed.

Michael loosened the knot of his tie.

"You know what else? We can also try to lie to God. We can tell Him we're OK when we're not. We can tell Him we don't need Him when we do. We can tell Him we aren't angry at someone when we are. We can tell Him we aren't angry at *Him* when we are! But He sees the heart. Trust me, He can handle your real feelings. They don't scare Him. No, they move His heart to compassion. So take off the mask!" Pastor Simms landed his closed fist on the podium like a judge's gavel.

When Pastor Simms gave an altar call for people to come forward for an honest conversation with God, Jennifer hoped Michael might respond, but he merely stood with the congregation as the choir offered up a mournful, penitent tune. He concealed much behind his handsome, frozen face, behind the mask, but he wasn't yet ready to remove it. Pastor Simms always cautioned his flock against applying sermons to other people, so Jennifer took a moment to pray that God would show her any ways she needed to be more honest with Him or others. Yes, she knew she needed a lot of inner reconstruction from the pain of her childhood. But she didn't really expect a response, because not only did the ways God spoke to people still waft of the mysterious and mystical, she also felt that some trash just didn't need sifting through before disposing.

Outside the church, the sun beat down on the asphalt as Jennifer stopped to confirm with Stella that they would meet at Chicken Express.

"Oh, no, honey, didn't I tell you? My cousin Reba invited us to dinner."

"OK ..." Jennifer's voice trailed off, uncertain if she and Michael were included and also fairly convinced Stella had mentioned Chicken Express just the day before.

"She has in a roast, and I'm not sure how many it will feed, you know. But you two should go on to Chicken Express, and we'd love to join you next week."

The sense of belonging evaporated like a drop of moisture on the pavement. "Oh."

Stella saw her reaction and took her elbow, pulling her a little apart from the others. She hissed in her ear, "You're all prettied up for that boy, now let him take you out, just the two of you."

Realization dawned. Stella was playing matchmaker. "Oh, no," Jennifer started to protest.

But Stella interrupted with a firm, whispered command. "Don't you miss this opportunity. Trust me. I see the way he's lookin' at you." So saying, she gave Jennifer a hug, then pushed her toward Michael, whom she also hugged and assured again of her delight that he'd come.

She told him she loved him every time she saw him now. Jennifer knew those gentle words would act over time like a wrecking ball on his emotional walls. Stella and Earl hadn't said them to her, *per se*, but she felt the words acted out in a way she had never known. Still, what a blessing for Michael to *hear* the words from so many people! Something in her soul sucked up the sound of them, like rain on parched ground, even if they were meant for someone else.

The moment Jennifer pondered that, Stella turned to her and clasped her forehead for a big sisterly kiss. "We love you, too, honey. Thank you for coming. Y'all have a wonderful time."

As the James family filed off toward their car, Jennifer stood stunned, her heart warmed but at the same time ... hurting. Why hurting? God had given her so much, showed her she was worthy of more than she'd ever imagined.

Michael waited on her. When she glanced at him with a flushed face, he held an arm out toward his truck. "Shall we?"

"Sure, if you want to."

"I'm starving."

"I know. It took me a while to get used to their services running so late."

Michael unlocked the truck and opened the door for her. She left it open until he got in and turned on the air conditioning. "I'm also sick of chicken fingers and sandwiches. I want some real food. What do you say we go to East Athens? DePalma's?"

"Sure."

He stared at her a minute, again like he was seeing a stranger, then put the truck in reverse.

"What did you think of the service?" Jennifer asked.

"I think Pastor Simms doesn't mince words."

She laughed. "That's true."

Mention of the sermon drew Michael back into his private mental morass. He spoke little as they drove toward Athens. Jennifer clutched her aching stomach, which possessed a strange case of hunger mixed with butterflies. She couldn't rationalize this outing as part of her job like she had the gala. But it could just be two hungry people getting lunch. It surely wasn't a date. Right? Right. She had never dreamed of dating anyone like Michael, and if she thought for a minute she was, she'd go into verbal lock-down mode and not know what to do with her hands, much less be able to eat in front of him. And she did want to eat, badly. DePalma's had the best Italian in town.

When Michael ushered her into the branch of the restaurant located in a strip mall, the dark interior enveloped them in a cool embrace. Heads turned as they walked past seated patrons to their booth. That was surely due to Michael, but Jennifer felt self-conscious nonetheless. She smoothed her skirt as she slid across the vinyl bench, thanking the waiter for the menu and smiling over at her companion.

"You really do look lovely. I know I said it before, but I can't get over it."

Jennifer couldn't hold his gaze, and she felt her cheeks burning. She pretended to peruse the menu. "Well, Rita and Jean are talented."

"They can't create what isn't there, any more than you could make an ugly house beautiful with just a coat of paint."

"OK, whatever."

"You're really bad with compliments, aren't you? Why is that?"

Gazing at pictures of fettucine and ziti noodles swimming in rich sauces, Jennifer chewed a hang nail and flipped the menu. "Uh, maybe because I don't believe them."

Michael reached out and pushed her hand down, causing her to look at him. "Why would I say it if I didn't mean it? What possible motivation could I have?"

"I don't know."

"Just say 'thank you.'"

"Thank you." She would say it gladly if it meant he wouldn't probe her insecurities and sordid past, or force her to reveal that the word 'lovely' had never once been spoken in description of herself.

Satisfied, Michael devoted his attentions temporarily to the daily selections, and by the time their waiter came with drinks, they were ready to order. The man conveyed their preferences to the kitchen. As he disappeared through swinging double doors into a realm of amazing smells, Michael sliced the bread set before them and asked, "Would you like me to pray?"

"Oh. Of course." Jennifer glanced at Michael, who smiled as if at ease, then at the people dining near them before ducking her head. She'd never prayed over her food before, much less in public. And certainly a guy had never offered to do so. Her employer's prayer thanked God for the morning service, their time together, and the food before them, short and simple, and so comfortable he clearly had prayed many such prayers his whole life. Jennifer sensed she glimpsed the Michael before pain brought guardedness. Unfortunately, she found him even more attractive!

Impervious to her embarrassing deliberations, he slid the butter toward her and took up a slice of his bread. "So have you given any more thought to your job situation? Not the one with me, of course, but what you'll do after?"

"I thought about it most of the time I laid awake last night, actually." Which had been a lot. Jennifer buttered her bread and added before taking a bite, "I think I'm going to leave the door open to both."

"You mean apply for the one in Savannah and tell Marian you'll interview for the one in Lexington?"

Jennifer nodded. "Right. It can't hurt to *talk* to both, can it? Then I can decide later. It's always been my dream to work in Savannah, but the thought of leaving …" She allowed her voice to trail off, unable to describe the empty sort of pain even imagining that brought … and also unwilling to examine fully why.

"People have really taken you in here, and no wonder. It's clear you have a heart for their community."

"I do. I don't even hate Calvin and his dog anymore. They're kind of funny." Jennifer chuckled.

"What does your professor say? I'm sure she has an opinion."

"I'm sure she does, unless I offended her too much by taking a step back. Maybe she has someone else lined up to recommend to the preservation firm now. It's not like I've totally cut her out, though. I texted her this morning before church, telling her how we got the apothecary sealed up and cleaned." Jamal and Gabe had returned to scrub the ceilings, while the men conducted a preliminary washing down of the walls. Jennifer assisted with the floors, moving from section to section while keeping her weak ankle extended. A more thorough cleaning could wait until after they knocked out the old plaster, since that would make such a mess. "I said tomorrow we'll move the shelving into the middle of the floor and the compounding desk into the middle room, in preparation for wiring and replastering. I also told her about attending the gala and meeting the county officials."

"Bet you didn't tell her about the Main Street position."

"Well, no." Jennifer dropped her lashes and folded her bread for a bite. Neither had she mentioned to Barbara that she had attended with Michael. "No need to poke a sleeping bear."

"No doubt she would consider such a position beneath you."

"Probably."

"Do you want to know what I think?"

Jennifer blinked. "About Barbara?" Did it matter? When he actually offered to open up that gold mine of private contemplation to her, did she care about the topic?

"Yeah."

"Sure."

"I think her focus lay more on making you who she thought you should be than discovering who you are meant to be."

"Hmm. Which goes right along with our sermon today."

"Right. About that …" Michael sat back from the table, halting his sentence as the waiter slid his baked ziti in front of him.

Jennifer waited until her fettucine chicken arrived, then, as she loosened the noodles with her fork prongs to release the heat from the entrée, she prompted, "You were saying?"

"Oh." Michael paused again, patting his napkin to his mouth as he finished chewing and swallowed his first bite. He looked dismayed at the interruption, probably for more than one reason.

Jennifer took pity on him. "It's all right. You can eat."

"No, I want to tell you." Nevertheless, Michael stabbed a meatball.

She waited and ate, too, trusting him to speak when he felt ready. An awareness that he prepared to say something important heightened her senses, causing her to notice every ting of glass on ceramic and every flash of passing color in the restaurant. But maybe that sensitivity came from trying so hard not to stare at her companion, knowing if she did, eye contact would create a silent connection she sensed him trying to delay.

Finally, he dove straight to the point. "I want you to know that if there are things I don't talk about, it's not my intention to be deceptive. This job arrangement has put us in close proximity, and sometimes things have come up that are, well, private to me."

Jennifer shrugged, trying to appear nonchalant. "I get it. There's no need for an employer to tell his employee everything about himself. I know what I need to know to work for you."

Michael frowned. "It's not just that. We've known each other long enough now that I consider us friends, don't you?"

"Well, sure. I guess so."

"I enjoy being around you. You're funny in that dry way of yours, and now that we figured out how to quit stepping on each other's toes, we have a good time together, don't we?"

"Yes. You're kind of funny too. And generally very thoughtful."

"Well, thanks." He flashed the crooked grin, then continued, moving his food around on his plate with his fork. "I guess at times I've felt like me not wanting to talk about those things has made you feel I think less of you, or I don't hold our friendship in high enough regard. I wanted to set that straight."

"It's OK. There are things I haven't talked about, either. Some things you don't just throw out there if the relationship is temporary."

"But now it might not be temporary." His blue eyes met hers.

"It might not?"

"If you stay in Oglethorpe County."

"Oh. Right."

"And today's sermon made me realize I really am guarded, and maybe I need to stop holding everyone at arm's length."

"OK."

Michael heaved a sigh. "You are *not* helping me."

Jennifer hid a smile behind her napkin. "I'm sorry, what am I supposed to be doing? I'm really bad at this."

"Yes, worse than me."

"Well, you had a great mom and dad to teach you."

"Point taken. I guess what I'm asking is, don't you think trust in a friendship should be reciprocal?"

"I do. I have no interest in friendships that are one-sided." She paused and waited while Michael stared at her. Finally, his meaning dawned. "Oh. You're saying *I* should be more open, too."

He laughed. "Yes, I'm suggesting that from this point forward, if we accidentally hit on a sensitive area like we seem to keep doing, neither one of us should clam up and act all angry or awkward. Not that we have to spill everything, but I think we can practice building a little trust like Pastor Simms suggested by talking things through."

"Wow, you really go for this sermon application thing."

"Well, when God puts something on your heart, it's hard to ignore." Michael grinned while the waiter refilled his drink, then he took a sip. "Are you stalling?"

"Yes, that would be stalling." Jennifer paused, thinking that part of her hesitation stemmed from simply making sure she heard him right. And from telling herself to be cautious about enjoying the warm fuzzy feeling this conversation and the focus of his intense gaze created. But at some point she must learn to respond in trust to what he offered, just like he pointed out. "Agreed. We will both be a little less mysterious, and next time Ashley comes up, you might just say who she was instead of storming off. Oops. I think I just said that name."

She didn't get the expected smile. Michael stared at her seriously, the moment broken only by a blink. Then he said, "Ashley was my wife."

"Oh." Jennifer's hand went to her chest in a sudden attempt to stifle the ache there. What was that? It was more than shock. With horror, she identified the foreign invader. It was jealousy. "You were married."

"Yes. While I was still at the university, in fact. That's where we met."

"Did she leave you?"

"She did. But not in the way you're thinking. Like my mother, she died of cancer."

That insane urge to take his hand flooded her entire body, but she resisted, just staring back at him. She could almost hear the pieces falling into place. The move to the middle of nowhere. The willingness to focus everything on the restoration of his great-grandmother's home. The morose introspection and distancing. And the sobbing in the woods. Wait. That had happened on Mother's Day. She had to ask. "You … didn't have any children, did you?"

Michael took the check the waiter offered him, then folded it in two. "Ashley was expecting our first child when she was diagnosed. The pregnancy didn't come to term."

Jennifer felt like a white hot poker had been shoved into her heart. "Oh, I'm so sorry." She could only shake her head, seeing Michael in a totally different light. He had been a husband, and he would have been a father. His grief went so much deeper than the spurning of a fickle girlfriend.

The crooked grin flitted over his rugged face. "See? That's what happens every time I talk about my life. This terrible shroud of darkness descends on any conversation or moment. I'm like the Psalmist David described himself, a dead man, out of mind, who people flee from when they see me. Can you blame me that I don't talk about it?"

"No, not at all, but thank you for telling me. Does Stella know?"

Michael shook his head.

"Well, you know she's realized for some time that heavy things from your past weigh on you. Would you mind if I told her? Or do you want to?"

He lifted a shoulder. "You can, if you think it will satisfy her curiosity."

"It's not that she's nosy. She's concerned about you. And this makes everything make a lot more sense now."

"Whatever you decide," he said, sliding out of the booth. Then he winked at her and added, "Well, *you're* still a mystery."

She followed him to the door. "My turn will come." Even as she said it to be fair, she dearly hoped not.

"Right. Now you owe me."

"Wait. Did you just pay for the bill?"

"Yes, is there a problem?" Michael paused, glancing back toward their table as he held the door open for her.

"I need to give you some money."

Michael pulled her out onto the sidewalk. "Of course you don't. Can't an employer treat his employee to a decent meal?"

"What happened to all this friendship talk?"

"I figured you'd be less likely to argue if I made it about the work."

"You're right." Jennifer grinned as she climbed up into his truck. "Well, thank you. It was delicious."

"You're welcome. Need anything while we're all the way in town?"

She shook her head. "Not that I can think of."

"Ice cream?"

"Nope." She experienced absolutely no desire to mix with the throngs at Wal-Mart or fast food places. How quickly she had acclimated to country life! Jennifer waited while Michael turned onto Lexington Road, then asked in a small voice, "Will you tell me about her?"

Michael glanced at her. "You mean I've not spilled enough yet?"

"Well, I understand if you need to be done."

"She came from Atlanta, from a large, Christian family. She was a very responsible person, very maternal. Maybe that's what drew her to me. She saw the wounded boy still hurting from the loss of his mother. She'd just gotten her nursing degree, and she planned on working with the babies in ICU. But the one thing she wanted more than anything was to be a mother herself."

Jennifer frowned. The description didn't line up at all with the blonde, cheerleader-type she had envisioned. The next question she asked veered from all logic, but she couldn't help it. "Do you have a picture?"

Surprised, Michael tugged his wallet out at the next stoplight and tossed it to her. "First photo."

Could he not even stand to look at it himself, still? Just like he wouldn't say her name, "Ashley?" Feeling invasive, she unfolded the leather and looked at the picture in the plastic flap inside. A younger, tuxedo-clad Michael leaned against a tree, a bride in white pulled in tight to his side. Ashley beamed into the camera, petite and dark-haired, with a radiance that came from sweetness rather than pride.

Something painful twisted in Jennifer's midsection, reminding her of the sensation after Stella told her she loved her. Ashley's radiance also sprung from being loved. And both moments, in the parking lot and here holding Michael's wedding day photo, reminded Jennifer of her lack.

In her mind's eye, a memory flashed of herself at seven. Crying after a spill on her bike, she curled her hand over a raw scrape on her shoulder even as her mother tried to pry it away to tend it. She was angry. The wound was her mother's fault, her father's fault, for not listening when she told them over and over the front bike wheel felt loose. For not caring. Now why that memory? She frowned, asking God for understanding.

To her surprise, it came. As much as she comprehended mentally that God her Father loved her, she didn't *feel* that love. The lack of human love from those most important in her life created that wound. Coming to God didn't automatically fix it. Healing required a process as painstaking as sanding down a rough spot and filling in the hole with a new bonding agent. But something stood in the way, like her tense, seven-year-old hand, holding on, holding. Angry.

She felt sick as she stared straight ahead, watching the miles roll away.

Michael watched her. "You OK?"

"Yeah." She stirred, closing his wallet and laying it on the console next to him. "She's lovely."

The barrier to Michael developing any interest in her beyond the platonic stretched far higher than she'd imagined, because only one kind of girl proved harder to compete against than peppy and beautiful, and that was one who had been sweet, pure and wholesome.

CHAPTER ELEVEN

At 8:36 a.m., Jennifer attached her resume and clicked the "submit" button at the bottom of Savannah Heritage Trust's online historic preservation manager application. Then, before even releasing the breath she held, she pulled up her e-mail. Dragging Marian Dukes' business card closer on her desk, she typed in the chamber director's e-mail address. In the subject line, she entered, "Main Street Director position." Then she proceeded to indicate her pleasure in meeting Marian at Historic Oglethorpe's Mid-Summer Gala and her interest in interviewing.

"Well, Lord, I guess this is how I'm supposed to make big decisions now," she murmured aloud. "It's in Your hands."

And it felt very foreign to leave it there. In consideration of potential disappointment from Michael and a more prestigious position on the table, Jennifer's old mode of operation dictated that she submit the Savannah application but leave Marian's card to gather dust in her file. But she'd spent a restless Sunday night examining the value of her other friendships and the inspiration she harbored for the future of this community. If that came from God, she didn't want to squelch it. And if God's will truly kept her best interests foremost, why would she want to resist? So Jennifer decided to place the situation in His hands as she took the next step available to her for both options.

After freshening up Yoda's litter box and petting the gray head as the cat followed her to the door, Jennifer gathered her tool belt and electric drill she'd laid out the night before. She locked her door and set out for Michael's house. On the front porch of the apothecary, she spied Stella, setting up to paint the millwork. She waved, and her friend waved back. Jennifer checked her watch. If she talked quick, she just had time to share her plan to address the repurposing of the old general store at next week's council meeting before Amy Greene arrived with shades and under curtains.

"Good morning!" Jennifer called.

Stella positioned her plastic drip cloth as Jennifer mounted the steps to the apothecary. "Mornin'! How did it go yesterday?" Her lips turned up in a sly smile. "You sure did look pretty."

Jennifer ascertained by her greeting that the men were not yet inside the apothecary. "Good, thank you."

"And you're not wearin' your glasses today, either."

"No, contacts will make it easier while we're looking up and down, putting up curtains." Still, at that very moment, almost as overpowering as an itch one shouldn't scratch, her hand twitched with the security gesture urge to adjust her glasses. Jennifer settled for adjusting the hammer and level in her tool belt instead.

"Mmm-hmm. Good for you. So what happened over lunch?"

"Well, I guess what Pastor Simms said really got through to Michael. He told me that while there are things he's still reticent to talk about from his past, he wants to strive for greater honesty and openness in our conversations."

Stella reached out and squeezed Jennifer's arm. "Oh, that's *good*."

"He also told me he was married before, Stella, and his wife died of cancer." Even though Michael had given her permission to share this with Stella, something in Jennifer's spirit checked at including the information that Ashley had been pregnant at the time of her diagnosis. That just felt like an unnecessarily lurid detail to throw out.

"Oh, no." In the throes of sympathy, Stella grasped Jennifer's hand as though Michael, and not Jennifer, stood before her. Jennifer understood the agony on her face. "So his wife *and* his mother. No wonder he's in pain, and guarded. He needs to let the Great Physician work on that, doesn't He?"

"Well, he did come to church and talk about the sermon afterwards."

"Yes, that's right. So he took some little steps. And he chose to talk about it with *you*."

Jennifer smiled, embarrassed. "I'm not sure that means much. He showed me a picture of his wife, Ashley, and she was so lovely. He describes her as this wonderful, selfless Christian girl. Even if he likes me as a person, Stella, how can I compete with a woman who was not only perfect, but her early and tragic death practically memorialized that perfection?"

"You don't have to compete, honey. God made you complete and wonderful just as you are. If you're the one for Michael, he'll come to see that."

Jennifer gave a nervous laugh and pulled away, her insecurities rushing up in the face of her perceived reality. "This is silly. He's given me no indication he likes me for more than a friend, anyway."

"But you like him, don't you?"

"Well, um … I came to talk about the town council meeting, and I don't have much time before Amy arrives."

Stella punctuated the humid morning air with a finger. "Fine, but know that I hear you, Miss Jennifer, and I hear what you don't say even more."

Jennifer balled her fists on her hips and fixed a fake glare at the woman before her. "*Fine*. This is more important. I got permission to raise the repurposing of the old general store at the next meeting. Hermon's mayor, Reggie Brown, thought the town might consider purchasing the building and renovating it as an art gallery and event facility if you were prepared to lease space there for lessons and showings. I need to know if that would truly prove feasible for you. I know you said you were interested, but are you sure you can support the lease?"

Stella moved her tray of white paint and a small, angled brush onto a section of rail covered by the drip cloth, staring off into the distance as she thought. "So I need to see if enough people will commit to lessons. I should e-mail all my former students and homeschool groups in the area, maybe run an ad in the paper, and put something on social media."

"Yes, and right away."

"I could do it tonight. I could also reach out to my artist friends to see if they'd want to do a showing there. I still have some contacts at UGA, too. Maybe they'd be interested in expanding the audience for their students past Athens."

"Great thinking! OK, sorry to pressure you, but if you get a good response, see if you can estimate what you might afford on a monthly lease. I'll put the tentative idea out there without naming your estimate and see what the council suggests."

"Oh, my land." Stella paused to look down the road, where little boys drinking RCs along the brick front of the former Gillen Department Store once taunted Georgia Pearl. "It's hard to believe such a thing could possibly come to pass."

Jennifer grinned and patted her hand, feeling better now that she'd escaped the hot seat. "Well, I think you'd tell me to put it before the Lord, and if it's meant to be, it will."

"Girl, you're learning," Stella said, laughing and swishing the finger at her.

At that perfect moment, Amy's Cadillac pulled into the driveway. The blonde woman waved from behind the steering wheel and eased the vehicle close to the house. Jennifer excused herself from Stella and walked over to greet the interior decorator as she bent into her back seat to corral an armload of curtain rods.

"Hi, want me to take those?"

"Oh, hey. I've got them, but you can carry the shades if you want."

"Sure thing."

"I'll come back for the curtains," Amy added. "I don't want to pick the lace. I can't wait to see them up."

"Me, too." Glad Michael had agreed to lace panels in the dining room, parlor and guest bedroom, even though he'd spurned them in his own chamber, Jennifer led the way to the front door.

Amy's heels took mincing steps over the pea gravel of the walkway. "The satin laine curtains should be ready next week. Then we'll really be able to see how good the windows will look." Her comment revealed that like Jennifer, she pictured fully dressed windows, which for the time period included inside shutters, a shade or "short blind" covering the lower half of the window; a lace or muslin panel; and the fabric curtain falling from a cornice. To simplify matters, even though most 1840s bedrooms favored cotton, chintz or calico for curtains, they'd selected a wool-silk blend for all the wall hangings. Most of the curtains would be golden-brown in color to harmonize with the paint, expect for the red-toned dining room and the blue-toned guest room, now James' room.

Jennifer paused to knock at the front door. When she heard James call for them to come in from the hallway, she opened the door. The older man just waved at her, having been alerted previously to Amy's visit. "We figured it was you. We're back in the kitchen, just cleaning up breakfast. Heading out to the apothecary soon. Do you need help with anything?"

"No, I don't think so. I see your ladder here in the hall, so we're good. We'll get the blinds and panels up and be over there, too, for Amy to match her swatches to the paint."

"Sure thing." James disappeared back into the kitchen, where Jennifer heard the rumble of Michael's voice. Her stomach did a little flip-flop.

She felt odd about going into the bedroom of either of the men while they were present, so she led Amy to the front parlor, where they put down their burdens. Then Jennifer arranged the ladder while Amy returned to her car for the lace panels. The parlor, with its triple windows in bay arrangement, would prove the most time consuming. Jennifer set to work mounting the spring-loaded shades first, while Amy returned to unwrap packages and hand the pieces up to her.

"I hope Michael will be happy with these," she said. "I tried to find the best quality I could."

"I'm sure he will be. He made it clear this is not a house museum, so no need to worry about details like pulley-operated shades," Jennifer muttered, more to herself than to Amy. "And you know he doesn't like to spend a ton of money. They'll hardly use these in the parlor, anyway."

"Right. Hey, I wanted to mention that I'd love to go with you this Saturday to the antique warehouse I told you about in Augusta. I can drive Horace's truck."

Raring back on the ladder to make eye contact with her guest, Jennifer held off on running the electric drill. "Really? Are you sure?"

"Yeah." Amy's eyes sparkled. "It will be fun. I can be here at eight."

"But you're not looking for anything, are you?" Jennifer couldn't get her mind around someone like Amy wanting to spend time with her just for *fun*. Had she and the interior decorator been high school contemporaries, she would have faded into the wall any time Amy swayed by in her designer jeans. True, Amy's birthday edged closer to Jennifer's mother's, but she wore her age well, retaining a confidence and sparkle that still made Jennifer feel lackluster by comparison.

"Mmm, nope, no clients up for antiques at the moment, and I'm sure I couldn't squeeze one more piece of furniture into our house without Horace blowin' a gasket. But I can take you to my favorite bistro for a late lunch, and I get to help *you* shop! So what are you lookin' for?"

Jennifer turned around to glare at the empty room behind them. "Parlor furniture!"

Both women burst out laughing.

"Yes, that kind of was a dumb question," Amy admitted. "And I'd be so excited to help find it. My imagination is creatin' all sorts of scenarios right now. This is an awesome room. Stella's faux wood graining on the baseboard trim fairly shines, and that mural ... I could stare at it forever."

Jennifer nodded. The painting had come off just as planned. The rapturous Hudson River Valley-style depiction of the Dunham plantation on the banks of Long Creek, including Levi's cabin, drew the viewer into a historic, gold-flecked green of late summer. Jennifer sometimes caught herself fantasizing that she could walk through it into the past.

"What are you ladies laughing at in here?" James demanded good-naturedly from the doorway. Michael stood behind him, gazing over his father's head.

"We're goin' quite bonkers with joy at the thought of shopping to fill this room with furniture," Amy told him.

Jennifer translated into language she knew the men would understand. "The Augusta warehouse opens Saturday. Amy kindly volunteered to take me."

"Oh, that's great," James said, while Michael rolled his eyes.

Jennifer shifted on the ladder, wondering if he found her appearance too Tool-time Tim. Did he notice she wore contacts? Looking away, she slid her hair behind her ear.

"Do you need to borrow my truck?" Michael asked her.

"Thanks, but Amy said we can take Horace's."

He nodded. "Well, if anything changes, you're welcome to it."

"I appreciate that."

After the men headed out the front door, Amy burst into girlish giggles. "You dig him."

"I what?"

"Oh, I saw the way you started acting the minute he appeared. Your whole aura changed."

Leave it to Amy to use "aura" over "demeanor."

"It did not ... I did not."

"Yes, you did. Oh, honey, who can blame you? He's a total babe." Amy swatted Jennifer's arm. "Makes you go weak in the knees, hmm? That's how Chad Fullerton did me."

"Your quarterback boyfriend in high school. The one Horace stole you from." Distracted, Jennifer drilled in the hook for the final curtain rod. If Amy picked up on her awkward awareness of Michael, did he? The possibility made her want to wilt like an unwatered Johnny Jump-Up.

Amy slid the lace panel over the rod and reached it up to her. "Oh, he didn't steal me exactly, despite what he likes to think. So I told you before how Chad got a football scholarship to the University of Florida. Of course he was hot stuff on campus, and I was far away startin' design school. Out of sight, out of mind, I guess. He broke up with me at Christmas break, freshman year. I cried for weeks. I mean, I thought I was gonna have that guy's babies! He said he'd stay in touch and still wanted to be friends and maybe go out some. *Whatever.*"

Jennifer gave a sympathetic grunt. She folded the ladder and led the way to the dining room, tilting her head toward Amy to make it clear she still listened. Amy trailed behind, arms full of rods and blinds.

"So Horace hadn't gone to college, right? His dad owned that property management company, which was boomin' at the time. He could make plenty of money in the family business. Someone told him Chad and I had broken up, so he called me. Pretty gutsy, right?"

"Yeah. He asked you out on a date?"

"Yes, to dinner. And to my lonely eyes, he looked pretty good. He'd grown up some from the scrawny punter on the high school team. He cleaned up pretty well, drove a nice car, and had great listening skills. And he held my door open and paid me compliments, stuff Chad never did. I came to like it, you know?"

Remembering Michael's considerate manners when she'd gone places with him, Jennifer nodded. A girl could get spoiled. "So you got together?"

"Not for a while. He was smart and played it cool. But then that summer, guess who shows up?"

"Chad?"

"Yep." With a delicate touch that spared her gel-tip nails, Amy unwrapped a blind and nodded. "Started comin' around. Horace got so mad. It was like watchin' a turkey when it spreads out its tail, you know? He got all protective. One day, Chad drove up to my house when Horace had just brought me home, and Horace had a few choice words for him. I really admired how he stood up to Chad."

"What did Chad do?"

"Well, after Horace left, he asked who I wanted around. And I said Horace."

"And that was that."

"Well, not quite. That next year when Chad blew his ACL, he went through a really rough time. I sent him a get well card, and he called me. Just to talk, he said. He sounded different, changed. Humble. He sounded the way I always wanted him to sound."

Jennifer hurried through hanging the shade and the lace panel, immersed in Amy's story now. "But wasn't Horace your boyfriend by then?"

"He was. We were talkin' about a future together. When I told him Chad was movin' home when he finished the semester, I've never seen Horace so agitated. He thought he'd lose me."

"But he didn't."

"No, that's when Chad disappeared. Like Stella said before, the police in Gainesville searched for him." Amy shook her head, pensive as she stood back to admire Jennifer's work, but Jennifer could tell her inner gaze focused only on the past.

Jennifer also leaned back on the ladder, spreading her arms to indicate the window. The lace curtain created a soft frame for the grape arbor and a dogwood tree just outside the glass. "Is this good?"

"Yep."

"Let's go up the hall to James' room."

"OK." Amy sounded automated, her gaze blank as she gathered her dwindling cache of supplies.

"Did they find any evidence?" Jennifer asked over her shoulder.

"No. He went missin' about two weeks before the semester ended. Took his car and a couple changes of clothes and told his friends he was goin' to check out his options."

"Wait, what did that mean, 'options?' He didn't say where he was going?"

"Not exactly, although he'd told several of them he planned to move back home."

"What had he told *you*?"

Amy bit her lip. "That he realized he still had feelings for me and he wanted to find a place to rent so he could attend the university. He knew I was about to graduate and gettin' serious with Horace. He asked me to reconsider."

"Did you?" Situating the ladder under James' window, Jennifer turned to face the interior decorator. "I mean, after everything with Horace?"

"I admit, I wavered."

"Amy!"

"I know!" she squealed, covering her perfectly made-up face. "It was totally dishonorable. But you should have seen him! One look from his eyes could melt me! And he was so different, so open to me for the first time. I told him I'd have to think about it. I was protecting myself, so I played it a little close to the vest. Later I thought I shouldn't have. Maybe I didn't give him enough assurance. I'll never know what happened, anyway, because that was the last anyone ever heard from him."

"But what about his car?"

"The authorities never found it, which leads me to believe he got cold feet, took off and never looked back. I'm guessin' the reason his folks never heard from him was he probably got into drugs or something else bad. He did some recreational drugs when he was younger, to help blow off the stress his dad put on him about football. Maybe he couldn't face not fulfilling their dreams."

"Oh, my goodness. How tragic." In the weighty silence which fell, Jennifer stood looking at her companion.

Amy just nodded and looked sad.

"I'm so sorry. Have you been … happy?" Was that something she should ask? Saying nothing seemed worse.

"Yeah, I got over it. Horace was there. I tried not to let him see how it affected me. He swooped in with a perfectly timed, very romantic proposal, and plannin' the weddin' really gave me something to focus on." She lifted a shoulder. "Horace was probably better for me, anyway. I can't complain. He's been a great provider, a faithful husband and a wonderful father to our son and daughter. He's bettered himself, and so have I, and we've supported each other through it all."

"I'm glad, Amy." Uncertain, Jennifer reached out to squeeze the other woman's arm.

Amy rallied, taking a breath and pasting on a smile. "Anyway, all that to say, girl, if you can get the hots and the sweets in one package, go for it."

Jennifer might have laughed had she not been so humiliated, and so unsettled by Amy's story. Her discomfort only increased when they entered Michael's bedroom, which he'd cleaned to perfection in anticipation of their curtain-hanging visit, but the scent of his aftershave still hung heavy on the shower-damp air. She worked as fast as possible to remove herself from his inner sanctum.

Carrying drinks and paint swatches, she and Amy proceeded to the apothecary, where Stella revitalized the porch paint trim and Michael and James labored to move the shelves out from the wall and the compounding desk to the middle room. Trying not to get in the way, the women matched the paint to Amy's samples, then the interior decorator went on her way, waving and confirming plans for Saturday.

Just as Jennifer stepped back into the front doorway, she heard James call in a matter-of-fact tone, "Uh, Jennifer, you're going to want to get back here."

"What?" She hastened to comply, a curious Stella at her heels. They stared at the men, who both knelt on the floor. The open-backed cabinet now sat in the middle of the room, the wooden clothes hooks it had concealed jutting out from the wall, and Michael clutched a bundle of sepia papers tied with a faded blue ribbon in his hand. "What did you find?"

James perused one unfolded paper. His shocked gaze lifted to meet hers. "Letters, it would appear, written just after the Civil War. This one is addressed to William Dunham and is signed, Charlotte."

Oglethorpe County, Georgia
1865

Stuart's green eyes locked on me as I brought the first mouthful of potato soup to his lips.

"'ll do it," he slurred.

"I don't think that's a good idea," I said. Weakness, partial paralysis and slight, intermittent palsy still commanded control of his right side. He would have to use his left hand to feed himself, a task he had not attempted before, and the lack of a lap tray would require me to hold the soup bowl.

"'ll do it!"

I hesitated, glancing at the small table I had just brought up beside the bedroom armchair where he sat. I repositioned myself with the bowl in front of him and the spoon in reach of his left hand. Leaning his head forward, he managed by angling the spoon and slurping. A trail of mashed vegetable and broth trickled down his chin. I wiped it and assessed him. His blonde hair looked darker than normal due to the fact that it needed washing again, also my job. The bandage covered a wound which closed a little more every day. Under it, his left eyelid drooped slightly.

Noticing me looking at him, he paused and growled, "Whaaat?"

"Nothin'." I pinched my closed lips into a smile. "I'll give you a wash and a shave in the morning."

"Notta cribble."

"I know that. But you need to be patient with yourself. You've been through a lot."

"Hell."

"Yes. And it will take a while to get back to normal."

He shook his head. "Nev'r."

"Don't say that. You've already improved so much under William's care in the three weeks you've been home. Before you know it you'll be walkin' with a cane, and frankly, it's a miracle you're even alive."

He made a huffing sound and bent for another mouthful of soup. His hand shook, and I moved to grab the spoon before the broth spilled. Rather than release it to me, Stuart flung the utensil across the room. His arm upset the bowl, sloshing soup over the lap of my dress.

"Stuart!"

The demanding voice came from behind me, and I looked over my shoulder to see William framed in the doorway. Startled to see him, I mopped at the mess. "What are you doing? How is Silas?" I asked.

Shortly after Stuart's return, his father's lassitude, weakened vision and neck pain translated to a case of the measles. The childhood disease sometimes latched onto the elderly. When William described Silas' rash as mild, I thought that a good thing. He corrected me that worse cases presented in that manner. Quarantining Silas to his bedroom darkened with a green shade, William tended him while delegating much of Stuart's care to Selah, the slave doctor and myself. William expressed confidence that his treatment of nitre and ammonia every four hours after the cough and fever abated would soon see Silas up and about, as was common a week after the eruptions ceased. So I expected the news must be good now that William stood in Stuart's doorway instead.

But William merely gave a quick shake of his head. "I want to try something new tonight for Stuart," he said, stooping to retrieve the silverware. He placed it back in the bowl and set the small tray he carried on the table. He bent to glare into his brother's eyes. "And clearly you need something to make you less surly."

"Whaaass . . ."

"Belladonna, according to Stille's 1860 *Therapeutics and the Materia Medica*." William spoke to Stuart as though his full mental faculties functioned. I doubted that, and I usually didn't understand half of what he said in medical lingo, but I respected him for the respect he showed Stuart.

"What is belladonna?" I inquired, moving out of the way. I turned the napkin over and sought the splatter remaining on the floor where the spoon had fallen.

"A narcotic plant used for epilepsy and neurological disorders," he told me, then focused on his brother as he gave Stuart a pill and raised a glass of water off the tray. "Hopefully it will help the shaking. I know you grow weary of that, Stu." Then he leaned in to tell Stuart something I couldn't hear but which sounded like a scolding for his earlier behavior. A surprising warmth bubbled up inside, the same as when I walked by William's bedroom last night, glanced through the crack in the doorway and saw him reading his Bible when I knew the man had slept less than a dozen hours in the last week. Since his return, I never saw him open a bottle of alcohol, either. Something in Atlanta had changed him from the intoxicated, sarcastic man I met before the war.

William helped me remove Stuart's dressing coat and get him into bed. He waited while I turned down the lamp, then followed me into the hall and down the stairs. I remembered he had not answered me about Silas and asked again how he fared.

In the night light of the gas fixture from Charleston hanging above the stairs, weariness and worry traced creases on my brother-in-law's face. "I think he contracted pneumonia."

I stopped in front of the grandfather clock, turned and placed a hand on William's arm. "Oh, William, I am so sorry. Are you sure?"

"Pretty sure. I just took him sassafras and pleurisy root tea. The sassafras will fight the measles and the pneumonia both."

"Then you'll have him well soon."

"I don't know." He shook his head. "He's very weak."

"I'm so sorry," I repeated. "I don't know how you're doin' this, takin' care of Stuart and Silas both."

"One does what one has to." His eyes penetrated mine, like he knew that statement applied to me, too.

I turned to go toward the kitchen, but under the portrait of Levi, he asked me to wait the dishes on the hall table and sit with him a minute in the parlor. Surprised, I followed him. Here the fancy Cornelius & Co. Girondole lamps remained unlit, while the embers in the fireplace maintained only a faint orange glow and one of my recently improvised rosin candles burned in a bowl on a banquet end table. I started to sit next to him on the rosewood sofa, but he put out a hand.

"Don't sit too close to me. I changed clothes after leaving Father's room, but we can't be too cautious."

I nodded and complied, sinking down on the occasional chair to his right. I had done away with my hoops in the days since Stuart's return. I asked, "You had something to tell me? Something besides what you said about your father?"

William nodded, ruffling his dark hair, grown too long now. "Yes, it's about Stuart. Selah sent Lettie to trim his hair the other day, and she claims he threw the scissors at her. I don't know what transpired since no one else was in the room. Did you hear of it?"

"No!" But I wasn't surprised.

"Well, Lettie's convinced he's what she calls 'tetched in the head.' She says he always has been, but now it's worse. She's been nagging Aunt Selah and Doc Jeremiah to make up a potion."

"A potion?"

"She and Aunt Selah would call it witchcraft, but don't be alarmed. I reviewed all the ingredients and find them helpful . . . parsley haw otherwise known as hawthorn, winter huckleberry, yarrow, St. John's Wort, elder and hazelnut, boiled in butter. Some of these old folk remedies do have merit. After the temper I saw on Stuart tonight, I'm in favor of letting them brew it up, with your permission."

"Stuart has always had a temper."

William's shadowed blue eyes squared with mine. "I tried to warn you."

"I know." My mind went back to the naïve girl at the ball, incensed at the rude interruption of her romantic evening, and great sadness swept me.

"I actually wasn't as aware of the temper. Growing up, he could be manipulative, controlling, arrogant. Then there was his penchant for anything in skirts."

I dropped my gaze, ashamed to address such things before any man. "Yes. There was all of that."

"Lettie and her daughters," he said. Then, "I'm sorry, Charlotte. I wanted to spare you."

My throat hurt like the measles might be coming on. I swallowed and said in a raspy voice, "Thank you."

The gentleness of his tone surprised me as he asked, "Has it been terribly bad?"

I'd reached my limit. I lifted my chin. "There's no need to speak of it now. He might throw scissors and spoons, but I doubt he could do much real physical damage in his current condition. But if you think the tea or whatever it is will improve his demeanor, I trust you."

"It should prove mildly sedative administered in the proper quantities."

"Very well. Is that it?"

"That's it."

I rose and clasped my hands before me, about to say goodnight when he spoke again.

"I was wrong about something, though, Charlotte."

"What's that?"

"You were stronger than I thought. He didn't make mincemeat of you. I'm sorry for saying that."

His praise warmed my heart. "That was a long time ago, and we've both changed. Would you let me make you up a plate in the kitchen? I don't recall seein' you eat. You must maintain your strength, William."

He shook his head, and perhaps it was a trick of the light, but I thought I saw his chin wobble. Oh, no. The man truly thought he might lose his father. Contagion or no, I couldn't just stand there all cold and proper. I walked over and placed a hand on his shoulder.

"It will be all right."

He nodded. "God will help us get through this."

"Is that what's helped you, what's changed you? You found God?"

William chuckled. "More accurately, He found me, July 22, 1864, during the fighting for Atlanta. Right in the middle of the yard of Atlanta Medical College where I operated alongside Dr. Noel D'Alvigny."

I sat back down, tucking my skirt under me. "What happened?"

"We worked out under the shade trees because the heat was so intense, but the bullets fell so thick around us we had to move back inside. I had just removed the arm of a sixteen-year-old boy when Dr. D'Alvigny's daughter called to ask me to help her carry her patient up the steps. I looked back at my own patient, who to my shock had come to after I bandaged the stump. But he said, 'I'll be fine.' So I went. When I came back, I discovered he had moments to live after a stray bullet had gut shot him. Do you know what he said?"

William's blue eyes were beautiful. I noticed that for the first time as I shook my head, my hand covering my mouth as I fought nausea.

"'I told you I would be fine. I know Jesus, Dr. Dunham. Do you?'" William dropped my gaze and stood up, adding in a quiet voice, "I realized then that I didn't know Him well enough to bet my eternity on it like that boy just had. I'd been running a long time from a God I thought disapproved of me the way I felt everyone else did. Traumatic times have a way of pushing you in one direction or the other. Thankfully, they pushed me into His arms."

I didn't know what to say. I remembered the early days of love and joy I'd experienced after meeting my Savior at the Methodist revival. In that moment, it hit me that I'd blamed God for allowing Stuart to steal everything good in my life, and Stuart for stealing it. The strength of my anger surprised me and ended our conversation that night, but did not stop me from observing William in the days ahead. He drew me like a fly to sugar water. I had to be close to see if this change constituted something real. Maybe the dearth of a man's approval and support had also starved me. I wanted it to be real.

"What are you readin'?" I asked when I found him one morning at the table in the kitchen, toast and coffee and his Bible again spread before him.

"About forgiveness. Matthew 18:21: 'Then Peter came to Him, and said, 'Lord, how oft shall my brother sin against me, and I forgive him? Till seven times?' Jesus saith unto him, 'I say not unto thee, until seven times: but, until seventy times seven.'"

I pulled up a chair as he flipped pages.

"And this, in chapter five. 'Therefore if thou bring thy gift to the altar, and there rememberest that thy brother hath ought against thee; leave there thy gift before the altar, and go thy way; first be reconciled to thy brother, and then come and offer thy gift.'"

"Are you thinkin' you need to reconcile somethin' with your brother?"

"More my father. I get the sense from this there may be another type of healing that's more important than physical. Maybe that even stands in the way of the physical at times. I know God may or may not heal him, Charlotte, because we live in a fallen world where sin, death and disease hold sway, but what if God can't hear my prayers because I hold a grudge against my father?"

Why was he asking me this? I shifted in my seat. "Might I ask, for what?"

"For treating me like a prodigal because I couldn't accept his decision to own slaves. I knew I was right, but I let that make me bitter toward him, self-righteous."

I nodded and laid a hand on the rolled-up sleeve of his cotton shirt. "Then you should settle that, and you both will have peace, regardless of the outcome."

William's eyes filled with tears. "He's not improving, Charlotte. I don't know what else to do."

"William, you've employed all your skills and diligence. No son could have served his father better. Whatever happens now is in God's hands."

He grasped my hand and squeezed. "You're right." He blinked the moisture from his eyes. "The Bible says we must honor our parents. It doesn't give conditions on that honor. It means honor their position even if they make wrong choices."

"Then you should go."

He nodded and left, leaving me sitting there with the cold nipping through my wool stockings despite the flickers of warmth from the cook fire … cold nipping like the realization that the Bible also said wives should honor their husbands. I had said the right things to William, but I was relieved he could not see the darkness in my heart.

That darkness swelled and magnified only hours later. I first heard the cry as I cleaned and put away the breakfast dishes. Anne labored behind me with the cook, preparing a stew for our lunch. But we both bolted into the hall when we heard William roar, "What did you do?" and a woman squeal in protest. He had Lettie up against the wall by her forearms. I always tried not to look at Lettie, but now I could not ignore the terror on her pretty face.

"William!" Anne and I both exclaimed.

He paid us no mind. "How much hawthorn did you put in that tea?" he bellowed at the maid.

I covered my mouth in horror.

"I didn' do it. Doc Jeremiah did it!"

William shook her. "Doc Jeremiah told me you've been watching him make the tea and taking it to Stuart. He told me he trusted you to take care of it today while he prepared medicines for Father. So don't lie to me! How much?"

A sob bubbled out of her mouth. "Double." But her gaze fixed on the chandelier.

He shook her again.

"Triple!" Lettie shrieked out the truth at last.

"Oh, God." William sagged and released her. He clasped his head in his hands, the knuckles tightening in his hair, closed his eyes and finished the prayer on an agonized whisper. "Oh, God, what do I do?"

Lettie's eyeballs bulged as she yelled, "Three heapin' handfuls, and I shoulda boiled the whole bush! That man deserve to die. He the devil spawn! You don't know what low, disgustin' things he do to me." Her gaze found me as I clung to Anne, weak with shock. Her finger stabbed the air in my direction. "To her! Only if he die can we be free. You know. Tell them." Lettie's panicked gaze entreated me to defend her.

Anne turned to look at me, her face twisted in disbelief and horror, but before she could speak, her brother rallied into action. "We have no time to lose! Build up the fire in his room. Make up a drink half lemon juice and half vinegar, and brew a cup of the strongest black coffee I brought back with me. Now!"

He ran up the stairs without waiting to confirm that Anne and I obeyed his orders. Of course we did. The whole household raced to assist the only functioning Dr. Dunham on the property. Even frail, black-clad Selah waddled into the house and up to Stuart's room.

During that day, as I did whatever William told me to try to rouse Stuart from the hemlock stupor and flush the poison from his body, I began to wonder … what if he died? Lettie spoke the truth. So many things bound would find release, things obvious, things nameless, things deep and secret. How could I not wish for that? Stuart's anger and impatience showed he did not want to live the way he was living. While I knew one should not take such matters into one's own hands, that such decisions belonged to God alone, did I really want Stuart to live? The horrible, horrible answer I found within myself sickened me.

By evening, Stuart's pulse, paralysis and breathing improved, and he began to stir slightly. William still listened to his lungs and heart every few minutes. Selah, who had attended Silas in the interim, appeared in the bedroom door to summon her grandson. She told him to make haste. When he grabbed his medical bag and bolted, my wide eyes met hers.

"It be the ninth day, and the fever's not broke," she said in an ominous voice. "And I did see the mocking bird yesterday. I was not sure who it was for. Now I think I will lose my brother instead of this one." Her small, shriveled head jerked toward Stuart, the gesture faintly condescending, then tears poured from her eyes before she turned and walked out.

I remembered in November of 1859 at his beautiful Lexington home, The Cedars, Governor Gilmer witnessed a mocking bird flutter and peck on his window. He took it as a portent of his own death, which indeed occurred several days later. Thinking of William, his impending sorrow, his selfless efforts to save both his brother and his father and all those mangled soldiers, tears flooded my eyes, too. I reached out and took Stuart's hand, wondering if anything selfless and noble remained in the younger brother, if the hands that had once expertly stitched broken lives back together could be raised in tenderness, not anger, could stitch our lives together again.

I sat by Stuart until almost midnight, when I heard weeping and moaning throughout the house and knew that Silas had left this world. One voice tore my heart so deeply I could not ignore it. I found William on the darkened servant's staircase, head in his arms, and drew him against me. I shushed him and stroked his dark head. When he leaned toward me, I put my arms around him. And when he raised his tear-stained face, I kissed him. And he kissed me back. Tenderness, admiration and desperation born of crisis mingled in the most poignant moment I'd ever known. Intense sweetness … and intense darkness … swirled.

I went up to bed without a word being spoken. I didn't need to. The kiss had said it all. But my guilty spirit pierced the heavens with a silent scream. *Oh, God, what have I done?* The darkness inside me mushroomed until it filled my head, my chest, flooding my brain with thoughts and my heart with cold, aching ice and making me grab my head and squeeze. But it didn't come out.

The next morning, we discovered Lettie had gone, taking Beulah with her. William speculated that she'd likely seek shelter in Union-held territory. When we were alone, he also told me that once he settled his father's affairs, he would leave, too. Short of doctors and supplies, Confederate soldiers still suffered and died in hospitals in Macon and Savannah. He had to go do something.

"It's me. It's me, isn't it?" I asked, clutching my chest where the searing pain threatened to make me lose all composure.

He wouldn't look at me, but his bloodshot eyes told me he had not slept, either, and the defeated slump of his shoulders told me I had wounded, not helped. "I don't blame you, Charlotte, but surely you can see, I can't be around you right now."

"I'm sorry, William. I'm so sorry." I ran from the room before my whole body crumpled in weeping.

That night I laid awake again. I'd never known such pain, not when Stuart hit me, not when he forced his way with me, not when he called me disgusting names. There was no pain like this. I thought it might eat me alive. I knew nowhere else to turn but to a Higher Power. "Oh, God, why? Why? Why did I fall in love with a man I can't have? And why did you let me be shackled to one who abuses me?"

As I wept, memories formed in my brain. All the little hints of Stuart's warped attitudes while he courted me. The unease I'd felt after I'd become a Christian, once Stuart came home from college. The words of William and Selah. God had gone out of His way to warn me, but I had been too preoccupied with position, wealth and the selfish desires of my own heart.

My crying quieted as I recalled the words William had spoken to me in the parlor and the day he'd read to me from the Bible about forgiveness and honor. Lettie's actions had forced me to look within and see the same fomenting bitterness within myself. I was far gone to darkness. I had to cut it out now, or it would consume me.

I slid out from under the covers and knelt by my bed. I asked God for forgiveness, and His peace descended over my shivering form like a warm quilt. Had danger been imminent, I should seek shelter in my own father's home. But I sensed that time was past. Stuart was now a broken man. I knew in that moment that even if Stuart never gave me what I needed, God would. My life might never be what I wanted, but God help me, from this point on, I would serve both God and my family—all my family, including my husband and my brother-in-law—with dignity.

CHAPTER TWELVE

The letters from Charlotte to William Dunham created the same disorienting effect in Jennifer's mind that the 1920 newspaper articles on microfilm at the Oglethorpe County Library had that spring, the sense that history nudged out modern reality, overtaking it, rewriting it. Those words from the past forced her to rethink things in her own life, things she preferred to ignore.

Granted, several important moments occurred the rest of that week. Marian Dukes replied to Jennifer's e-mail, delighted with her interest and assuring Jennifer she planned to discuss a potential hiring package for a new Main Street director with Lexington Mayor Alton Wilson right away. The mail collected from the Hermon post office box that same day included a letter from the National Register Staff Board stating that due to a satisfactory review of their nomination, no site approval visit would be necessary. Their property now appeared on the docket for the February meeting. Huge news.

Jennifer, Michael, James and Earl knocked out the apothecary's old plaster using hammers and ripping bars. Whomever completed the original job possessed great skill, for while the single coat had been coarse and not residential standard, the plaster still stood several inches think. Chunks of the lime-based, horsehair-laced compound fell between the framing of the walls, requiring them to remove several rows of the thin lathing near the baseboards so that they could reach in and scoop out the mess. They shoveled three trailer loads full of rubble. Friday morning the electrician hired for the apothecary arrived and went to work at the service entrance box.

However, the week's accomplishments only registered on the surface of Jennifer's consciousness. Its depths swirled instead with memories of sitting on the apothecary floor with Michael, James and Stella, pouring over letters written by Charlotte Ormond Dunham to her brother-in-law, Dr. William Dunham, between 1865 and 1870. Since no letters from William appeared in the bunch, they conjectured that William himself had saved Charlotte's letters and hidden them between the frame of the cupboard and the wall in the apothecary.

Saturday morning, Jennifer felt grumpy as she sloshed across the yard to Michael's F150. The rain now slowed to a faint drizzle, but she still did not relish driving to Augusta by herself in an unfamiliar vehicle. Michael had handed her the keys the night before, when he told her he needed to remain home in case the electrician returned. Stella couldn't accompany her because of some school-related function. At least they *had* an excuse. Jennifer fought irritation toward Amy for cancelling at the last minute. She said Horace insisted she accompany him to meet a new client in hopes that the man would engage her interior decorating services for the historic home he was moving into.

Well, getting blown off was nothing new, Jennifer reminded herself as she backed the truck into the turn-around and flicked the wipers on low speed. Taking a minute to acquaint herself with the vehicle's controls, she felt confident to proceed onto the main road. At least the early hour would ensure many other motorists stayed home.

Talk about getting blown off. Charlotte Ormond Dunham sure had. But either her good attitude or the strict proprieties of 1860s correspondence veiled any resentment Charlotte might have borne toward her brother-in-law for leaving her in charge of her wounded husband Stuart's care only about a month after his return home. Charlotte even referenced William's departure as "noble." At first Jennifer and her companions had assumed that referred to his return to doctoring wounded soldiers in the last days of the Confederacy. Later, it became clear there might be more to the story.

That first letter began a string of discussion about Stuart's medication, care and progress, lasting several years. Terms and prescriptions foreign to the modern readers peppered the delicate, looping script. Each missive also referenced pertinent events in the region. Just following the war, Charlotte described Union occupation and thievery by displaced slaves in Athens. She also wrote of new residents of the county, South Georgia refugees who camped at the Crawford train yards and citizens of East Tennessee escaping Yankee sympathizers to dwell in The Glade near Madison County. Some of these stayed. As Franklin College reopened and Georgia began the long struggle toward readmission into the Union, many attempted to pour new life into local economy, like Samuel Bailey, who worked in the Athens armory during the war and then drew the pattern for the first Y switch of the railroad after its destruction by Union troops. He came to Hermon to establish the first fertilizer plant in the South, eventually winning a State Agriculture Society trophy for his wheat crop and introducing the "Nellie Rich Strawberry." Augustus Brightwell returned from the war to aid his father William at his farm and grist mill. James Smith, ex-soldier-turned-peddler, began buying up thousands of acres near Madison to create a convict labor plantation.

But what stayed foremost in Jennifer's mind from Charlotte's letters were the things unsaid, or merely hinted at. Only required to slow for one light in Union Point, Jennifer had plenty of time to replay those things during the hour and a half whizzing by pine forests en route to I-20.

William returned to Atlanta later in 1865. He must have contemplated a Christmas visit that year, for in November, Charlotte told him, "Please do not hesitate on account of what passed before. You will find the peace of our Lord reigns in the household. Stuart's progress is indeed marked by occasional fits of ill temper. That he will never be what he once was some days creates angst. But Anne and I settled into your latest suggested remedy and nurse him with patience and diligence. With God's help, I forgave Stuart right after you left for the way he treated me before the war. Nothing here should cause you grief."

How had Stuart treated Charlotte? Had he been neglectful? Unfaithful? Abusive? Whatever it was, it must have been bad for Charlotte to mention it in a letter to William. Jennifer also wondered what "passed before" concerning William. Perhaps a rift with the family. Something caused William to return to a practice in Atlanta rather than the Athens area, and something induced him to remain there even though his brother suffered from post-war head trauma.

But Charlotte's favorable opinion of William shone through. "Please see that you take adequate precautions," she urged him during an autumn 1866 smallpox epidemic. "I know your tendency to work yourself into exhaustion. You must not let yourself get to that state lest you give the dread disease a foothold."

Then, the following year, one of Charlotte's letters responded to what must have been a worried inquiry, for she assured her brother-in-law of the family's safety. "It is true that Mr. Hawkins organized the Oglethorpe Klan after the war, with his wife supporting as honorary member. Those who joined endured a 'Crucial Test' with a strict oath to secrecy. I hear over five hundred joined to quell insolence by

Negroes incited by Northern Republicans. The 'better blacks' are told they have nothing to fear. The Federal government sought Mr. Hawkins, and he hid out for a while. Recently soldiers with fixed bayonets charged a mob of a hundred armed black men gathered in Athens. Also a group of Negroes with sticks and clubs invaded Franklin College, but a professor managed to dispel the mob. Understandably, the black man agitates for his right to education and vote. But I think the trouble is in hand, and I hear many of the former slaves begin to migrate West. Never fear. The county has been quiet, posing no need for you to return home, although you should know, William, while we are proud of your work in Atlanta, you are always welcome here. A ready clientele of patients would welcome you, as would your family."

Jennifer sipped her coffee as she auto-piloted down miles of straight roads, remembering how Charlotte's tone changed toward the end of the decade. "Stuart's condition grows worse. The headaches, dizziness and convulsions come more frequently. This week he fell into what I believe you would term paralytic shock, lying unconscious several hours. Aunt Selah rallied him, but he is not the same. The strides he had made with his left side are retarded so much that he again requires aid in dressing and feeding himself. His vision dims. And William, there are times he thinks the war is still going on. Most alarming, last night he began screaming about something dark and terrible he saw in the corner. I must ask you to come to us."

The last paper in the bunch had not been a letter, but a single sheet of stationery folded around a ticket to John Robinson's Great Combination Circus, Menagerie and Aviary in Athens, dated Thursday, May 12, 1870. Unfamiliar writing scrawled on the edge reflected the theme of the show: "When I look at you, my spirit flies free." On the paper, in Charlotte's handwriting: "You asked if you spoke too soon today. You asked if my heart still contained affection for you. My answer is that God has given strength for years, but today His gift of grace left me speechless. My answer is yes. Yes, a million times, yes."

Jennifer picked up her cell phone. One dot indicated questionable reception, but she dialed anyway. Grace Stevenson at the Oglethorpe County Library answered on the second ring. "Grace? Hi, it's Jennifer Rushmore. Listen, I'm driving to Augusta, so I might lose you, but would you be willing to look something up for me?"

"Well, of course, Jennifer. What is it?"

"Dunham marriage licenses for 1870 and 1871."

"OK, just give me a minute. I'll put you on hold while I go check."

"Thank you so much!"

Noticing an increase in the spitting from heaven, Jennifer switched the wipers up a notch. Allison Winters had said that William was the son who built the Hermon apothecary in the 1870s. If things panned out as Jennifer hoped, following years of serving a wounded, unworthy husband, Charlotte had joined William there in a happy ending. Her heart beat sped up as a rustling sounded and Grace came back on the line.

"Jennifer? Here it is! And I must say it proved easy to find, because the marriage took place on January 1 of 1871. I'd say William Dunham and Charlotte Ormond Dunham knew how to start the year out right!"

"Oh, Grace, that's—"

Jennifer did not get to finish her statement, for a large buck leapt out of the woods and over the bank toward the road. Dropping the phone, Jennifer slammed on the brakes hard and jerked the truck over the yellow line to avoid him. The brown body darted back toward the cover of forest, and heart hammering, she braked again. But rather than offering her the security of solid resistance, the pedal eased toward the floor.

"What? What in the world?" Panicking, Jennifer pressed the pedal down harder, but her speed only decreased fractionally. A glance told her that the straightaway ended in an upcoming curve. Quickly she reached over to downshift manually. The engine hummed into a new gear.

"Oh, God help me," she said aloud as she continued to pump the brakes. Then she remembered the emergency brake was not connected to the brake lines, which had to be leaking fluid. But how? Concerned with getting Michael's truck off the road while on a safe stretch, Jennifer transferred her right foot to the brake and practically stood up like a rider in stirrups to simultaneously depress the emergency lever. As the vehicle finally slowed to a crawl, she steered onto the grassy shoulder, just shy of the curve.

She sat breathing hard, heart hammering. "Oh, Lord, what just happened?" She covered her face with trembling hands. In that moment she experienced a flash of realization that her stepfather Roy's automotive teaching actually proved helpful. An example of God using something bad for good? "Thank you, thank you, for helping me get off the road safely."

Finally, Jennifer lifted her head to look up and down the highway. No cars approached. She consulted her cell phone. Not only had her call to Grace been disconnected, but the dot grid at the top of the screen revealed no cellular service. She fought down panic. This could be worse, as she'd already recognized. Someone would come along, probably in a matter of minutes. She just had to pray it was the right person. In the meantime, she needed to look under the hood.

Turning on her flashers, Jennifer hit the release and climbed out, going around to the front of the truck. Under the hood, all looked normal, and no suspicious smells mingled with those of damp earth and pine. She unscrewed the lid on the brake fluid reserve and peered inside. Nothing. A groan escaped her, and she knelt on the damp asphalt. Sure enough, clear liquid dripped from behind the tire.

Jennifer raised her head at the sound of an approaching engine. A beat-up Chevy truck came from the direction of I-20, a man's shaggy head and shoulders silhouetted in the driver's seat. A chill of fear purled down her spine as she recalled that, should she need to defend herself in this barren stretch of wilderness, she possessed no weapon, not even pepper spray. As she stood up, she willed the man to keep driving. But he pulled off the road, nosing his grill up to hers, and leaned out of the window.

"Havin' trouble, miss?" The stranger sported a deep summer tan under a dingy ball cap and long, dark hair shot through with silver. His arm resting on the side of his truck measured twice the size of hers.

Jennifer felt sick with blood-pumping apprehension. She tried to inject a casual carelessness into her voice as she waved and called back, "No, nothing serious. Just heard a strange noise under the hood, and thought I ought to check it. No need to worry, but thanks!"

"Maybe I should take a look for you," the man offered.

"I think everything is fine."

"Still, just to be sure ..." He got out of the vehicle and closed the door, approaching the open engine of Michael's truck.

At that moment, Jennifer followed a strong instinct without wasting time agonizing over its lack of sociability. "I'll just wait in the car. Thank you," she called out as she hopped up into the cab. When she shut the door and threw the lock, her heart thudded. The man's head jerked up, but she could not see his expression. Awkward, yes, but the strong, familiar sense of potential danger and entrapment overruled niceties. Her companion bent under the hood. Then he did as she had and investigated under the engine, where he doubtless realized in seconds she was a sitting duck. At least he'd have to break a window to carry out any sinister intentions. Of course, she'd need to lower that window to receive his report when he decided to walk back and talk to her.

Jennifer swallowed and whispered aloud, "Jesus, if you see me now, please send someone else. Fast." Just in case her prayer didn't register in time, she picked up her cell phone and tried punching Michael's number. Her call hung in the atmosphere, suspended in orbital silence. Still, she kept the phone there at her ear, trying to make it look like she was talking.

Then two things happened at the same time. The man started toward the driver's side door, and a small, boxy vehicle approached from behind. Jennifer rolled the window down far enough to allow her arm out the top, and she made a big, slow, waving gesture in an attempt to flag down what she now recognized as a mail truck. *Oh, please stop.* Then she saw with great relief that the vehicle slowed and edged in behind Michael's F150.

"You're leakin' brake fluid," Chevy man told her through the crack in the window. "I could see a bleeder bolt's totally missing. It's a wonder you didn't run off the road. You musta done some smart driving."

"Yeah, well ..." Jennifer smiled deprecatingly, glancing in the rear view mirror, where she beheld a tall, older man getting out of his truck. He, too, approached her window. Sight of his official uniform settled her discomfort, but he looked far too buff to be a mailman, a fact that proved especially surprising since he must be around sixty. *Lord?* She sent the inquiry upward, and while no voice answered, she felt calmer, like the intended solution had arrived.

"Ma'am, there's no way you can drive this truck safely," the dark-haired man said.

"What's the trouble?" the mail carrier asked.

Jennifer's initial visitor reiterated what he'd seen under the hood. "Did you have your brakes serviced recently?" he asked her.

"Well, it's not my truck, so I really don't know."

The guy in the ball cap shook his head. "OK, well, you can't get back on the road like it is. Did you call somebody?"

Jennifer thinned her mouth, then admitted, "I couldn't get reception."

"Yeah, this stretch is particularly bad," the mailman observed, glancing down the road. He lifted his hat and swiped at his silvery-gold hair.

The Chevy driver said, "There's a service station off the interstate exit. I'm friends with the mechanic there. I can give you a ride." His eyes pierced through the slit in the window.

Friendship with mechanics bestowed no special status in Jennifer's estimation. "But you were going the opposite direction."

"That's no problem."

"Well, I'm headed toward Crawfordville," the postman interrupted. "It would be no inconvenience."

"Thank you." Making her decision, Jennifer reached for her purse and phone.

"I'm happy to take her. No need for you to be late to work," argued Chevy guy. Then he affected indifference, shrugging and lifting his arms. "But hey, whatever."

"No worries. I won't be late." As soon as the mail man heard Jennifer unlock her door, he opened it, then stood to the side, between her and the other man, as Jennifer climbed down. His presence had the opposite effect on her as that of the driver of the Chevy. And she noticed he smelled particularly good, like unusual, sweet spices.

"I appreciate the offer and the help, but since Mr. ..."

"Lowe. David Lowe." He lifted the U.S. Postal Service name badge on his shirt to verify.

Jennifer nodded. "Since Mr. Lowe is already going in the right direction, I'll gratefully accept his help. But thanks to you, also."

"Suit yourself." The dark-haired man turned and stalked back to his truck. As they watched, he turned over the ignition and revved his engine as he took off down the road.

Not commenting on the driver's sudden ill humor, David smiled and gestured toward the open driver's side of his truck. "Sorry, but I'm afraid you'll have to climb over and perch inside. They intentionally made these buggies one-seaters."

"Oh. That's no problem." Jennifer grinned and climbed in. She found a place on the floor to sit cross-legged between David's seat and the reassuring clutter of mail trays and packages. I guess he could still be a serial rapist or killer. The Mail Man Murderer. After all, Ted Bundy was handsome, rich and educated. The girls getting into his Volkswagen probably didn't think twice. He could still kill her and throw her body out in the Georgia pines and nobody would be the wiser. But somehow the idea seemed ridiculous, even disrespectful.

It helped when, right after starting down the road, he said, "You should get reception in a mile or so. You can try your phone again, call someone to come meet you at the station."

Jennifer brightened "Oh. Thank you. So do you like your job? I mean, it must be one of the few in these parts, right? But I'm surprised they make you work on Saturdays."

David chuckled. "Oh, I just like to get ahead sometimes. And yes, I love my job. I'm usually bringing good news, right? The more rural the area, the more people appreciate the messenger."

"I can imagine that would be true. Well, thanks so much. I hate to say it, but that guy kind of gave me the creeps."

With a glance back over his shoulder, David admitted, "Me, too."

"Oh! I got one bar." Jennifer blew out her breath and dialed Michael's number. When he answered, she surprised herself by tearing up. Responding to the thickness and anxiety of her voice, he expressed immediate alarm, which only increased as she related her tale.

"Did you have the brakes serviced recently?" she asked him.

"Definitely not! There's no reason that bolt should have been loose. I can't think how it could have gotten loose enough to fly off when you hit the brakes. Something's not right here."

"Well, I'm fine. This nice postman came by and is giving me a ride to the station on I-20. Can you come get me there?"

David leaned over to interject in a quiet voice, "If you don't need a mechanic, I could take you some place in Crawfordville. It would be a much nicer wait. That service station is run down, remote."

That sounded imminently more appealing. "Hold on a minute, Michael." Jennifer cocked her head and asked her driver, "Any historic sites in Crawfordville?"

David grinned. "You bet. The whole downtown's historic, as featured in the movie 'Sweet Home Alabama.' And there's Liberty Hall, home of Alexander Stephens, Vice President of the Confederacy."

"Is it open on Saturday?"

"Sure is."

Jennifer nodded, then asked Michael to meet her at Liberty Hall and to text when he arrived. Michael agreed, assuring her he'd leave the house immediately in his father's car and would call roadside assistance on the way, to tow the truck back to Lexington. "Are you sure you're OK? And safe with this mail man guy?"

"Yes, I'm sure." Jennifer doubted David would have let her call Michael if he intended her any harm. Besides, the atmosphere in his mail carrier just felt, well, warm and safe, and that faint odor of pleasant spices hovered when the damp air from the open side of the vehicle did not whisk it away.

"Well, stay put at that old house. This makes one too many accidents recently. I'm also going to call Stan."

"Don't call Stan. We don't even know what happened yet."

Michael refused to discuss it further. "Just stay at the old house in Crawfordville, OK? I'll be there as soon as possible."

"Don't get a speeding ticket." He'd already hung up before she finished speaking.

David smiled down at her. "You've got a man who really cares about you."

Jennifer gave a laugh and made a dubious face. "He's my boss."

"His tone of voice didn't sound like a boss. Here, you want a water?"

Jennifer took the bottle he offered with thanks, checking to make sure the top remained unopened before she took a swig. *Thank you, God*, she prayed. Soon the preserved-in-time appearance of Crawfordville welcomed her, and as David let her off at the drive of beautiful, green-shuttered Liberty Hall, she pondered how what could have been a disastrous, even fatal, day, had turned out so unexpectedly well. She made her way over pea gravel to the rear office entrance where tickets were sold, then turned, expecting to see the mail truck ready to pull out onto the main road. To her surprise, it was nowhere in sight. Come to think of it, she hadn't even heard it drive away.

Silly, she told herself. *You just weren't paying attention*. Yet when she entered the gift shop and told her story to the elderly lady behind the desk, the small woman's eyes opened wide behind her plastic frame glasses. "Honey, I can't imagine what mail carrier you saw. There's only one mail carrier in Crawfordville. His name isn't David, and I can guarantee you he doesn't work on weekends."

Jennifer had to sit down. Had David said he worked in Crawfordville? Maybe his route centered on another town nearby. Only by accepting an offered granola bar and assuring herself such an old lady could be senile did she generate strength to accept the woman's offer of a tour. Well, and she *was* curious about the preservation of the 1875 mansion. By the time Michael texted as they stepped out of the attached kitchen, the beautiful walnut furniture and smell of old volumes in the statesman's personal library had calmed Jennifer again.

Michael did not share her frame of mind. To her surprise, he hugged her when he first walked up, causing her cheeks to flame in front of her tour guide. After Jennifer expressed thanks for her tour, he drew her away under the shade of some massive oak trees. There he told her, "I stopped to look under the hood of the truck and take some photographs on my way down. I didn't see anything else wrong with the truck except the bleeder screw, just like you said. But Jennifer, those don't come loose on their own."

"I know that." Jennifer eyed a small grave site with interest, wanting to walk over and ignore the discussion Michael forced her to have. Something uneasy stirred in her gut.

"I need to ask, and this sounds stupid, I know, but did you make any enemies during your time at UGA?"

She looked into his concerned face and gave a snort of a laugh. "Yeah, someone jealous of Professor Shelley helping me get the Savannah job is trying to kill the competition."

"I'm serious, Jennifer. You said something about pushy guys once. There are no obsessive ex-boyfriends?"

"Michael, really. Do you think a guy would ever be *that* obsessed with *me*?" When he looked pained, she regretted saying that, and chewed her lip. To fill the silence, she attempted to change tacks. "It's *your* truck. Do *you* have any enemies?"

"For someone to loosen that screw, they'd have to have done it last night or early this morning. That would mean the person would have known you were driving the truck."

"Not necessarily. They could have wanted to get to you, and I just got in the way."

Michael spewed out a breath. "OK, never mind. The last time I had work done on the truck was about eight months ago. I guess the screw could have gotten loose then and gradually worked its way out. That makes more sense than supposing someone wants to hurt or kill one of us enough to sneak over on a rainy night to crawl under the truck with a wrench. Regardless, I told Stan, and he can ask the questions from this point on. Let's just not argue." He reached out to take her elbow and guide her toward the parking lot. "Are you hungry for lunch? I saw a Country Café downtown."

Jennifer grinned. "I would love a big, juicy, old-fashioned hamburger about now."

Minutes later, seated at a table draped with a stiff checkered cloth and surrounded by the hum of conversing locals, Jennifer told Michael about David's rescue and abrupt disappearance, then what the woman at Liberty Hall had said. "I was really praying during the whole episode. That first guy who stopped really made me uneasy. Then when David came, it was like I knew I could trust him. I wonder what makes you sense that. Do you think it was the Holy Spirit?"

"I think it can be. The Holy Spirit enhances our natural intuition and makes it on target."

Jennifer hesitated, nibbling a corner of her burger, then wiping her fingers and mouth. Eating in front of Michael made her nervous, but hunger won out. Her next question also made her nervous, but curiosity won out. "So ... have you ever felt like the Holy Spirit ... spoke to you?"

Michael swirled a fry in ketchup and glanced up at her. "Aloud?"

"Well, maybe not aloud, but directly."

"Like hearing direction inside your head, when you know you didn't think it?"

"Exactly!"

"Sure. A number of times. Sometimes it's just a feeling of caution, kind of like what you just described, or a prodding to speak up and say something to someone. Or to be quiet." Michael laughed unexpectedly. "I got that one a lot, with Ashley. I was really stubborn when I was younger, if you can't imagine."

Jennifer grinned. "Your poor wife."

"So do you feel He's been speaking to you lately?"

"Sometimes." Jennifer took a sip of her Coke, then poked at her ice with the straw, avoiding his gaze. Discussing spiritual matters felt intimate. Stella would be easier to talk to about such things, but Jennifer found herself curious to know where Michael stood, what he thought.

"What's He been saying?"

"Uh ... mainly that He's working on me a lot like I'm working on Dunham House. A restoration project. You know, clean out the mess, fill the holes, put on a new roof, strengthen the structure, that sort of thing." Jennifer's cheeks burned. She dabbed her fries in her ketchup as long as she could to cover the silence, but eventually she had to look up. Michael stared at her intently. "What? Did that sound stupid?"

He chuckled, but without mirth. The dry sound came from deep within. "No. It sounded right on target."

"But you didn't like it."

Michael sat back from the table, playing with the paper from his straw, like he wanted to withdraw, divert. "Well, sometimes when we suddenly get what God is doing, we don't like it. His renovation projects are painful."

"That's what you said that day in the yard, after Bryan Holton's interview, that God won't stop until He gets you where He wants you. Wait, has God been telling you the same thing, about yourself?"

"No, but you just did. And when you said it, I knew it was true."

"You had a moment, right? Like when things suddenly came clear? Isn't that good?"

"I guess." Michael balled the straw paper up and flipped it across the table with an index finger.

"OK, you just got all withdrawn. What is it?"

Michael sighed.

"Stella said you were running from something, and running from God."

His eyes flicked up to hers. "She did?"

"Yeah."

"Man, she's a walking spiritual radar. It's really annoying." He laughed, then blew out a breath. "OK, I can see how neither of us are at Dunham House by accident. I can see that the process of restoring the property and all the people that involves is His set-up to do His work on us. But I've been there before, when my mom died, and again when Ash died. At both of those times, a lot of supernatural stuff went on. Things like hearing God speak into my heart, and people bringing messages I knew were from Him. I had this pastor who always said births and deaths were the times the veil between the worlds was thinnest."

Jennifer nodded, and he continued. "What I said about God getting you where He wanted you was true. But first, we have to be willing for Him to work on us. I didn't want to hear from Him anymore. I was angry about the way God took both of them. You'd know what I mean if you've seen someone die from a painful form of cancer. No one should have to suffer that way, especially two of His sweetest, most faithful servants."

When Michael seemed unable to continue, Jennifer nodded and sat back from the table, clasping her hands before her to avoid reaching for his. Michael chewed his lower lip, then rasped in a broken tone, "He could have stopped that."

OK, she had to reach out now. Maybe that urge was the Holy Spirit anyway. She curled her small fingers around his big, rough ones. "You know what Stella would say about that."

"Yeah." He nodded and pulled back, balling up his fists. "But to heal the scab has to come off. Ripping it off too early isn't pretty. I don't know if I can do that yet. Can you?"

Jennifer squirmed under his level stare. He knew she hid things in her past. "I don't know," she admitted. "I just know I really like feeling that Someone bigger than me is looking out for me, like I did today. I've never felt that before."

"That is a benefit. I don't know what to make of your mail man. But Jennifer, I know something else, and that's that when God's at work and God stuff starts to happen, there's always opposition."

She looked up again. "You mean Satan?"

"Yes, and those he can use. Even if there are logical explanations for some of the things that have happened to put you in harm's way, I can't shake the feeling that I need to look out for you."

She grinned. "So you're going to help God out?"

"Yes, I am. Next weekend is Labor Day. Dad and I are going to the lake, no family, just us. Lots of cooking out and fishing. I want you to come with us."

Reminded of Michael's assuming manner the first time she met him, Jennifer bristled. "Are you asking me or telling me?"

He sighed. "I am asking you. While Stan does some investigating, please come to the lake with us."

Jennifer sensed a negotiation opportunity. "I need to get some stuff done, too. Like finding antiques. If I take that extra time off over Labor Day, will you drive me on down to Augusta this afternoon?"

"It's getting a little late for that, and the electrician is working at the apothecary today. I'd like to get back in time to check over his work before he leaves. So no. But there's an antique store in Lake Oconee you could check out."

"With *you*?"

Reluctantly, Michael wobbled his head, then agreed. "Come on. We all need a get-away."

It was Jennifer's turn to nod. He looked grimly satisfied while he went to pay the bill. As he waited at the counter with his back turned, Jennifer grabbed the remaining half of her burger and scarfed it down fast.

CHAPTER THIRTEEN

"So are we going to the antique store first?" Jennifer asked Michael and James as the new F150 Michael brought home that week hummed down Greensboro Highway. The Lexington mechanic had added brake fluid, replaced the bleeder screw, and pronounced the older truck fit earlier that week. But Michael promptly traded it at the Ford dealership, saying simply the vehicle had seen better days, and as much hauling of not only goods but people as they were doing now, he felt the need for an extended cab. Jennifer had to admit the new truck was much nicer, but just to be safe, Michael himself performed an exacting check of the tires and under the hood before they pulled out today.

As wary as the potential awkwardness of close proximity to the men made Jennifer regarding the weekend at the lake, excitement stirred, and not just when she considered a new antique store. Charcoal cookouts and fishing sounded pretty good, too, especially after the week spent cleaning the apothecary, replacing missing lathing, and reinforcing curved shelving, flimsy once they moved them away from the walls to which they had been nailed. Another bonus, Yoda now curled on her lap. The comforting, now-purring fur ball refused to stay in her cat carrier in the back, where James sat, having insisted Jennifer ride up front. Yoda's constant meowing insisted she did, too.

"My vote is to get it over with," Michael said. At her incredulous look, he added, "The cabin's address is Eatonton, not that close to the Lake Oconee retail area. Once we get to the lake, I'd rather stay at the lake."

"Despite your ungracious manner of suggestion, I'm not going to argue about hitting the store first. But we have a problem," Jennifer pointed out.

"What's that?"

Jennifer wiggled a finger in the direction of Yoda's head. "What are we going to do with the cat? It's far too hot to leave her in the truck."

"There's an ice cream shop next door," James suggested.

Jennifer said, "They won't let you take her in there."

"No, but someone could wait while I go in and get a double scoop, then I'll be quite content to sit in the truck with Yoda while the two of you look for buried treasure."

"That would work," Jennifer agreed, while Michael murmured, "Oh, goody."

As traffic picked up, Jennifer admired brick walls and signs and handsome landscaping with spurting fountains marking entrances to lake developments. A new hospital and movie theatre, small but state-of-the-art, along with trendy shops and restaurants, attested to the affluence of the area's residents. By the time they pulled into a brick strip mall, Jennifer observed aloud, "Not much hope of finding a bargain here."

"Well, I hear double chocolate and pistachio calling my name," James retorted as he climbed out of the cab's rear door.

"Yuck," Jennifer laughed.

The older man waggled his eyebrows and took off toward the business called "Scoops," where the sign displayed bright yellow and pink half-moons of ice cream dripping down a waffle cone.

Michael turned to her. "Well? Why are you still sitting there? There's no need for both of us to wait on him. You could be scouting everything out. Maybe by the time I come in, you'll have already determined we can't afford anything."

Looking at him, Jennifer drew her bottom lip in and let out a sigh. Transferring the cat to Michael's lap, she reached for the door handle. She adjusted her shirt and capris as she walked toward the entrance, feeling underdressed. Despite the authority designated by her current job position, part of her feared the shop owner would sniff out her disadvantaged background.

Not among the jumbled junk variety of antique store, the place indeed displayed its wares with style. Furniture and accessories clustered in room displays on either side of a wide, open aisle, classical music swirled as Jennifer opened the door, and a faint floral fragrance wafted out rather than the typical musty scent of age. She blinked in the brightness of sunshine reflecting off glass display cases and polished silver tea sets as she focused on the petite lady behind the counter.

"Welcome," called the woman. "Is there anything particular I can help you find today?"

"Um, thank you, I think I'll just take a stroll through your store. Are you the owner?"

"I am indeed. Myrtle Dee. And you are?"

Jennifer shook Myrtle's hand over the counter and introduced herself. She decided to briefly explain her business. The shop owner responded with enthusiasm. "A bachelor, you say? American Empire parlor furniture? I have just the thing."

Casting quick glances to the right and left, Jennifer followed her hostess down the aisle, afraid to hope. But when Myrtle stopped in front of a living area and held her hands out toward a low, flamed mahogany sofa, the thick, curved sides of which supported cushions reupholstered in a golden-brown velvet, Jennifer's chin dropped. Rolled, elongated pillows nestled against each arm. Then her eye zoomed in on the probable deal-breaker: the tiny, white price tag floating from the side. Jennifer edged up and peeked. A thousand dollars.

"Um, Miss Myrtle?"

"Yes, dear?"

"Is this price firm? I'm on a budget." Jennifer turned to present the store owner with her most winning, pleading smile.

"Wellll, let's see. That sofa has been dated to 1840, so it's a special piece. However, if you might be interested in that Gothic arm chair next to it, I could sell you both for ... twelve?"

There sat the exact Gothic emphasis piece she'd envisioned, complete with carved, pointed top and striped gold and red material. She swallowed. She mustn't appear too eager. "Let me consult my boss."

Seeing Jennifer coming, Michael stepped onto the hot sidewalk while James licked his ice cream in the truck. Jennifer couldn't help herself. She grabbed Michael's arm. "I've found it. Before we go in, act cool, like you're not sure. But it's perfect." She described the sofa and chair in detail. "I'd like to see if we can get her down to eleven. If you approve of the furniture, would you agree to that? Knowing that if you do, you could get away with a modern reclining wing chair to complete the grouping, thereby saving money elsewhere?"

An eyebrow went up.

"Oh, just come see, and let's have a secret sign, like a discreet thumbs up or something."

"A secret sign? Really?"

"Yes, I'll take you to see it, and if you like it, you give me the sign. But we'll say we want to think about it as we look around. We'll rotate through the whole store, then make our offer. *Capiche*?"

"Have we joined the Italian mob now?"

"OK, just remember that you're going to spend most of your leisure time lounging in the sun room. These two pieces are key to the authentic setting of the parlor. You'd only have to tolerate them on occasion."

Jennifer pulled on the door, not waiting for Michael to agree. His teasing already told her he found her machinations amusing and would play along. Michael made a big show of sitting in various positions on both pieces of furniture, muttering about the low height of the sofa and the straight back of the arm chair, like they might not accommodate him. Myrtle watched with an expression of concern, then pointed out the solidity of the mahogany furniture. As they expressed their thanks and desire to think it over, she returned to her counter but cast surreptitious glances as they cycled through the other displays.

"Don't you love it?" Jennifer hissed.

"I can live with it."

Given the fact that Michael employed her, she resisted the urge to pinch him. "Let's see if we can find some accessories that could strengthen our bargaining power."

He laughed out loud. "Right. More like finding more accessories decreases my bank account."

"But is necessary. What are you gonna do, put swimming trophies on the mantle? Look at this. This urn is a little earlier period, but it goes with the sofa. Mmm, I can just picture it with pussy willows or feathers sprayed out the top." Jennifer held up the item in question, searching for a price sticker on the bottom.

"Am I having a bad dream, or did you really just say 'pussy willows and feathers?'"

"OK, fine, it would look good by itself, although peacock feathers were all the rage during that time period." Ignoring Michael's choking sound, Jennifer encouraged him to help her locate a potential mate to the vase. "These often came in pairs."

Minutes after accomplishing that mission, Jennifer found a squared, gilded mirror which Michael agreed he preferred over the mantle to artwork. In that particular room, they both wanted to limit visual competition with Stella's mural.

"See, it's so much easier when you're here with me, making these decisions," Jennifer pointed out. As she turned around from inspecting a whale oil lamp, she felt something settle on her head and reached up to touch the scratchy edge of a big-brimmed straw hat Michael perched there.

Before she could remove it, he said, "Wait. It's cute." He tucked a strand of hair behind her ear and gestured to a nearby dresser mirror, where she caught sight of herself.

"Reminds me of a hat I wore for special events at Westville," Jennifer admitted. "I always liked hats."

"As much as I hate shopping, I like seeing you get excited." Michael smiled.

Her heart pitter-pattered as she lifted the hat from her head and smoothed her hair.

He must have sensed her embarrassment, for he added, "That's why I hired you, right? So you could get excited about the things I don't?"

Right. "Uh, let's discuss a figure we want to offer Myrtle for the sofa, chair, urns and mirror, OK?"

Minutes later, after arranging a time to pick up the furniture, they emerged from the shop, Michael carrying the mirror and Jennifer a box containing the carefully wrapped urns. The truck's air conditioning whirred, spewing a hot current onto the already steamy asphalt, as James leaned out the window and said, "I take it the prices were better than anticipated. I just woke up from my nap, and I think your new truck's about to overheat, Michael."

"No doubt." Opening the rear door to settle the mirror and boxes inside, the younger man frowned at the sound of the laboring engine.

"I'm sorry, James," Jennifer apologized. "I'm afraid I got carried away with our purchases. It's too hot out here for you to have waited this long."

"Nonsense," he replied. "I was just giving you a hard time. Go on into Scoop's and get yourself something for the road."

That did sound appealing. "Are you sure?" Jennifer asked.

"Yeah, go on! Just don't be quite as long selecting your ice cream flavor."

That proved no problem at all. As soon as she leaned over the frosty counter to peruse the circles of decadent temptation below, Jennifer exclaimed, "Mmm, mocha latte! And vanilla caramel truffle!"

"We'll both have a double scoop," Michael told the employee, then turned to smile down at Jennifer. "So more than antiques and old houses gets you going?"

"You should see me in a coffee shop." As they waited, Jennifer related her vision for Mary Ellen's store, then asked, "What do you think?"

He laughed out loud. "I think Mary Ellen would blow the place up trying to figure out how to steam lattés!"

Picturing that, they were still laughing as they exited the ice cream shop. James gave them a strange look as they climbed into the truck.

"What?" Michael asked him.

"Nothing," James said, smiling.

As Michael eased the truck back onto the highway, Jennifer asked brightly, "So, are there any more antique stores in Lake Oconee?"

"Nooo!" both men yelled in unison.

"But don't we at least need to stop and get some groceries?"

"A local lady cleans for us before we arrive," Michael explained. "She knows what we like available in the fridge and pantry and picks everything up for us."

"Wow, how nice!"

Licking her ice cream cone, Jennifer couldn't remember the last time she'd enjoyed herself so much. Maybe at the gala, though that experience had been tempered by anxiety, and that had also been with Michael. The moments of happiness had been so rare in her life that she scarcely knew how to behave when one came. She only wished if Michael didn't like her he'd quit making the sort of comments and giving her the sort of approving looks that made her heart race. She managed to settle its rhythm some as they crossed the lake into Putnam County, then turned off by a bunch of mailboxes on a post onto a narrow, asphalt road.

"What, no fountains at your entrance?" Jennifer teased.

"Ha. Don't get your hopes up. This is the old-fashioned kind of lake house, not the *Southern Living* model," Michael replied.

Trepidation stirred. "It is more than one room, right?"

"You're sleeping on the porch. The good news is, it's not far from there to the outhouse."

Jennifer couldn't resist swatting him.

James chuckled from the back seat. "Don't worry, Jennifer. It's three bedrooms, and two bathrooms."

Both men under-described the beautiful cedar cottage that came into view among the pines. True, it had probably been there a good twenty or thirty years, but the chalet-style windows glinted in the sun, and rockers awaited them on a wide porch. When James unlocked the front door, the cedar smell welcomed them into a wood-paneled living area with high ceilings, exposed beams and a wall-length, stacked rock fireplace. The open floor plan revealed a kitchen with updated granite counter tops and stainless steel appliances.

"This is so beautiful," Jennifer gasped.

"It's a split floor plan," James told her, setting Yoda in her cat box down near the kitchen, opening the carrier door, and gesturing Jennifer ahead of him to the right. "We'll put you in the master, and Michael and I will take the two bedrooms on the other side."

"Oh, no, I couldn't take the master," Jennifer protested, knowing the other rooms were probably smaller and shared a bathroom.

"Nonsense." James showed her into a bedroom with a king-sized bed and walls paneled half-way up, then sheet-rocked, punctuated by nature-themed artwork in heavy wooden frames. He turned on the ceiling fan in the indented trey ceiling. "Bathroom's through that door."

Jennifer peeked in to admire a tiled glass shower and garden tub. "Wow. I just might move in here."

"You see why we like to visit often. Come have a look at the back yard. It's the best part."

As she trailed the men, Jennifer paused in the living room to pick up Yoda, who had climbed out of her carrier to cautiously sniff at the brown leather sofa. She petted the silky head as she stepped onto a screened-in porch complete with table and chairs, cushioned rockers and ceiling fans. Metal artwork decorated the wall, while looking out from the cabin, a stone-trimmed trail wound through pines and hardwoods toward a dock on the shimmering lake, where a pontoon boat was moored.

"Wow, this is fabulous," Jennifer said. "How many acres do you have here?"

"Six," James replied. "We preferred not to be able to have a conversation from our dock with the neighbors on theirs." As she nodded in appreciation, he added, "Well, why don't we rustle up some sandwiches for a late lunch?"

"Oh, goodness, I don't think I could after that huge ice cream cone!"

"Well, how about if Michael gets the grill going for some burgers?"

"I'm good with that," the grill master agreed, ignoring Jennifer's look of disbelief.

James rubbed his hands together. "All right. By the time I have them ready, maybe you'll be hungry, Jennifer. Then when the sun gets down a little, we can take the boat out. Do you like to swim?" he asked her.

The moment she'd dreaded had arrived. "Um, no, I really don't like to swim in lakes." Or at all, for that matter. She felt over-exposed in even the most modest swimsuit, especially in front of a man like Michael.

"Because they're dirty?" Michael asked her as he went to the kitchen to rummage for a lighter and a bag of charcoal.

She recalled their previous conversation on the topic. "Yeah, something like that."

"Not my favorite, either, and this time of year there's a little brown on the upper lake. But as hot as it is today, I could do an open water swim."

James grinned when he found hamburger in the refrigerator and began to locate various spices in the cabinets. "Do you float, then? I have a big tire inner tube I can pump up down at the dock."

She could wear water shorts and just dangle her feet. She'd look like a wimp if she just sat in the boat. "Sure, that sounds fine."

Michael paused at the door to the back porch and pointed at her with the lighter. "Let me guess, mountains, not beach."

"Right. You called it." She laughed as he waved dismissal and went out. "James, let me put this kitten down, wash my hands and help you out."

"Sure, honey, you can slice this tomato and get the other condiments ready."

A warm tingle of belonging made Jennifer flush with pleasure, quite an opposite reaction to her typical response to a casual endearment. She could almost pretend ... but that was silly. As considerate and protective as these men were to include her in their Labor Day at the lake, their interest would not extend to her past her employment on their property. She would never be part of their family. She'd do well to remember that. Still, she had a hard time ignoring the intense desire to be near Michael out at the grill instead of in the kitchen getting lunch ready.

"So Michael told me Stan called yesterday. Did he give you the report, Jennifer?" James asked as he worked bread crumbs and dried onion into the meat.

Jennifer took a deep breath. "Yes, he said Stan interviewed the neighbors, and no one saw anything last Friday night or early Saturday morning. Then again, it stormed most of that time. It doesn't surprise me that folks stayed indoors."

"Did he also tell you that Stan talked to Horace and Amy?"

Jennifer turned to stare at the older man. "No, why?"

"Well, since Amy was supposed to go with you originally, in Horace's truck."

"That's just silly." Jennifer shook her head. "I've never met two such nice people. I hope he didn't offend them."

"He assured them he was just doing his job. Amy said they both stayed home all evening, with Horace in his workshop."

"Well, I'm sure they did," Jennifer said, indignant. "I really hope they don't think we put him up to asking."

"No, Stan said Amy sounded very concerned about your safety," James assured her.

Jennifer's internal sensor pinged the moment Michael stepped back over the threshold. "Are we talking about the brake incident?" he wanted to know as he made a bee-line for the platter of burgers his father had prepared.

"Yes, we are," James said.

"I don't like it," Michael told her. "I'll check your Civic regularly to make sure everything is OK."

Jennifer laughed, signaling for Michael to wait the platter so that she could add several unwrapped cheese slices to the edge. "There's no need. My stepfather and brother are mechanics, remember?"

"Fine, but you have to look everything over before you go anywhere, especially anywhere far away."

Jennifer's response to being dictated to remained the same. She shot back as she crumpled the plastic wrappings in her hand, "Well, you'd best do the same."

"I will. But I want you to tell us if you ever feel uneasy about anything on the property. We've got to keep a sharp eye out now."

"You really love to tell, not ask, don't you?"

Toe to toe, they glared at each other. James cleared his throat, causing Michael to step back.

"Sorry," he mumbled. "We just don't want you in any danger, do we, Dad?"

"We most certainly don't."

Jennifer began to soften at Michael's apology when he added, "In fact, we were thinking it might be best if you stayed in the house with us for a while, or at least in the camper out back."

"Are you kidding?" Jennifer couldn't imagine giving up her freedom and privacy almost as soon as she'd laid claim to them. "No way!"

Michael let out a sigh as he headed back toward the deck. "Suit yourself, but we can't look out for you as well there."

"I don't need anyone to look out for me," Jennifer stated, then added belatedly, "except God." She didn't think Michael heard that part, as he slammed the door while she was speaking. She addressed James with a deflated air. "Was he always this protective towards women?"

James shrugged and turned back to wash his hands. "Only those he cared about."

CHAPTER FOURTEEN

They enjoyed their burgers under the whir of ceiling fans on the back porch, with Yoda chasing her favorite ball of yarn under the table. The lingering hint of charcoal smoke on the sultry air, the distant sound of a ski boat motor and the juicy drippy-ness of the meat combined lured Jennifer to forget to be nervous in front of Michael as she ate. For a not hungry person, she sank her teeth into the ripe cantaloupe she'd diced and quickly polished off the deli potato salad.

Finally, she sat back and wiped her mouth with her paper napkin, eyeing the men as they launched into their second burgers. Since they'd be occupied for a while, Jennifer figured conversation fell to her. "So did I tell you about the town council meeting I attended Thursday night?"

Michael paused and looked up as a tomato slice slid from the bun he held onto his plate. "No! The one where you talked about the old general store?"

"What's this?" James asked as he speared a pickle.

Jennifer laughed when she realized he was cutting it up and adding it to his potato salad. She caught the older man up on the repurposing of Gillen's, then concluded, "So that's pretty much what I explained to the council. Then I presented a renovation estimate based on what I determined when Mayor Brown walked me through the building again on Tuesday."

Michael asked, "Is *that* where you went when you bugged out on me sanding the apothecary shelving? I thought you said you were going to Lexington to pick up the oil-based paint."

"Well, I did that first. I met Mayor Brown after hours."

"And you whipped up this whole estimate between Tuesday and Thursday?" James' eyes bugged out.

Jennifer smiled and admitted, "Bryan Holton and Barb gave me some starting points when they were here. I just followed up. I made it clear what I quoted them was not official, but a ballpark idea."

"That's still amazing. So how did it go?"

"Good at first. I brought notes to speak from, but I forgot to use them. They got caught up in my suggestions and started having ideas themselves!"

"That's great, but what about the lease terms?" Michael asked. "Ideas are useless if the cost is unreasonable."

"Well, that's just what Bryce Stevenson said," Jennifer admitted, sinking forward with her elbows on the table.

"He was there?" James asked in alarm, pausing with a barbeque chip hovering in mid-air.

"Yes, and having never met him, I didn't know it until that point in the meeting. He looked like a harmless old man with a cane. But then he spoke up, and I felt like the flaming arrows of hell were shooting at me." Jennifer cringed as she recalled the old man's acid tongue. "He asked why the other council members were so quick to follow a pie-in-the-sky outsider who came in trying to force her grand ideas on everyone. He reminded them of failed past business ventures. And he warned them that they would just lose money in another crazy scheme."

"What did you say?" Michael wanted to know.

"Well, I reminded everyone that the mayors of Hermon and Lexington, the Chamber director and the Rails to Trails chair all supported the idea. I also told them I'd be willing to start paperwork on a public use restoration grant and a tax exemption that could save them up to $300,000."

Michael swallowed his last bite of burger and asked, "Did that win them over?"

She rolled her eyes. "Mr. Stevenson's next question was what was in this for me."

"That sounds about like him, according to what I've heard," James agreed. "He's convinced everyone is a money-grubber."

Jennifer nodded. "He does seem the perpetual glass-half-empty type. But Stella was there with me, so I didn't have to come to my own defense. She said, 'Mr. Stevenson, Jennifer's proposal is truly made in the community's best interest. She's not going to benefit in any financial way from giving the old department store new life. Now, it's true that I could, but I also believe many others will benefit as well. Jennifer provided you all with a proposed floor plan. Now may I put before the council what I'm prepared to offer as monthly rent for my portion of that space?' And she went on to name a hundred dollars below what I knew to be her top price."

James clapped his hands together. "Good for Stella!"

Michael drew in his lips as he folded his napkin, shaking his head. "She's going out on a limb with this. I have to admit it worries me a little."

Steepling her fingers, Jennifer assured him, "I know, and I've asked her several times to make sure she really wants this. She says she's prayed up and feels peace about it. And she's done her homework. She got a good response from potential clients, plus a contact at UGA helped her create projections for hosting two shows a year, one featuring local talent and one student work. The town would supplement by renting out rooms for special events. She explained it all at the meeting with great clarity and persuasion."

She went on to tell how the council did not accept or reject Stella's number out of hand, but asked for Jennifer's list of contractors to contact in the next month. Based on Stella's proposal and what those companies estimated, the council would vote in the next month or two whether to make an offer on the old department store.

"Who owns the department store? Do we know that?" Michael inquired.

"I guess the owner's a private party represented by a local lawyer. Folks say the lawyer has fronted all negotiations in the past."

"Huh. It's weird that people don't know, in a town where everybody knows everything."

"Maybe the owner just doesn't want to be heckled by potential buyers," James suggested.

"Even if the owner proves reasonable," Jennifer concluded, "Bryce Stevenson still could be a big problem. Mayor Brown silenced him by taking over the meeting after Stella spoke up, but I could tell he was stewing over there. After the meeting, a couple of people told me that some folks might feel uneasy because Bryce's son George, Grace's husband, is the manager of the only bank in the county. Lots of councilmen and women bank there. He could deny future business loans or call in favors or whatever, if he bowed to pressure from Bryce."

"Ugh," James said. "All that trouble from a grumpy old man resisting change. I call that a real spirit of control. But the good news is … he doesn't have the control. If the Lord wants this idea to come to pass, nothing can stop it. We just need to pray that all opposition will be brought down."

Jennifer nodded. "I'd appreciate that. In the meantime, if you're seriously thinking of starting an Oglethorpe branch of Johnson Construction, I'd suggest you put together a crew. It would be perfect if Stella's studio could become your first project."

Michael and James looked at each other. "I've spoken with about three guys Horace recommended over the past couple of months," James said. "Their qualifications impressed me. The timing could prove just right, and what an investment in the community, and a family member at that."

"I'm willing," agreed Michael with the lift of one broad shoulder. "Why don't you call them back and see if they'd be interested? If they are, I'll approach Mayor Brown."

Jennifer shrugged her shoulders forward and gave a stiff grin. "If you don't hear from him first."

"What? You already talked to him about it?" Michael's brow drew down over his blue eyes.

"Uh … I put a little note at the bottom of the contractor list mentioning you and your dad might represent a possible source."

"Jennifer! You should have talked to us first."

She showed her teeth again, like the cringing emoji on her phone. "I put a question mark by it. Sorry. It hit me in the middle of the meeting, and I got so excited I just jotted it down."

"You and your excitement!"

Leaning back and folding his napkin, James started to chuckle. "I think we can agree, Michael, that Jennifer has everyone's best interest at heart. If overenthusiasm for her work and the community are her biggest faults, I believe we can forgive her." He leaned over to pat her hand.

Jennifer gave him a grateful smile.

Michael shook his head and rolled his eyes, starting to rise from the table with his cup and plate in his hands. "We'll talk about it later."

"Yeah, time to get the tackle box ready!" James paused and rubbed his stomach. "Hmmm. Maybe after a little nap. Would you mind, Jennifer?"

"Of course not. Why don't you guys go lie down? I'll clean up the mess."

"But you're our guest!" James protested.

"Please. It's so thoughtful of you to have me here this weekend, I have to do something to help. Besides, I'm not much of a daytime napper."

They'd used paper plates and cups, but as Jennifer put away the condiments and washed the platter and tongs from the grill, her mind turned as it often had during the past week to Charlotte's letters. James and Michael had put them in an airtight box, and she'd asked James to bring it this weekend. She wanted to read through them again, slowly, once the initial shock and excitement faded, to see what impression remained.

Jennifer opened a can of Fancy Feast for Yoda and placed it in a bowl, then checked the stack of belongings the men had brought in and left in the hallway between their rooms. Faint snores and heavy breathing issuing from behind partially closed doors broke the silence of the cabin as she ascertained that the box indeed sat among duffel bags, coolers and tackle boxes. By the time she'd brushed her teeth and changed into her bathing suit under water shorts and a tank top, Yoda had finished her meal and sat in the middle of the kitchen, uncertain of what she should do next in the strange environment. Jennifer scooped her up and settled with the box on the sofa. Lulled by the sound of birds chirping in the trees and Yoda's soft purring as the kitten fell asleep, she slipped back into the 1800s.

Half an hour later, when Michael emerged from his nap bleary-eyed and ruffle-headed, Jennifer looked up and asked, "Will you come sit down and give me your opinion on something?"

Michael smoothed his hair and shuffled over. "Sure, for whatever it's worth," he mumbled as he sank down at the other end of the sofa.

Yoda's head lifted at the sound of her master's voice, and Jennifer curled a hand over her so the cat wouldn't upset the delicate papers. "Are you awake enough?" Having never seen him in the fuzzy vulnerability of the recently returned to the land of the living, she tried not to stare.

He leaned back against the cushion, his long legs stretched out in front of him. "Shoot."

Jennifer held up the letter in her hand. "So I've just reread the letters from Charlotte to William, and I keep getting hung up on these two sentences. 'I forgave Stuart right after you left for the way he treated me before the war. Nothing here should cause you grief.' It seems like the two were tied together, the way Stuart treated Charlotte and whatever caused William grief. So I'm guessing Stuart treated Charlotte badly, and she had not forgiven him for it. Do you think that made William angry enough to decide he couldn't be around them?"

Michael reached out to finger the yellowed aviary ticket which peeked out of the paper lying next to Jennifer's leg on the couch. "We have what we think is William's handwriting on this, don't we? If it is, William had feelings for Charlotte. I doubt those developed out of years of letter-writing."

"You think he left because of those feelings?"

A sad smile flitted across the shadowed jaw of the man opposite her. "If William found Charlotte's treatment of his brother lacking, he probably would have confronted her. But if it were the opposite, only now his brother was an invalid ..."

Jennifer filled in the blank. "Maybe something happened between them." She sighed and folded the letter. "It's eating me up that we'll never know for sure."

"Men don't run because they're angry. They run because they're hurting. And yeah, something probably happened to bring that pain into focus."

Jennifer stared at him, then finally released the kitten to trot over the cushions and into Michael's arms, right where Jennifer herself wanted to be in that moment. As Michael bent his head to pet Yoda, she carefully placed the papers back in the box. "If what we think is true, I feel bad for Charlotte, having to live with a man who mistreated her in some way, then having to tend him as a semi-vegetable for what ... five years? While having fallen in love with his brother! Man, what a prison sentence."

"I can only think of one thing to get someone through that. Charlotte mentioned it in the letters. She wanted William to know God had given her peace."

"I still think it would be almost impossible to not only forgive someone for the past but to treat them with so much grace. I would have shoved his care off on a nurse or servant and taken an extended European holiday," Jennifer half-joked.

"'For if you forgive men their trespasses, your heavenly Father will also forgive you,'" James quoted from the hall doorway to the bedrooms.

Jennifer experienced a sinking feeling as she realized she had not forgiven her family, not one of them. Worst of all, none of them would ever admit to any wrongdoing, much less ask her forgiveness. "But since Charlotte didn't mention any change in Stuart, he probably never asked for her forgiveness," she pointed out.

James' gentle smile indicated he guessed Jennifer spoke about something more recent than a one hundred and fifty-year-old case. "Doesn't matter. Forgiveness is meant to free us, not the offender. The chapter of Matthew before that one I just quoted tells us if we come to the altar bringing a gift to God and remember a brother with something against us—not even us against someone else—we must leave our gift and immediately try to be reconciled." Reading Jennifer's expression of disgust, James added, "When something's not our fault, only God the Holy Spirit inside us can give us the humility to initiate forgiveness. A lot of people mistake humility for being a doormat, but forgiveness is not excusing the wrong. It's choosing to give the wrong into God's hands. That takes strength, not weakness."

Never having heard the concept of forgiveness put that way, Jennifer digested that in silence.

"I've heard it said that not forgiving someone is like dragging a corpse around on your back," Michael put in.

"Same thing when we don't forgive God."

The room went silent. Michael's back grew stiff as he bent over the cat. To break the sudden discomfort, Jennifer stretched and sat up, latching the lid of the storage box. "Well, I'll put Charlotte and William to rest with history. Sorry to make everything so serious when we're here for fishing and cooking out."

James clapped his hands together. "Right you are. Michael, come help me sort through this stuff. The crappie will be lying low this time of year. I'm thinking about Jiffy Jig Super Grubs." Groaning over his aching knees, he knelt to open a tackle box.

Michael put the cat on the floor and rose, saying, "I want my Net Boy football jig, the green pumpkin one with the big twin trailer." As he joined his father, Yoda loped behind him.

"Whoa!" Jennifer threw her hands up to her ears. "You totally lost me. I speak preservation, Allison Winters speaks herb, and you speak fishing!"

Michael turned back to her with a quizzical expression. "Didn't you used to fish with your stepdad and brother?"

"Yeah, but we used live worms and minnows. If they ever had the plastic stuff in the box, they never named it except for 'worm' and 'bobber.' I think I'm in a whole new league. You probably have rich boy depth finders, too, don't you?"

James grinned. "A Lowrance HDS. Can't locate the crappie hiding among the submerged trees in this lake this time of year without it. Hey, cat, these aren't kitten toys." Everyone laughed as Yoda batted at the tail of a lure James held up, and he shooed her away.

CHAPTER FIFTEEN

With Yoda settled in the guys' bathroom with litter box and toys and the door closed, they headed down to the pontoon boat. As he started the motor, Michael explained to Jennifer that as it was a little early for fishing yet, they would take her on a tour of their area, then find a place to anchor for swimming and floating until the sun sank lower. Jennifer hoped she manufactured the expected amount of enthusiasm.

As they cruised over the water, memories returned of the last time she'd been on a lake, at Lake Walter George and Lake Eufaula, on the Alabama-Georgia border. Roy liked to launch his aluminum fishing boat with trolling motor from Florence Marina State Park, where they tent camped. The scenery differed, more Spanish moss, egrets and herons there, but the sensations of the wind in her hair, the sun on her face and the smell of the water felt similar. Along with those rose a faint unease. Something bad was coming. She knew it, she just had no idea what, or why.

Jennifer tried to shake the faint sickness as she climbed fully clothed onto her inner tube from the ladder of the pontoon. She managed to land rear end first, her feet flying up in the air, with only a slight splash. If Michael and James thought her weird, they had enough grace not to point it out. James kicked back at the table with a spy novel, a Coke and peanuts, while Michael stripped off his T-shirt and, in his traditional swim shorts, executed a near perfect dive from the bobbing rear of the boat. Her inspection shaded by sunglasses, Jennifer watched him come up and, without taking a breath, synch into a perfect free style toward a nearby island. It wasn't a short swim. She leaned back and closed her eyes, attempting to relax into the lapping of the waves. But the cool water on her feet and the warm sun on her skin didn't succeed in uncoiling the tight springs of her muscles, and the pit at the bottom of her stomach wouldn't go away. What was wrong with her? Did Michael really make her that nervous?

Before long she heard him returning, but the splashing sounded different. She lifted her head to see his upper body pull out of the water as his arms came forward in a straight, simultaneous stroke, then his feet kick like a dolphin tail. "What's he doing?" she called to James.

"Butterfly. Hard to do on a lake, but he earned one of his medals at state in the one hundred fly," Michael's father replied without even a glance up from his novel. Apparently he recognized the stroke by sound.

Even now, years later, Jennifer could see why Michael won that medal. To her consternation, the man's trajectory carried him not toward the pontoon, but right up to her inner tube. She squeaked as a final stroke produced a spray of water, then Michael's head bobbed up and he caught onto the edge of her float, torqueing her sideways. "Hey, let go," she protested.

Water ran down from his dark hair into Michael's eyes as he grinned at her. "I won't sink you," he assured her, kicking to provide buoyancy.

"Who are you, Michael Phelps?"

"I used to wish. I can assure you my times were not as good as his."

She wanted to shove away the tan arm touching hers. His attractiveness created enough of a challenge without him increasing it with athletic demonstrations. "But it's obvious you still love to swim."

"Yeah. I love it," he panted. "How do I describe it to a non-swimmer? It's ... like riding a bike, after you've put in the effort and your heart is racing, when you get that perfect downward slope, and suddenly you're flying."

"Ha. Literally. You should join a team or something."

Michael wiped his face. "Like Master's?"

"I don't know what it's called."

"Do you know how much time I'd have to spend driving into Athens to train? And to be only half as competitive as I used to be?"

Tugging up the top of her shirt, Jennifer shifted in an attempt to get a little farther away from him. "But is that really the point, if you love it? And you're still very good."

James, who must have been listening from afar, put in, "You think that was good, I'll show you the video of the state meet tonight. We keep our VHS tapes at the cabin since we have a player here."

"Oh, geez. Dad, no!" Michael yelled out.

"I'd love to see it," Jennifer called to James, if only to antagonize the man hanging onto her inner tube. When she grinned at Michael, he pulled on her float as though threatening to dunk her. A water battle ensued. Not wanting to appear the fainting female, she refrained from screaming but splashed him in the face and kicked her feet in an attempt to flee. In retaliation, he reached under the tube to tickle her sides. An immediate memory of another man doing the same thing as a step toward domination put iron in her voice when she said, "Stop, Michael. I mean it. *Stop.*"

The sound of her genuine distress kept Michael from reacting with sarcasm, but caused him to tread water, watching her with concern. She had forgotten that memory. It hovered like a sick presence above them as Jennifer fought to keep it from expanding, from remembering the rest. Worst of all, he couldn't have missed the way tears thickened her voice. The fact that she'd clued him off to her vulnerability threatened her more than his anger would have.

"Sorry," he said a minute later. "Since I'm given to picking on people, I forget you don't like to be messed with."

Relief flooded her that he'd chosen to simplify the matter. "It's OK."

"You ready to get back in the boat?"

She didn't want to be defeated by her insecurities. The idea of immersing herself in the cool water beckoned, but the idea of Michael being near her, touching her in any way, ruined the chances of that going well. "Sure," she said. Maybe things would improve while they fished.

Michael held her tube for her to get out with the assistance of the ladder at the back of the pontoon. As she floated submerged to her waist, she felt him close behind her and hurried to pull herself up. James waited with a towel, which she gratefully wrapped around her lower body. She also accepted the drink he offered. They trolled for a while, the men discussing the revelations of the depth finder in low tones. The sun kissed the horizon with tongues of orange and silver by the time they settled on a cove, killing the Yamaha four stroke motor where the top of a submerged tree reached within ten feet of the surface. The silence soon swelled with the lesser sounds of cicadas, crickets and lapping waves.

Michael marked the spot with a buoy as James set up Jennifer's line. "Now you've got to watch it close," he instructed her. "The bite can be very light. If there's a school of fish, they often hit on the first drop."

They didn't. Rusty in her fishing techniques, Jennifer watched Michael work the water eight to sixteen feet down by lifting and dropping his jig. She tried to bounce and twitch her bait like he did. On her second drop, she got a hit.

"Hey!" James cried in approval as he helped her reel in a decent sized crappie.

"I can do it," she told him when he started to remove her hook from the fish's mouth. She didn't want James and Michael to think her a complete wimp. Taking the fish off the line, she carried it to the cooler and released it into the aerated water.

Leaving her to her own devices, James hurried to bait his hook. Soon after that, both men kept busy reeling in their catches. Jennifer worked her line for a bit, bringing in a couple more crappie, but she didn't experience the satisfaction evidenced by the guys' congratulations and laughter. When she excused herself to sit on the net front of the boat, James asked, "You OK?" She waved and told him to enjoy himself. Ignoring Michael's furrowed brow, she made her way around the pilot house.

A few minutes later, James explained that since the bites were slowing, they wanted to ride up the lake a bit to check for another spot. Was that OK with her? She assured them it was.

As dark wrapped its humid cloak over the lake, James anchored the pontoon under a bridge and hung a light over the side. With limited visibility, Jennifer wrapped her arms around her knees, but the gnawing feeling in her gut only increased. It felt like something cold and palpable lurked under that bridge. In the back of her mind, she pushed against a memory of slippery hands touching her, hot breath on her face, a hissed warning to keep a secret. Her stomach lurched and she whimpered, trying to think about something, anything else. The panic of being stuck on that boat with the men as the specter from the past stirred made Jennifer's heart race.

She felt the boat shift and a body lower next to her. Michael sat in the middle of the pontoon's front, facing her, Indian-style. "Something's wrong," he said simply. When she didn't speak or raise her head from her knees, he gently placed his hands on her arms. His crossed legs butted up against her feet. "Something about today upset you."

She tried to deny that, but all that came out was a small sound.

"Talk to me."

Jennifer's breath came fast. "I can't."

"This is about more than overly aggressive college boys, isn't it?" he asked.

She managed a nod.

Michael's arms went around her, bent knees, bent head, back and all. Part of Jennifer's brain acknowledged with surprise that the gesture felt non-threatening, holding her together rather than undoing her. She heard him whisper, "I'm sorry."

"You didn't do anything," Jennifer told him.

"I know. But someone did."

Thank God that in the dark he couldn't see the tears that overflowed and ran down her face, falling through the net and into Lake Oconee.

Later that night, lying under the quilt in the cabin's master bedroom, Jennifer couldn't recall making her way from the boat to the house. She knew James had asked from a distance if they were ready to go in, and Michael had answered in the affirmative. James must have taken care of the rods, for the only memory she had after that was of Michael's arm anchoring her to his side as the pontoon purled through the dark water.

Now she regretted allowing that. She worked for Michael, after all, and as the coordinator for the projects on his property, she needed to maintain respect and professionalism. Yet she'd thrown both out the window the minute a repressed memory blew in. How incapable and immature she'd acted. Jennifer wished herself back at her solitary double-wide, where if she had to fall apart, she could do so in privacy.

Whomever or whatever held her brain in a feverish grip didn't let up now that she was alone, either. Questions and suggestions hissed in her mental ear. *Why did you come up here? Were you hoping something would happen? Just like you hoped it would with Roy. You'd do anything for a little attention. Slut. You were a slut even when you were a little girl. Your own mother knew who you really were. Now Michael and James do, too. They know you're dirty. Why would upstanding people like that want you in their lives? Just do the job and move on. That's all you're good for.*

Jennifer flipped to her other side and put a pillow over her head. *Stop it*, she told the voice. *This is stupid. Why does this always happen at night? I'm talking to myself.*

Then a fragment of a sentence rose in her mind, something she'd read in the Bible Stella had given her. "*There is now therefore no condemnation.*" She was not talking to herself. Stella had called Satan "the accuser of the brethren." She said he would do anything to keep people from committing their lives to Christ, but once they did, the battle had only begun. Despite the lies of Satan, Stella said Jesus' blood washed the stains of a person's past clean, that He died not only to conquer sin, but all pain, death and disease as well. That blood also gave believers power over their spiritual enemy.

Jennifer sat up and said aloud, "'There is now therefore no condemnation toward those who are in Christ Jesus,' so in Jesus' name and by the power of His blood, leave me alone!"

As the heavy press of darkness receded, Jennifer let out a breath. It even appeared lighter in the room. Perhaps the security light outside the cabin experienced a sudden surge of energy. Or perhaps this spiritual stuff worked just like Stella said it did. She laid back down and pulled the covers up to her chin. Maybe now she could sleep, so she wouldn't have bags under her eyes in the morning.

She did sleep, and she dreamed. Her shoulder hurt. Maybe she slept on it wrong. No, she'd fallen off her bike. How could she forget that? Her mother pulled on the hand which covered the flaming gravel brush burn.

"Jennifer, let go! Let me see it!" Kelly insisted.

"I told you about the loose wheel, and you didn't believe me!"

"I have to see it to fix it."

Jennifer relaxed her hand. Maybe her mother did care. Kelly's bleached blonde head bent close as she worked to stop the bleeding and cover the wound. It did feel a little better.

Then Kelly said, "Yuck, all this blood. Why did you have to go bleedin' everywhere? There, I think I fixed it."

When her mother moved back, Jennifer saw that she had stuffed tufts of white tissue into the area where the skin had torn away. She would never heal like that! If that tissue remained, it would only require another painful procedure later! What kind of mother wouldn't know that? She hated her mother. She hated her.

Jennifer startled awake. In the same moment that she acknowledged the scope of betrayal and anger against her mother, like a large piece of a puzzle dropping into place, she recalled everything that Roy had done to her that first time at the lake when she was eleven years old. And disgust and hatred pumped her out of bed like dual levers, driving her out in search of air, in search of relief from the pain inside. Moonlight slanted through the chalet windows in the living room, its silver coldness mocking her. She grappled at the bolt on the back door and pushed out onto the screened porch, gulping down lung fulls of fresh air. She bent over, holding her middle, not sure if she would be sick or not. Finally, she crumpled onto the scratchy indoor-outdoor carpet. Jennifer shoved a fist against her mouth to hold back the sobs. Some escaped anyway. She rocked in agony, praying, *God, please take this pain away*.

The door scraped, and someone stood over her. Please let it be James.

A second later, Jennifer knew the body that folded on the floor next to her was too long to be that of the older man. "Oh, no," she moaned. "Please just go, Michael."

"What kind of person would I be to ignore someone in so much pain?"

Jennifer drug an arm across her face but angled away from him. "A normal one. I'll be fine."

"Are Dad or I in any way responsible for this?"

"Of course not." He had no idea how much effort it took right now to speak. If he did, he would leave like she asked. Jennifer wanted to sink below the concrete slab and pull the rubble on top of her. A strong sense of vulnerability ran through her like an earthquake, producing a shudder, followed by tremors with no regard for the sultry late summer night.

"You're shaking." He made a move toward her, then stopped. "May I?"

There was only one way she could answer that question and retain any dignity. "No."

"Why not?"

Anger flared in her voice. "Because you're a man, you're my employer, and I don't want you to!"

"I'm also a human with half a heart, and more importantly, a Christian, and I don't believe you." Moving very slowly, Michael inched his arm around her shoulders. When she didn't bolt, he maneuvered them to where their backs rested against the cabin's exterior wall. Then he looped his other arm around the front and joined his hands on her far shoulder.

Jennifer didn't lean into him, and she certainly didn't put her head on his shoulder, but his nearness did calm her trembling. She'd always longed for someone to sit beside her when the night terrors came. She hadn't experienced such attacks of fear and pain since praying to accept the Lord, so tonight confused her. At the same time, she felt ashamed Michael saw her need.

"I shouldn't have come here," she mumbled.

"Of course you should have. Whatever this place has shaken loose has happened for a reason. Remember what we said about God being like a tracking hound?"

Though he hadn't used quite those terms before, Jennifer nodded.

She heard a quiet, mirthless laugh next to her. "A Scripture is coming to my mind. It's actually been coming all day," Michael admitted. "I've been trying to ignore it, because I know it applies to me, too, but I think it's for you right now."

"What is it?" she croaked.

"It's in the Psalms. 'He heals the brokenhearted and binds up their wounds.' Isaiah says something like it: 'the Lord binds up the bruise of His people and heals the stroke of their wound.'"

Jennifer paused to absorb that before saying, "That's funny. I just had a dream about falling off my bike and my mother putting tissues in the wound rather than cleaning and bandaging it properly. Like she didn't want to deal with it. She took a shortcut. That really happened, with the bike … and other things."

"You told her what happened to you?" Michael asked in a quiet voice.

Jennifer nodded. "She pretended she didn't believe me, but her comments showed she really did. It was just easier for her to sweep it under the rug. Put tissue on it. So I think you're saying God's allowed this to surface so He can clean and bandage the right way."

"Yes."

"I shouldn't be talking to you about this."

"Have you ever talked to anyone?"

She gave a brief head shake, unable to look at him.

"Then you need to talk to someone. God often uses His people to help others. Many believers have been through something similar. Even me." Michael gave a short laugh of recognition. "I wasn't abused, but I sure know what pain is. God turns heartache into something helpful to other people. Those trials make us stronger, more empathetic. He'll do the same for you." Michael paused, then asked, "Why don't you want to talk to me? Because I've been a jerk?"

Jennifer scoffed. "No."

He tilted his head a little closer. "Then why?"

"Because it's embarrassing." Also because the night terrors and dream had left her shaken and vulnerable.

A long silence ensued. Then, just when she began to hope that he'd given up on making her talk, Michael blurted out, "It was your stepfather, wasn't it? Roy?"

She shuddered. "Please don't say his name."

"And you have a bad memory at a lake."

Bitterness loosened her tongue, eroding judgment. "Bad would be an understatement. And yes, it started at a lake, although I have a whole chain of delightful recollections, from the time I was eleven until I left for college."

"Oh, no, Jennifer," Michael whispered. "Being at the lake brought the memories back?"

"I used to think it just happened when I was a teenager, at our trailer when Mom was gone, or when he took us camping. But today I remembered that the really bad stuff started a lot earlier than I'd thought." Feeling Michael's arms stiffen, Jennifer waited for him to react, then said, "It's OK, you can let me go now and tell me I'm disgusting. I know, what kind of idiot eleven-year-old wouldn't be suspicious of a grown man's invitation for a night swim?"

Michael turned to her and took both her shoulders in his hands. With his eyes boring into hers out of the dark pools of his sockets, he said with emphasis, "You're not disgusting. And don't ever blame yourself. Do you hear the blame in what you're saying? That's what God needs you to let go of."

Realizing all she'd revealed, Jennifer covered her face with her hands. "I can't talk about this anymore. It's not helping."

Michael sucked in a deep breath. When she glanced at him, his gaze focused on the forest outside, but his lips moved faintly. In prayer? Finally, he said, "I understand why you wouldn't want to talk to me, but you need to talk to someone. Stella? Maybe she could go with you to Pastor Simms or his wife, someone qualified to help. Please, Jennifer? This has come out for a reason. If you don't deal with it now, you'll just be doing what your mother did and stuffing tissue on it. Do you know what I mean?"

Jennifer gave a slow nod. "I do."

"So you'll talk with Stella?"

"I guess."

"Good. And there's another thing."

She wrapped her arms around herself. "What?"

"I think we found Charlotte's letters for a reason, too. Remember our conversation earlier on forgiveness?"

Jennifer started to turn her head back and forth. "I can't do that."

"No. You can't. But the Holy Spirit through you can. This wound will never heal without that forgiveness. I don't know what that will look like for you, and I know I'm the last person to be spouting platitudes about something like this, but will you pray about it? See what God says?"

Jennifer heaved a sigh, and, pulled by the weight of the invisible emotional anchor she carried, her chin dropped to her chest.

"And will you let me pray for you now?"

Surprised, she cut her eyes to him. "You want to?"

"Yes, I do, although every single word I'm saying convicts *me*. I'm the least likely person to be praying for someone else, seeing how far I am from God right now myself."

Jennifer gave a chuckle. "I seem to keep putting you in that position. Sorry."

"Don't apologize. Let's just pray." When Jennifer bowed her head, Michael began: "Lord, tonight … we just bring our pain before You. We just … put Jennifer's past before You. We can already see that You've begun a healing work in her. We ask for the strength for her to take the next step, that You will send what she needs to become whole again … that You Yourself will come." Michael's voice faltered, and he stopped.

Jennifer sucked in a quiet breath, for in the moment he spoke, she felt a change in the atmosphere. She stopped shaking. Her heart's painful thudding returned to a normal rhythm. And the ache inside her chest dulled to bearable. For the first time she felt the promise that inhuman pain wouldn't always hover just a word or a memory away from returning full force.

"Finish what you started." The wobbly statement hung in the air, then Michael whispered, "In Jesus' name. Amen."

In the electric silence after Michael's prayer, Jennifer hesitated to speak. Finally, she murmured, "Thank you."

He gave a nod, still looking out toward the lake. "I think if you'll talk with Stella and the pastor, you might move toward forgiving your parents."

And Rab, for not standing up for her like a big brother should have. For saying nothing when he noticed Roy's midnight absence from his tent. For not asking Jennifer why the sound of her tears penetrated the thin trailer walls of his adjacent bedroom night after night. For preferring a false father figure to manning up himself. But she said none of that to Michael. She'd said far too much already. Even if he wanted to help her, he had to look at her in a different light now. As broken, not strong.

"By the way," Michael added in sheepish tone, "earlier, when you thought I was disgusted, I was angry. My first thought was to get in my truck, drive to Stewart County, and punch his lights out. And I almost called him a bad word just now, mere seconds after praying."

With an unexpected laugh, Jennifer's defenses sagged. Michael's reaction exactly mirrored what she'd desired from her brother. Only as Michael reached out and covered her hand with his, Jennifer realized she wanted Michael to be much more than a friend, or a brother, or a brother in Christ. And she had probably just blown it.

CHAPTER SIXTEEN

Part of Jennifer hated to see the old plaster in the apothecary gone. She'd become attached to the rustic look of the faded walls cracked in places to reveal the intricate lathing. Some areas had lacked whole chunks of the filler. But as fascinating as it proved to examine the apothecary's secrets, if the building were to become functional and not just remain a monument to the past, the mess must be torn away and fresh compound mixed and applied … two coats down to the baseboards, to be exact.

Jennifer didn't miss the ironic parallel that as fresh plaster recovered the building's bare "bones" in early September, Stella came knocking on the door of the double-wide. Michael had told her about what had happened at the lake. She prayed aloud first, then asked if Jennifer might be ready to unburden her heart.

"Now don't think I'm huntin' any gory details, sweet girl," the older woman said. "You just tell me enough so's another person knows what you've been bearin' all these years. Then I'll go to the pastor and his wife with you, if you want, and we'll all figure out what to do together." With that, Stella sat back and folded her hands, her tea cooling forgotten in front of her.

Jennifer shared how, as a young girl aching from her father's abandonment, she longed for her stepfather's notice. When Rab's boyish enthusiasm for Roy's favorite pursuits produced an instant affinity, Jennifer weaseled her way into whatever her stepfather and brother did, even if it meant putting aside her Barbies and dresses. She learned to hunt, fish, cheer for drag racing and football, and work under the hood of a car. She rubbed Roy's shoulders when he came home from work and brought him hot chocolate. She comforted him when he and Kelly fought, something that happened more and more frequently. Like her mother, Jennifer learned never to provoke Roy into one of his drinking binges, and she learned denying him anything led to hurting his feelings. When Roy's feelings were hurt, he mastered the art of ignoring the object of offense so entirely they might as well not even be in the room. To a child starved for affection, the withdrawal of all attention seemed like the worst possible outcome. She was wrong about that. As she sat on his lap when he asked her to, and laid beside him when he was "too tired" to get up in the mornings, things went downhill from there.

When Jennifer related this part of her story to Pastor Simms in his church office, he startled her by exploding, "Jennifer, he groomed you!"

She paused in confusion. "Well, yes, he sometimes did my hair if my mother—"

"I'm not talking about brushing your hair, young lady, but about emotional grooming. It's a characteristic of many predatory relationships, especially those with children. He prepared you for what he intended by control and manipulation. You were on his hook long before the trip to the lake."

Jennifer's mouth fell open as she considered all the ways this had been true. Then she jumped as Pastor Simms pounded his fist into his hand. "And it makes me *mad*! And what's more, it makes God mad." The reverend's voice reached such a low tone on the last two words that Jennifer's stomach trembled like jelly. In that moment, she felt glad she was not Roy sitting in front of this man of God.

Mrs. Simms, a tall woman with glowing dark skin and thick lashes, patted Jennifer's hand in reassurance. "Pastor Simms is not mad at you, Jennifer," she clarified.

Jennifer squeaked, "I know. I guess I've just never seen him angry before."

"This sort of sin should make everyone angry," the man across the desk exclaimed. "Jennifer, were you a teenager still in this predator's home, I would advise you to tell the authorities. That is still part of your decision-making process, but you can know that whatever you decide, God promises to bring the perpetrator to either repentance or justice. As fearsome a thought as this might be, Jennifer, I've seen Him start that process with a confrontation by the victim."

She quaked to the tips of her Mary Janes. "Oh, I could never do that," she said, then went on to explain how her childhood attempts to confide in her mother had failed.

"But you're an adult now," Mrs. Simms urged, "and a child of God. Your voice carries much greater authority. You have a Heavenly Father who gives you what you need, but breaking your silence can be a powerful tool. What if you wrote a letter to both Roy and Kelly? Disclose what occurred, then grant them your forgiveness?"

Jennifer turned wide eyes from her to the reverend, who extended an entreating hand across his desk. "Let's start with talking of forgiveness, Jennifer," he said. "Of yourself, God, and your family members."

During the month of September, Jennifer met with the pastor and his wife weekly. They sent books on abuse survival, forgiveness and restoration home with her. Pastor Simms encouraged Jennifer to look up everything in her Bible on related topics. She also joined Stella's new Wednesday Bible study, held in her parlor over tea and cookies. There she learned how others also worked to metamorphosis from pain to joy, bondage to freedom, making her feel less alone. During this process, the Lord brought back repressed memories, not of her abuse, but of things she had heard Roy and Kelly reveal about their own fractured pasts. Moving toward seeing them as broken people desperate for God's grace, not monsters, provided a step on Jennifer's road toward forgiving them. Most of all, Jennifer knew she did not want anger and bitterness to foment in her own heart, causing her to run the risk of one day becoming like them.

"It's that more than anything that makes me willing to consider writing the letter Mrs. Simms wants me to write," Jennifer told Stella from the apothecary's middle room as she swiped polyurethane sealer over the walnut-stained top of the compounding desk. "I want all that darkness out of my heart. I don't want any left to grow unseen."

Stella stood on a ladder, applying dark green, oil-based paint to the ceiling of the front room. Amy had delivered it earlier that week, the same day a crew had drilled holes in the side of the shop and blown in insulation. She worked around the curved shelving that Michael and James had strengthened and which now awaited Jennifer's primer coat. The doors at either ends of the building opened onto a cooling day of early autumn, with touches of gold in the trees. The fresh air helped dispel their paint fumes. "What does Michael say about the letter?" Stella asked.

Jennifer shrugged. "He thinks it's a good idea, that or a phone call. I don't think I can do a phone call, though. Just hearing the man's voice would make me lose my nerve."

"Well, honey, you just keep praying it over. I'm praying with you. When the time is right to act, God will let you know."

Setting aside the sealer can, Jennifer sighed and moved around the edge of the desk to access her own tray of dark green paint intended for the main portions of the desk. The truth was, Michael expressed his opinion when she asked, but since handing her over to Stella and the Simms, he had backed off discussion of Jennifer's personal life. True, she mostly wanted it that way, but it also made her fear the correctness of her initial impression.

"What you huffin' about back there?" Stella asked.

"Oh, I don't know. I guess I wish Michael hadn't seen me in that state. I'd rather he not know all my yuck."

"Well, did he not tell you he wanted more honesty between you two?"

She gave a mirthless laugh and said, "Yeah, but I'm pretty sure he didn't know what he was asking for! Now he probably sees me like some broken piece of pottery, sure, able to be glued back together by the Master Potter, but never that attractive, flawless piece he would pick for himself." She mumbled something about Ashley and perfect pottery, then realized Stella stood in the doorway. And, uh oh, her hands balled into fists on her hips.

"Now you listen here, missy. Jesus tells us through the prophet Isaiah that He will give us beauty for our ashes, the oil of joy for mournin', the garment of praise for the spirit of heaviness, so that means you ain't no broken piece of pottery! You're a finely garbed child of the King! Now don't you go forgettin' that again!" Stella punctuated her declaration with a pointed finger.

The woman left no room for argument or self-pity. As a slight motion caught her attention, Jennifer's eye traveled downward, and she cried out, "Stella James, you're about to drip paint on the floor, and that spot is not covered with plastic!"

Too late. "Oh, my Lord, I got to deliver Your message to this girl, but I don't need to ruin the hardwoods in the process!" she cried out, jumping back onto the plastic in the front room and placing her brush on the tray. She grabbed paint thinner, sloshed a dab onto a strip of old T-shirt, and went to work to repair her damage. As she scrubbed, she continued, "Now as for Michael, don't you worry your head about him for one minute. God will help you come out of this even stronger and more beautiful in his eyes. All the bad will be put to good use. If Michael's the one for you, that past of yours will hold no more water with him than it does for God."

"You're so confident of all that, Stella."

"Well, I spent my whole life learnin' lessons, honey. I have a lot of confidence now in who God is and what He can do. Mind you, I didn't always."

Jennifer sighed. "Yes, I'm new at this. I guess it will take me time to develop my faith, heal and change the way I think and act."

"Sure it will. But didn't what Pastor Simms told you about grooming help you transfer some of that guilt?" Stella looked up at her, then rose to her full height.

Jennifer nodded. "Yes, it did."

"Good. That's one small step, then. Now let me ask you another question. As we've all been praying for your healin', have you been able to feel God's love more than before? Do you feel Him close to you, wrappin' around you like the insulation they just put into these here walls?"

Jennifer cocked her head. "Since you put it that way, yes. I have felt more secure, and sometimes when I pray at night, it feels like a protective cloud surrounds me."

"Well, praise Jesus!" Stella cried, and reached out to embrace Jennifer.

Jennifer laughed and hugged her back with one arm, attempting to keep her paint brush raised in the air. At that moment, the cell phone in the pocket of Jennifer's jeans buzzed.

"Lord help us if that's Barbara again," Stella protested.

But Jennifer looked at the display screen and grinned. "It's not." She slid the answer button and said, "Hi, Tilly. Do you have good news for me?"

The voice of her former roommate came across the line, bright and cheerful. "Yes, we've got the new latté machine up and running. The old one is taking up space in the storage room, which makes the boss grumpy. Is there any way you could come get it today?"

Jennifer's gaze swung to Stella, even though the older woman waited with eyebrows raised, having no idea of what was going on. "Today? I'd have to check with Michael. I'll need him to help us load and unload using his truck. But are you free later?"

"I get off at four."

"And you don't mind driving out to show Mary Ellen how to work the machine?"

"Not a bit. I'd love to see what you've been doing out there. But I'll need dinner. Can you feed me?" Tilly asked.

Jennifer laughed. "Of course, as long as you don't expect anything fancy." When she disconnected the call a moment later, Jennifer squealed and did a happy dance. "Just in time for fall! Just in time for fall!"

Stella smirked and shook her head. "You're always plotting something, girl. Does Mary Ellen even know what's comin'?"

"Well, she'll have a little surprise this evening, but I know she'll love it. Granted, she's going to have to move some things around to create a seating area, and she'll need to order supplies and flavor shots, but think of it, Stella!" Jennifer grabbed the older woman's arms and stared off into the distance with a dreamy expression, then waved a hand to encompass her vision. "Lots of pumpkin spice is in my very near future!"

Two weeks later, Jennifer stepped back from the mirror to admire the new, autumn-colored, rayon wrap dress hugging her petite form. She slipped a layer of red-brown hair behind one ear and smiled at the reflection of the fifteen-minute face she'd just applied. If Tilly had found her altered the day she and Michael picked up the latté machine, she'd really spew the clever comments tonight.

Jennifer couldn't get over how everyone had pulled together to plan this evening in such a short amount of time. Another one of Jennifer's ideas had struck as she watched Mary Ellen chortle with joy while brewing her first cup of steamed coffee with Tilly's help. Why not introduce Mary Ellen's coffee bar to the community in grand style?

That night, ideas flew. And after that, things happened. Tilly set Mary Ellen up with a flavor supplier. Michael, James and Mary Ellen's husband, Bob, cleared the space behind the counter for the machine, as well as a spot for the mini-fridge Mary Ellen purchased at Lowe's the very next day. Jennifer and Stella helped rearrange displays, moving a big rack of vintage clothing to the rear. After putting in a profitable call to a very excited Montana Worley, Jennifer also cleaned out the glass display case. Mary Ellen commandeered furniture odds and ends from her store room, including a sofa and two tables and chairs, to create a sitting area running from the front window to the end of her counter. She found room in her budget for the purchase of two small outdoor tables with umbrellas. Finally, Michael crafted a wooden sign for the window painted with the brown word "coffee" and a steaming red mug.

For the sake of practicality, Jennifer slipped her feet into her Mary Janes, but her reflection told her the label "Plain Jane" no longer fit. In much the same way her training enabled Jennifer to revitalize a dilapidated building, she now knew God created each person to shine. Life in a fallen world damaged and dulled, but the Master Renovator always finished His plan for those willing. Jennifer looked forward to seeing the completion of that plan in her life.

Filling Yoda's bowl and petting the gray head, Jennifer slipped out the door and hurried across the lawn. She found Allison Winters setting up in the apothecary. The sight that met her eyes there, so much like a window into the past, warmed Jennifer's heart. During the last half of September, they sanded, stained, and varnished the now-glowing, six-inch heart pine floors twice, moving the furniture around as their limited quarters demanded, then spent two days applying poly-urethane to create a natural but protected appearance. An antique reproduction wooden chandelier Mary Ellen located hung from the ceiling. The refinished shelving again curved against fresh plaster. On the yellow and green compounding desk, Allison arranged a display of her homemade soaps, bagged fresh herbs, and teas, which also now supplemented the coffee options at Mary Ellen's. She'd even created a flier announcing the Halloween opening of Hermon Apothecary Herbals.

"It's all under control here," Allison assured Jennifer.

"OK, can I get you anything?"

The graying brows waggled. "If you can get Mary Ellen to put some hot water on a pouch of my jasmine tea and add a squirt of honey, it would oil my voice to talk all evening about the apothecary's history ... and future!" She winked.

"Done," Jennifer said, waving as Allison gave her a thumbs up sign.

Bringing Allison a cup of tea didn't begin to repay the herbalist's commitment to the project at hand. As Jennifer left the building, she glimpsed the tiny plants of the rock-bound herb garden thriving in September's lingering but gentle warmth. When Jennifer had visited Allison's nursery to purchase them, Allison had Jennifer dig and transplant the herbs herself but refused payment. Jennifer planted according to Allison's directions, but the older woman showed up the next day with tiny wooden name plates for each garden resident. She also brought signs for the herbs she transplanted in the adjacent woods. Allison assured Jennifer and Michael she intended to maintain the garden as well as provide certain spring additions.

The white mini-lights Stella had used to frame the antique store's windows winked a welcome as Jennifer jangled the bell on the door. A chorus of greetings sounded. She took a minute to appreciate the oil lamps Mary Ellen had lit and placed on the tables before Montana bounded up to her and almost knocked her over with a massive waist hug-tackle.

"You look so pretty!" the tween cried.

"Yes, she does," Tilly agreed from behind the counter, her agreed-upon station of service for the evening to relieve Mary Ellen's nerves. "I'm glad you people finally got her to take my advice and get rid of the lame hair and glasses."

"Haha, *lame*!" Montana crowed.

Jennifer pinched her cheek. "That's not funny."

"Well, you look a lot better now. Michael's goin' to ask you to marry him, and you'll get to stay here forever."

Jennifer made a shushing sound as Montana squeezed her in another rib-crunching but blissful hug. Laughter floated from behind the counter, where Rita continued to put out Montana's culinary creations while the baker lapsed into delinquency.

Montana grabbed Jennifer's hand. "Let me show you what I made for tonight!" she cried, pulling Jennifer over. "Check it out. Cinnamon streusel muffins with cream cheese inside, mini-cheesecakes, pumpkin oat bars, peanut butter cookies and apple dumplings!"

In a dramatic gesture, Jennifer slapped a hand over her eyes. "I can't take it! It's a veritable fall goody sampler. The temptation is too much! I simply cannot choose."

Montana giggled and slid a bar cookie onto a napkin. "I know you want pumpkin, and you want Mary Ellen to make you a pumpkin spice latté."

Taking a bite of the scrumptious treat, Jennifer closed her eyes. "I think I'm gonna cry. But before I get that coffee, I've got our first order up. It's a jasmine tea for Allison."

"Oh, I can do that!" Mary Ellen called with confidence. She grabbed a thick paper cup, dropped in a tea bag, and held it under the hot water feed, then extended it to Jennifer with a flourish. "Wa-la!"

"Honey," Jennifer reminded her.

Mary Ellen added a squirt and swirled the concoction with a skinny, wooden stir stick. As Jennifer took the cup, Mary Ellen stopped her with a hand over Jennifer's. "Jennifer, if I didn't tell you what all this means to me, let me do so now. Thank you. I'm so excited, I think I'm the one who's goin' to cry."

Jennifer shook her head. "Mary Ellen, *you* did it. You bought the equipment and made the space and learned how to make the coffees."

"But I never would have if you hadn't given me the nudge. So thank you."

"Well, you're welcome." Jennifer blushed, then she felt Montana attach herself again.

"And you made my dreams come true, too!" the child exclaimed from below.

"Oh, Montana, this is just your start."

"No, no, she has to stay!" Mary Ellen insisted. "She can never move out and start her own bakery. I would lose all my new customers."

Montana chuckled. "But we haven't even opened yet, Miss Mary Ellen."

"Well, I predict a huge success. Jennifer, turn that open sign over on your way out." Mary Ellen took a deep breath, blew it out with a sound like a steam whistle, and gave her rounded shoulders a Zumba shake. Then she opened her arms in a welcoming gesture. "I am ready for the masses."

Jennifer laughed. Before she could do as Mary Ellen requested, a ginger-bearded gentleman clad in a plaid shirt and cowboy hat stuck his head in the door. "Are you Ms. Rushmore? I'm the fiddler with the band, Rusty Cowper. My guitar player will be here in a second. Where do you want us to set up?"

"Oh, just right outside the shop. See where I've placed those chairs? Thank you so much for coming."

Jennifer's call to the number on the band's card from the gala had paid off. These two musicians lived locally and agreed to serenade guests for tips in the hopes of booking future gigs. Jennifer had also peppered Mary Ellen with future events suggestions, from a youth poetry reading to historic storytellers to guests like the local author who tonight would treat customers to a selection from her upcoming novel. Jennifer herself had a surprise for the community, hidden behind Mary Ellen's counter.

Once the cars started to pull in, Jennifer stood at the shop's entrance, listening to bluegrass tunes, her hands clasped in joy when she wasn't greeting guests. Michael joined her there as the overflow parking in the grassy median began to fill. He looked resplendent in khakis and a button-down striped shirt, his wavy hair slicked back and kissing his collar. He shook his head at her.

"What?" she asked, confused by the approval in his gaze.

"You've done it again."

"What did I do?"

"Amazed me."

Silence fell between them, as Jennifer's heart seemed to swell into her throat. "I'm just happy for Mary Ellen and Montana," she finally managed to say with humility. "This is their night."

He leaned in close to her, and she caught a whiff of cologne as he whispered, "Then why are you the one shining?"

With that, she did feel positively electrified. The energy hummed in her veins long enough to give her the courage to introduce the local author half an hour later.

"But before I do," she told those gathered around, some sitting crossed-legged on the floor and others standing behind the occupied sofa and chairs, "I'd like to give a little reading of my own."

Questions and murmurs rippled through those gathered as Jennifer held up the magazine she clasped against the front of her dress. "This is the October issue of *Old Houses*. Many of you know that one of the magazine's writers, Bryan Holton, visited Hermon this summer. His article featured the restoration of the Dunham property, but as it turns out, it featured much more than that. Listen to this portion: 'The restoration of the Dunham property reflects not only the training of The University of Georgia's Master of Historic Preservation graduate Jennifer Rushmore, but a concentration of community effort and interest. The best of Oglethorpe County and the tiny town of Hermon invested sweat and skill into bringing this historic doctor's house and apothecary back to life, from the local fireplace restoration, roofing and exterior painting crews, to the exacting strokes of painter Stella James' brush in stenciling and trimming the interior of the home. Her project *piéce de resistance*, a parlor mural of the historic Dunham plantation on Long Creek, showcases her talent even more richly than her individual offerings, which are sold at Mary Ellen McWhorter's next-door antique store. With discussion of expanding the antique store to appeal to the coffee lover's palate, opening a complementary shop in the Dunham apothecary, and renovating the historic Gillen's Department Store into an art gallery and event facility that could house James and her students, add Hermon to your next Georgia ramble to gauge how this former railroad town resurrects!'"

As the room erupted into applause and enthusiastic cheering, Jennifer paused. Her cheeks ached from the size of her smile. She turned the magazine around to show everyone the photographs Bryan had chosen, including Stella's mural and one of her paintings. Stella herself, standing at the back of the room, smiled and nodded, receiving congratulations in her typical calm manner. Earl squeezed her shoulders.

Once the reading began, the attentive guests sipping their coffee in a cocoon of cultural awareness, Jennifer slipped out. Checking on things at the apothecary, she heard Allison engaged with a small group in a discussion of herbal medicine. No need to interrupt that.

Jennifer needed a minute alone with God to tell Him thank you for all that had come together tonight. As gratefulness bubbled up in her heart, she wandered onto Michael's lawn, gazing up at the stars. Then she heard a voice call, "hey," and noticed Michael himself sitting on his front porch steps. She walked over and sank down beside him, turning her knees toward him and clasping her hands in the lap of her dress.

"What are you doing, hiding over here?" she asked.

"Well, it's not like I could fit in that antique store," he joked.

"Right. I guess that's a good problem to have, though."

"It's a great turn-out, Jennifer, and the first of many special evenings. I don't care what you say about it being Montana's and Mary Ellen's night. It happened because of your big heart."

Surprised by Michael's generous words, Jennifer ducked her head. "Thank you. But you know, I don't deserve all that praise."

"Why not?"

"I still haven't written that letter forgiving my parents."

Michael blew out a soft breath, then said, "It's OK if you need time."

Jennifer tilted her head, listening to her own spirit, or rather, the Holy Spirit, then straightened. "No. I don't think I do."

"What's that?"

"I think tonight has given me the strength. I think I'm ready. God has showed me that my life is in His hands. I'm no longer at the mercy of my family. I no longer need to be at the mercy of the enemy, either." Jennifer pressed her palms onto the brick steps as she turned to her companion. "If I go write that letter right now, will you come with me?"

Michael's eyebrows raised. "Now? To your double-wide?"

She worried her lip. "Yes. It's just—maybe the scariest thing I've ever done, short of … well, short of telling you." A nervous little laugh escaped her.

Michael reached out and took the hand she moved back to her lap. He squeezed it as he said, "Jennifer, I think you're very brave. I want you to know that. I'm so proud of you for doing the right thing."

Love for him surged in her heart, but at the same time, fear. Fear of being vulnerable, fear that he wouldn't want to get close to her, fear that he might. Boy, however far she'd already come, her future held some indisputable emotional land mines! Putting that aside, she squeaked out, "So you'll come?"

"Uh, do I have to help write it?" Michael looked exceedingly uncomfortable at the idea.

She laughed. "No, of course not. If you'll just sit in the living room with the cat, that will be enough. And pray. You do have to pray." Somehow she thought if Michael would do this, the enemy would be less likely to deluge her with the horrible memories that always accompanied thoughts of Roy. Alone, those memories possessed the power to suck her under a drowning tide.

"OK, I'm good with that." With his trademark statement of agreement, Michael stood up, brushing off his khakis. To her shock, he then reached toward her again. He wanted to hold her hand?

Jennifer slipped her palm into his grasp, and with her heart fluttering like the moths attracted to the porch light on her double-wide, they made their way across the lawn together. This could just be a gesture of support, she reminded herself. But as Michael glanced over and smiled down at her, did she glimpse admiration in his expression?

Unlocking her front door, Jennifer flipped on an extra light to supplement the lamp she'd left aglow. Yoda loped over and went straight for Michael's pants. As he greeted the playful kitten, she started for her bedroom to boot up her computer, but Michael called her back.

"Wait," he said unexpectedly. "Let me pray for you before you start."

She tried to hide her trembling chin by tucking it down. Now that the time was here, her anxious insides churned like wet cement in a mixer truck. Michael placed a hand on her shoulder and prayed aloud that God would give her strength and the right words, that He would prepare the hearts of Kelly and Roy, and that nothing would oppose the work God wanted to do in the situation. By the time he finished speaking, a soft mantle of peace settled over Jennifer's spirit.

The e-mail flowed out of her with amazing ease and matter-of-factness, releasing years of pent-up pain, but amazingly, without anger or accusation. Truth marched across the screen in its own bold power. Then she told her mother and stepfather how God had begun a healing process in her life that provided her with the strength to forgive them for their abuse and neglect, and that she hoped one day they might experience that same forgiveness and restoration through Christ.

A few minutes later, Jennifer came out and stood before Michael, hands clasped before her, taking in the most beautiful sight she'd ever seen, the man she now knew she loved with his head bent, praying for her. "You can say 'amen,'" she told him in a quivery voice. "I pressed send."

Michael looked up. Putting the cat down, he rose and took her hands. "You're shaking."

"Yes, but somehow I never felt stronger. Something that's not me is flowing through me."

His eyes misted. "I can tell," he said, then pulled her in, not forcing her, but drawing her, like Someone Else she now knew. He bent his forehead to hers, hands on her arms, just breathing the same air. Adrenaline flowed through Jennifer's veins, but instead of the usual urge to flee, she leaned in, safe enough to want to be closer. "And you're beautiful," he whispered just before he sealed her lips in their first, soft, simple, but ultimately perfect, kiss.

DISCUSSION QUESTIONS

Historical Section and Chapters One, Two and Three

1. In the first historical account of Charlotte Ormond Dunham, what warning signs of abusive behavior by Stuart does Charlotte ignore, and why? How do subtler patterns prove effective in entrapping women? Have you ever encountered "an angel of light?"
2. What makes Charlotte uneasy about Selah? William? Why has William parted ways with his family?
3. Why does Jennifer feel the need to exert independence from Barb, yet find that difficult?
4. What about her double-wide home makes Jennifer happy? Have you ever had a place that imparted a sense of security? Why do you think that was, and did it last?
5. Why do you think Michael warns Jennifer that her life as a new Christian might not continue to feel warm and fuzzy?

Chapters Four, Five and Six

6. Throughout the story, Jennifer evolves from introspective, guarded and task-oriented into someone better able to care about and relate to others. What does she see in Allison Winters that she applies to herself? In what ways do you see Jennifer's increasing trust and affection for others manifest?
7. What do you make of Barb's reactions to Michael and Stella? Why do you think Barb tries to stay in Jennifer's life?
8. During their conversation at the antique shop, what type of affirmation do Stella and Mary Ellen give Jennifer? Why is this so meaningful to her?
9. What did you think about Michael's comment that "sometimes evil spirits take up residence where bad things happened?" How might his observation tie in with what Jennifer thought she saw in the apothecary attic?
10. How does Michael take Jennifer's over-reaction when he tries to carry her? How does she attempt to explain herself? Do you think he buys that?
11. How do the armadillos serve as a foil for Jennifer's relationship with Michael? What prevents the two of them from making steady progress?

Chapter Seven, Historical Section, and Chapter Eight

12. What can the relationship between Jennifer and Montana teach us?
13. In the second historical flashback, did you agree with Charlotte's mother that Charlotte should return to Stuart when he returns home wounded? Do you think Charlotte's "imprisonment" is improved or worsened after his return?
14. What deeply seeded line of reasoning from Jennifer's childhood does her makeover expose? Does her reaction surprise you?
15. Michael's attempt to act like a gentleman throws Jennifer into a further tailspin. What confusing emotions does she experience? What concept does she struggle with and why?

Chapters Nine, Ten and Eleven

16. In what ways does the historic gala advance Jennifer's relationship with Michael?
17. How does the sermon preached by Pastor Simms affect Michael? What does Michael suggest he and Jennifer do? How does Michael's behavior over lunch make him even more appealing to Jennifer?
18. What kind of reaction does Stella telling Michael she loves him and seeing Ashley's photo provoke in Jennifer? What does she realize she is missing? How does God use a mental flashback to give Jennifer a picture of the spiritual work He wants to accomplish? Has God ever approached something in your life similarly?
19. Why does Jennifer feel she has no chance competing against the memory of Ashley?
20. What does Jennifer do at the beginning of Chapter Eleven that demonstrates she is increasingly seeking God's will for her life? How does that go against her natural inclination? Has God ever asked you to do something similar?
21. Supported by her story about Chad, what advice does Amy give Jennifer?

Historical Section and Chapter Twelve

22. In the third historical section, how could Charlotte have justified her actions using her circumstances? How does Lettie's action cause Charlotte to look at her own heart?
23. How does William's testimony to Charlotte provide a counterpoint even amid trials? How is sin often begun in both "intense sweetness" and "intense darkness?"
24. What does Charlotte realize about God's role in both her past and future, and how does that change her heart?
25. Do you think there are natural explanations for the oil spill in the apothecary and the missing brake screw, or that something more sinister is going on? What do you think about the mail man who came to Jennifer's rescue? What does Michael say to expect when "God stuff" is going on?

Chapters Fourteen, Fifteen and Sixteen

26. How do the letters from Charlotte to William open a modern day discussion on forgiveness? What reasons to forgive do James and Michael point out?
27. What causes Jennifer's memory of her earliest abuse to surface? How do the spiritual forces of darkness come against Jennifer that night, and how does she combat them? How does Michael help? According to Michael, why does God allow the memory of abuse to surface, and how does God use the dream of Jennifer's mother?
28. What "grooming" tools preparatory to abuse did Roy use on Jennifer? Stuart on Charlotte?
29. What makes Jennifer willing to move toward forgiving her family? What steps do you see her taking, with the help of others, to break the bondage of her past?

AFTERWORD

While the restoration process and buildings in The Restoration Trilogy are based on an actual project, and the Dunham doctors are based on an actual line of historic doctors, names and facts have been changed to suit the story line of *White*, *Widow* and *Witch*. You'll find the series cradled by the real county of Oglethorpe in Piedmont Georgia, with larger towns and topographical details unaltered … but rest assured, no real characters from the series exist. That said, I wrote The Restoration Trilogy with the same goal in mind as The Georgia Gold Series: to weave an entertaining, fictional story among the sturdy framework of history, with its true-to-life people, places and events. I hope you enjoy it! And remember, real history is often the most shocking part of any story!

I would like to thank several local experts consulted by interview for The Restoration Trilogy, including: Susan K. Goans, restoration artist; Jim Carter, 1800s architecture and interiors; Debbie Cosgrove, herbs and herbal medicine; Dr. Allen Vegotsky, historic medicine; and Bill Summerour, log cabins. Also, my thanks to the helpful staff of the Oglethorpe County Library. For readers interested in further study on the topics touched on in The Restoration Trilogy, I include a list of sources consulted. These are offered not in MLA format, but merely in the order I consulted them, through the completion of writing *Widow*. Many historical threads overlap and interweave in all three books of the series, but in bold are the sources most pertinent to *Widow*.

Sources:

The Travels of William Bartram: Naturalist Edition, University of Georgia Press, Athens, GA, 1998

Bartram: Travels and Other Writings, Literary Classics of the United States, Inc., NY, NY, 1996

***The History of Oglethorpe County, Georgia*, Florrie C. Smith, Wilkes Publishing Company, Inc., Washington, GA, 1970**

Woman of Color, Daughter of Privilege: Amanda America Dickson 1849-1893, Kent Anderson Leslie, University of Georgia Press, Athens, GA, 1995

***The Story of Oglethorpe County*, Lena Smith Wise, 2nd Ed. by Historic Oglethorpe County, Inc., Lexington, GA, 1998**

Scull Shoals: The Mill Village That Vanished in Old Georgia, Robert Skarda, Fevertree Press, Athens, GA, 2007

White Flood Red Retreat, Robert Skarda, Old Oconee Books, GA, 2012

***Antebellum Athens and Clarke County, Georgia*, Ernest Hynds, University of Georgia Press, Athens, GA, 1974/2009**

***College Life in the Old South*, E. Merton Coulter, University of Georgia Press, Athens, GA, 1983**

***Confederate Athens*, Kenneth Coleman, University of Georgia Press, Athens, GA, 1967/2009**

Cotton Production and the Boll Weevil in Georgia: History, Cost of Control, and Benefits of Eradication, P.B. Haney, W.J. Lewis, and W.R. Lambert, The Georgia Agricultural Experiment Stations College of Agricultural and Environmental Sciences, The University of Georgia, Research Bulletin Number 428, March 2012

New Georgia Encyclopedia: History & Archaeology: Progressive Era to WWII, 1900-1945, online: World War I in Georgia / Athens / Oglethorpe County / Ku Klux Klan in the Twentieth Century … and many other online resources

An Hour Before Daylight: Memories of a Rural Boyhood, Jimmy Carter, Simon & Schuster, New York, NY, 2001

Behind the Mask of Chivalry: The Making of the Second Ku Klux Klan, Nancy MacLean, Oxford University Press, New York, NY, 1994

***Dr. Durham's Receipts: A 19th Century Physician's Use of Medicinal Herbs*, Debbie Cosgrove and Ellen Whitaker, 2008**

City of Maxeys Historic Interest Group Interview Report, Bereniece Jackson Wilson & Regina Jackson Wilker by Dennis and Faye Short, April 13, 2014

The Negroes of Athens, Georgia, Thomas Jackson Woofter, Phelps-Stokes Fellowship Studies, No. 1, Bulletin of the University of Georgia, Volume XIV Number 4, December, 1913

Send Us a Lady Physician: Women Doctors in America: 1835-1920, "Co-Laborers in the Work of the Lord: Nineteenth-Century Black Women Physicians," Darlene Clark Hine, W. M. Norton & Company, New York, NY, 1985

A Pioneer Church in the Oconee Territory: A Historical Synopsis of Antioch Christian Church, Billy Boyd Lavender, 2005

***A Scythe of Fire: A Civil War Story of the Eighth Georgia Infantry Regiment*, Warren Wilkinson and Steven Woodworth, HarperCollins, NY, NY, 2002**

***Resources of the Southern Fields and Forests, Medical, Economical, and Agricultural*, Francis Peyre Porcher, Charleston, SC, 1863**

BOOK THREE OF THE RESTORATION TRILOGY:

Having restored Michael Johnson's ancestors' house and apothecary shop and begun applying the lessons of family and forgiveness unearthed from the past, Jennifer Rushmore expects to complete her first preservation job with the simple relocation of a log home. But as her crew reconstructs the 1787 cabin, home to the first Dunham doctor, attacks on those involved throw suspicion on neighbors and friends alike. And while Jennifer has trusted God and Michael with the pain of her past, it appears Michael's been keeping his own secrets. Will she use a dream job offer from Savannah as an escape, or will a haunting tale from a Colonial diary convince her to rely on the faithfulness of his love?

ABOUT THE AUTHOR

DENISE WEIMER

Native Georgia author Denise Weimer holds a journalism degree with a minor in history from Asbury University. Her writing background prior to The Restoration Trilogy includes numerous regional magazine and newspaper articles, romantic novella *Redeeming Grace*, and the Georgia Gold Series (*Sautee Shadows, The Gray Divide, The Crimson Bloom* and *Bright as Gold*, Canterbury House Publishing), sweeping historical romance with a touch of mystery. *Bright as Gold* won the 2015 John Esten Cooke Fiction Award for outstanding Southern literature. Denise is a wife and the swim mom of two teenage daughters.

CPSIA information can be obtained at www.ICGtesting.com
Printed in the USA
LVOW08s0616200816

500918LV00004B/5/P